DRAGON ABOVE!

Then the dragon spread his wings and jumped into flight. His first blast of fire struck Baron Swordfern, and the dead, dry lower branches of a big alder. His second blast burned three other warriors, and kindled some dry brush. His third blast burned a pitch-pine split by lightning . . .

They shot at him, but few arrows found their mark, and none hurt him seriously, and before they could crank up again, he swooped low to hit them with blasts of flame, and his dragon laughter echoed in their minds.

He landed, and quickly gulped down the fallen and the dead.

Ace Books by Carl Miller

DRAGONBOUND
THE WARRIOR AND THE WITCH

THE GOBLIN PLAIN WAR
(coming soon!)

THE WARRIOR AND THE WITCH

CARL MILLER

ACE BOOKS, NEW YORK

This book is an Ace original edition,
and has never been previously published.

THE WARRIOR AND THE WITCH

An Ace Book/published by arrangement with
the author

PRINTING HISTORY
Ace edition/March 1990

ISBN: 0-441-87343-X

Ace Books are published by The Berkley Publishing Group,
200 Madison Avenue, New York, New York 10016.
The name "ACE" and the "A" logo are trademarks
belonging to Charter Communications, Inc.

PRINTED IN THE UNITED STATES OF AMERICA

10 9 8 7 6 5 4 3 2 1

Thanks to Holly Sweet and Shayla Briner

*"Dancing in the Garden" is for Donna Armistead,
"The Refugees" is for Darlene Glebow, and the
pooks at Treeworm's house are for Susan Protter*

AUTHOR'S NOTE

This book, *The Warrior and the Witch,* which takes place between the 194th and 199th year of humans east of the sea, begins the story of the fall of Newport, telling how Rockdream the Warrior and Coral the Witch lead a small group of refugees to safety when the dragon Riversong attacks the city.

The Goblin Plain War, in preparation, which takes place between the 199th and 202nd year, concludes the fall of Newport, telling how General Canticle's army of refugees attempts to conquer Goblin Plain, how the goblins resist, and how Coral the Witch and Drakey the High Shaman help both peoples find a new peace.

Dragonbound, previously published, which takes place in the 202nd and 203rd years, tells the story of Periwinkle and Bellchime, a warrior and a storyteller dragonbound to the young dragon Distance, who plan to battle the dragon Riversong when Distance reaches majesty, but are forced into this battle much sooner.

Each book, though part of a larger history, tells a complete story in itself.

CONTENTS

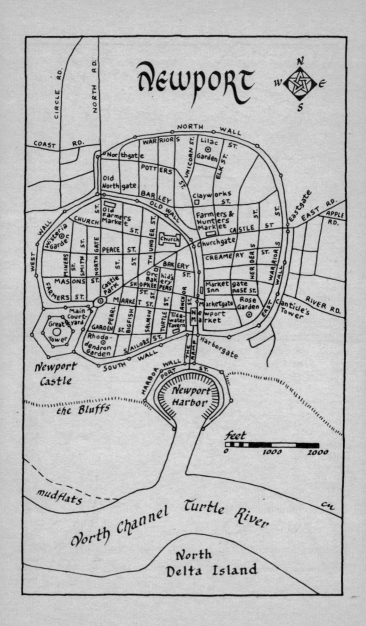

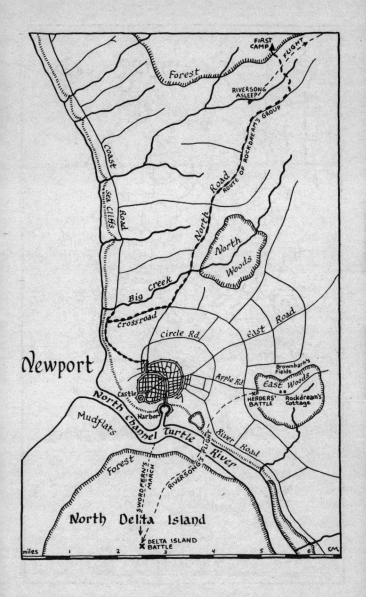

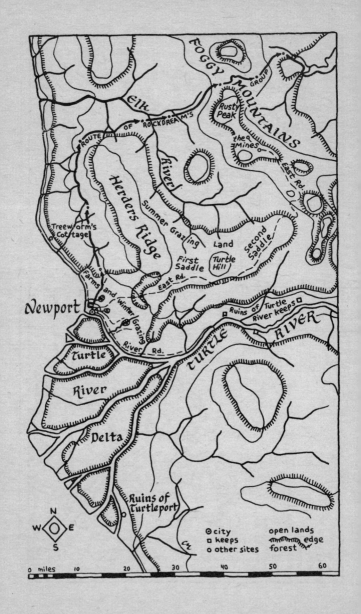

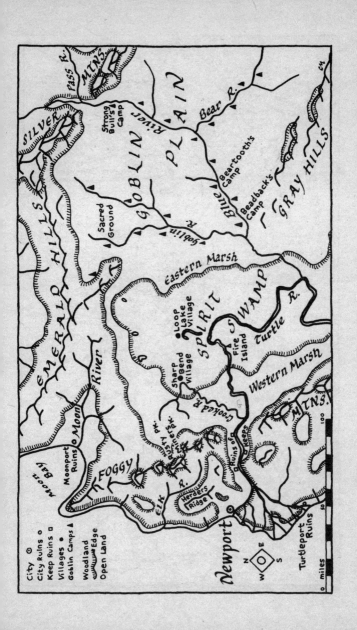

PROLOGUE

Newport was the largest human city east of the sea, and it was built to endure.

The castle's great tower was five stories tall, ninety feet in diameter, and stood on an outcrop of solid rock. It was surrounded by two curtain walls, three and two stories high, with sixteen lesser towers. The castle's outer wall was one with the city walls, which were five miles long, with another thirty towers. Even the harbor was fortified; this wall had another eight towers.

In the older part of the city, all of the buildings were made of stone and roofed with lead sheets or clay tiles, even the private dwellings. Houses in the newer part of the city were mostly made of brick. Only outside the city walls were there any homes of half timber with thatched roofs such as humans built in other cities, and there were fewer than a hundred of these.

Ten thousand humans lived within Newport's walls. Farmers and fishcatchers went out each morning in season, to work in their fields and boats, and returned each evening. Merchants sent ships along the coast or across the sea to other ports near and far, and riverboats up the Turtle and Blue Rivers to inland places. Miners went out for days to work the ore pits in the nearby Foggy Mountains, and smiths worked in the city forging tools and weapons from the ore. Masons and sculptors remodeled buildings and carved statues to adorn the many fountains and parks. Minstrels and storytellers entertained in court and tavern, and also served the children as teachers of language and history. Priests and priestesses of the Church, sworn to celibate devotion of the Holy Family, led public chant and prayer ceremonies each day at sunrise and sunset, and twice more on market days, and also bound marriages and other agreements of love and trust, healed the sick, and in private did much prayer and meditation.

Perhaps half a thousand humans lived immediately outside the city walls, and among these were all sixty or so of the city's known witches and wizards, most of whom made their living treating serious illnesses, which they did better than most priestesses or priests. But they were not completely trusted, and were forbidden to live inside the city, though allowed and even encouraged to practice their arts there if they did so openly and honestly, but they were forbidden to enter the castle at any time.

In the castle lived Lord Herring and Lady Whitewing, their four sons, Oakspear, Pelican, Swordfern, and Drill, their only daughter, Lupine, and their many grandchildren. A good ruler had a general's sense of strategy, a priest's sense of what was right, a storyteller's understanding of human nature, and a merchant's understanding of economy. Lord Herring was considered a good enough ruler, and his oldest son, Oakspear, was expected to be even better.

In the castle and also in the towers of the city wall lived most of Lord Herring's thousand warriors, the women and men who day and night patrolled the ramparts of the castle and city, armed against dragon attack with crossbows and deadly steel arrows.

East of the sea, humans did not fight wars with each other, and except for some keeps isolated in the wilderness east of the Silver Mountains, they also kept peace with the goblins. Dragons were the one great enemy of all human cities, especially seaports, and uncommon as they were, they were devastating.

A dragon, a particularly large and fierce male dragon who called himself Riversong—a name likely given to him as a dragonling by his first dragonbound human because he was the copper-green of a mountain river—completely destroyed the city of Moonport despite a vigorous defense by its warriors, and devoured and scattered its people and livestock. This was in the second year after Herring became third Lord of Newport, and the 182nd year of humans east of the sea.

Some survivors of the fall of Moonport fled south, to swell Newport's population, and Lord Herring listened very carefully to their stories to learn what he could. Then he spoke to his sons and daughter and council of advisors, saying:

"We are very fortunate that this dragon chose to attack another city, but even though he will likely spend the rest of his life in Moonport and is no direct threat to us, what he has done, another dragon may learn to do.

"Riversong's tactics were both uncommonly cautious and contrived to spread despair. He could hear the very thoughts of the Moonport warriors, and though he only attacked on foggy nights, there are many of these, and he always came when and where he was least expected, which put the warriors under constant stress.

"We cannot do much to fortify our city against such an attack that we have not already done, so we must fortify the resolve and skill of our warriors. We must have more tournaments and contests of skill, and we must have more difficult tests for the trainees. When war swoops down on us suddenly from the sky, we will be ready, and we will win, and our city will stand."

1

WARRIOR'S TEST

1.

"For my warrior's test, I will go to Spirit Swamp and kill a drakey," said Rockdream. The young man breathed slowly, trying to be strong and calm while he faced the baron, the two warriors, and the priest.

"What weapon will you use?" asked Baron Swordfern, third son of Lord Herring, and commander of the Old Wall. His face was stern, his dark beard cropped short, his blond hair trimmed evenly at the shoulders.

"I will use my crossbow and four steel arrows."

"And how will this prove your skill?" asked Windwater. She was Rockdream's master of archery, and though her gray hair was turning white and her face was wrinkled, her eye and aim were still good enough to hit small birds at maximum range.

"Though a drakey is a large target, it is extremely sensitive and perceptive to the presence of a hunter, and difficult to kill."

"And how will this prove your courage?" asked Canticle. He was a very ambitious man, who in his twenty-fifth summer was already lieutenant of the second tower south of Eastgate. His skin was swarthy and his hair and beard dark brown.

"If I do not hit the drakey in a mortal place with my first shot, it will likely turn to attack me, and I will have to crank quickly for my second shot."

"And how will this prove your wisdom?" asked Father Stonelight, who wore the deep red velvet hooded robe of a midpriest. His face was ageless, and inscrutable.

"I say that my choice of a test proves my wisdom. Dragons, rare as they are, are the city's only real enemies, and of all animals, a drakey is most like a dragon."

"Of all animals, a monkey is most like a human," said Father Stonelight, "but would killing a juggler's pet prove that you could fight a warrior?"

Rockdream sighed. "No, facing a drakey alone would not prove I can face a dragon alone. But facing a drakey alone in the swamp without a longbow might be a comparable danger to facing a dragon from these walls and towers, together with all the other warriors of Newport."

"That it is not," Swordfern said firmly. "But no one expects a warrior's test to be as severe as a battle."

Windwater said, "You may stand in the corridor while we discuss your proposal."

Rockdream bowed to each of the four examiners, and stepped out into the hallway, closing the door behind him.

"Pst!"

Rockdream looked down the hall, and there was Salmon, peering out of a doorway, covering her mouth with her hand to choke back a giggle.

"Not yet," Rockdream whispered irritably.

She motioned him to come to her. He frowned and shook his head, but she smiled and beckoned, and glancing at the closed door, he stepped lightly down the hall to her.

"Who are your examiners?" she whispered. "What did you tell them?"

"No," he whispered, and stepped back to the door.

At that moment the door opened, and Windwater called Rockdream back inside.

Swordfern said, "We accept your chosen test with these changes: You must arrange and pay for your own transport, and you must have no weapons but your crossbow and two steel arrows."

"Two arrows?" said Rockdream, feeling his face become pale.

"We are certain that you can do it with two arrows," said Windwater.

The priest said, "When you return, we will listen to your story, and we will know if it is true."

"You may set out tomorrow morning," said Swordfern.

"Yes," said Rockdream.

"If you would like a purification ceremony, come to the evening chant and prayer at the Church, and we will do the ceremony afterwards, so that you may know that the Lord of Light and Darkness is with you," said Father Stonelight.

"That might be good," said Rockdream. "I want to pray in particular to that part of god who is Wind the Hunter, the First Daughter."

"Her light will be brightest for you. It is three days to the full moon," said the priest.

Rockdream bowed, and left the room again, hoping that Salmon was no longer lurking in the hallway. Her face was pretty, and her long brown hair even nicer, but she was sort of fat, and she was always around, even when Rockdream did not want her to be around.

"Did they make it hard for you?" she asked him in a low voice.

"Two arrows," he whispered.

"How many did you ask for?"

"Four."

"Bloody death! I told you to ask for six."

"If I had asked for six, they might have allowed me only one," he said, starting down the stairway.

"Who was there?" she asked, following him.

"Swordfern and Canticle, if you can believe that, and a powerful midpriest."

"Blood!" said Salmon. "I hope my test is easier. Still, someone must think you are very good."

Rockdream walked down another hallway to the courtyard door and past the guard, and Salmon followed.

"You know, there are some times when I need to be alone," Rockdream said irritably.

Salmon's voice became very serious. "Tomorrow or the next day, you are going to be very alone, and you might not come back. I thought you might like to—" she hesitated "—do something fun with me."

Rockdream touched her hand. "Salmon, I must pack my provisions, and tonight I want to go to Church. I need a purification ceremony."

"Do you want to become a warrior, or a priest?" Salmon asked mockingly. "If the Church had its way, we would have men defending the north walls, women defending the river walls, and married couples on the Old Wall, or something."

"That could never happen, and would never be proposed," said Rockdream.

"Oh no? Did you know that freedomwort is on the Church's List of Proscribed Herbs?"

"That is because priestesses are celibate. Why would they need to chew freedomwort root?"

"My mother says they do not want other women to use it either."

"Oh, that is nonsense. But even if it was true, the Church does not make the laws; Lord Herring does."

"You might say so, but since when did priests become involved with warrior's tests? Since Herring became Lord of Newport thirteen winters ago is when. More and more, he accepts the Church's ideas. Could you imagine Lord Herring's grandparents, Wentletrap and Pip, undergoing a purification ceremony before setting out to kill Mugwort the Dragon? Bloody death, no! They were making love all night in the Upriver Tavern."

Rockdream sighed. "Salmon, you and I will never agree about the Church."

"It is your test," she said. "Prepare for it any way you wish."

2.

Rockdream returned to the room he shared with two younger squires, and packed his woolen blankets, some hard cheese, smoked meat, and dried fruit, his water pouch, and enough silver and copper coins to cover the cost of his boat ride to Spirit Swamp, his donation to the Church, and any incidental expenses.

When he passed his test, he would be a warrior, and would move to his own room in one of the city's many towers. Canticle's Tower? Possibly, but if a baron was examining him, he might be offered a position in the castle itself. This was what he hoped, for he had come to love the castle.

This made him think about Salmon. Did he or did he not want her for his lover and his wife? If he did not do something about it soon, he would likely be separated from her; they might end up in towers across the city from each other. The way he felt half an hour ago, this might be best. Now he was less sure.

He inspected his crossbow, cranked it up and released it once unloaded. It was in fine condition. He picked up two of the four arrows he had painted red, and put them in his quiver. Painting them red was his own idea. If he missed a shot completely, he would have a much better chance of recovering the arrow.

Then he put on his pack and quiver, picked up his crossbow, and walked through the familiar maze of tapestry-covered common rooms and torchlit corridors, and everyone he passed wished him good luck.

To his surprise, the same happened outside the castle, while he walked down Castle Street across the old part of the city. But he was a young warrior alone on foot with a large pack, and it was not hard to guess what he was doing.

He passed the green oval of Castle Park, with its single large cypress tree, which was there long before the city was built, and its fountain and flowering shrubs, which were added in Wentletrap's time. He passed many homes and shops, all built of stone and glass, with roofs covered with lead or clay tiles, for it was the wisdom of Newport's lords that city buildings should be strongly built, of substances that would not burn. The dragon Riversong's destruction of Moonport twelve years before showed what could happen to cities made of half timber and thatch, however stoutly their warriors fought in defense.

Rockdream stepped inside his favorite bakery shop. To his delight, Birdwade was at the counter. She had a round face, upturned nose, big brown eyes, and curly black hair, and was about three years older than Rockdream, and married to a farmer named Brownbark, who now raised much of the grain for her parents' bakery.

"I guess you will not want cinnamon rolls today," she said, smiling.

"Well, I would like one to eat right now, but what I came for is two loaves of waybread," said Rockdream.

"I know," said Birdwade, reaching into one of many breadboxes below the counter. "I baked two loaves myself, just for you, and made them a bit sweeter than waybread is usually baked, with a pinch of cinnamon too."

"Will this cover it?" he asked, handing her a silver eightstar.

"And then some. You have some pennies coming back to you."

"Give them to me in pastries when I return," said Rockdream.

Birdwade laughed. "A generous person is often someone in love. Did you and Salmon finally—?"

"No," said Rockdream with a sigh. "We just had a big argument because I want to go to Church tonight."

"On the night before your test begins, that is only proper," said Birdwade.

"Her arguments were so absurd. She said she thinks that the Church wants to take over the city and make everybody celibate."

Birdwade chuckled. "She just says things like that because she wants to sleep with you. You cannot keep her waiting forever. How would she stand it? I was cuddling and kissing and having even more fun in my thirteenth summer. How can you stand it, for that matter?"

"I think if she was more—" Rockdream hesitated "—like you, I would be glad to be her lover. But she can be so irritating."

"My husband often says that about me, but he loves me very much."

An older man and woman, fishcatchers most likely, came into the shop asking for longbread and biscuits.

"We got our catch early, and sold it right away," the woman said to Birdwade.

Rockdream put the waybread in his pack, and Birdwade wished him luck.

"A warrior's test?" asked the man.

"He is going to shoot a drakey," Birdwade said.

"Oh, I have done that," said the woman. "Aim for the wing where it meets the chest, and the drakey will be crippled, and crash. But do not think too much about your shot, or he will sense you and fly away."

"That may be hard for me, because I am only allowed to use two arrows, and this kill is important."

"I know what you can do," said the fishwoman. "Just think of kissing your lover's breasts as soon as the drakey comes into sight, and you will not think too hard about your shot. Those kinds of thoughts can draw a drakey closer to you, in fact."

"Truly?"

"We fished the swamp for sixteen years before we got our seaboat," said the man. "Killing a drakey is not hard, if you think the right kind of thoughts."

"Where are they most common?" asked Rockdream.

"I would say they are all over the swamp," said the man.

"Not so many in the open reeds," said the woman. "They like the trees better. Good luck to you. You may not believe what I say now, but try it out if your drakey does not come near enough for a good shot."

"Thank you for your suggestions," Rockdream said, and put on his pack and stepped back into the street.

"Good luck!" Birdwade called after him.

Now Rockdream wondered whether he was doing the right thing by going to Church. To these fishcatchers, killing a drakey with one shot was no hard task; just think about love-making and aim for the base of the wing.

But when he thought about Salmon, he felt confused, and confusion was a sign of impurity, so going to Church probably was his best choice. The spires of the Church that loomed above the buildings across Castle Street seemed to be beckoning to him.

3.

It was still hours before the bells would ring for the evening chant and prayer, when Rockdream walked up the steps to the main doors of the Church.

"Welcome, and bless you," said a voice at the small door. "How may we serve each other?" He was a young priest, with shaven head and face, wearing a light red robe.

"My warrior's test begins tomorrow, and I want the purification ceremony."

The priest smiled. "Yes, that may be done after the chant and prayer. Do you come for solitude and meditation first?"

"Yes," said Rockdream. "Where do I put my things?"

"Outside the door of the meditation chamber." He motioned Rockdream to step into the vestibule, and rang a small bronze bell, which had a soft high purifying tone, and a few moments later, another priest stepped up to the vestibule from a stairway.

The two priests whispered to each other, then the second one asked Rockdream which names of god he wished to call upon.

"Wind the Hunter," said Rockdream.

The second priest motioned Rockdream to follow him down a gloomy stairway. He opened a closet and took out a statuette, a bronze bell, and a small lamp, which he lit with a sparker. He led Rockdream through a maze of corridors and down another flight of stairs. Here was a low corridor with many doors, some few with possessions piled outside. The priest stepped inside the first open door, placed the statuette, lamp, and bell in the simple stone altar, came back out, motioned Rockdream to step inside, and closed the door.

The room was four feet wide, and less than seven feet deep and high, with walls of dark unpainted stone. It was cold. Rockdream sat cross-legged on the mat staring at the statuette and holding the bell in his hand. He would ring it whenever he had thoughts he wanted to release, and its tone would help clear his mind.

The bronze statuette depicted Wind as a mature woman in tunic and pants, wearing a quiver and holding a longbow. If he sat there long enough with silenced mind, the goddess might speak to him.

She might have said, "Listen to your own heart," but he might have imagined this.

Rockdream doubted that he knew his own heart, and tried ringing the bell. His restlessness changed to sleepiness. The minutes seemed like hours, but eventually even the hours passed, and faintly he heard far above the great bells chiming for the evening chant and prayer.

He bowed to the goddess on the altar, set the bell beside her, picked up the lamp and walked out, back down the low corridor, and up the steps to the other corridors. A priest saw him, took the lamp, and directed him to a different stairway that led to a door to the main sanctuary, where thousands of people were gathering for the ceremony.

Soon the Church was full, and the lesser priests robed in light red led the congregation in chanting many hymns and canticles of praise and power. Then the midpriests in dark red offered prayers for fruitful farming, safe return of ships, invincible warriors, and continuing peace. Father Stonelight offered a prayer for the success of a young warrior taking his test, and other midpriests offered prayers for the health of certain people who were sick.

"We ask that these prayers be granted to bring the best good to everyone concerned, in the name of the Lord of Light and

Darkness, who is embodied in Father Sky, in the Nameless Mother of All, in the Three Sons, Thunder the King, Cloud the Messenger, and Mountain the Priest, and in the Three Daughters, Wind the Hunter, Fire the Warrior, and Lake the Lover, so be it."

Then there was a time of silence, followed by the Canticle of Fortune, which was the canticle Rockdream liked least. In a time of despair it might be heartening, but in a time of prosperity it was a grim reminder of disaster. Rockdream moved his lips, but could not bring himself to give voice to the words of the reprise.

Then the entire congregation chanted the sixty-four greater names of the Lord of Light and Darkness, and the bells rang again.

A priest was waiting to pull Rockdream aside from the slowmoving flow of people leaving the Church. He was led downstairs once more, this time to a richly furnished room about twenty feet square, with upholstered chairs and carpets of rich twilight blue, which even in the lamplight made a vivid and beautiful contrast to the red robes of the three other priests. There were two empty chairs; the priest escorting Rockdream took one of them, and he took the other.

One priest spoke, beginning the purification ceremony by invoking the Lord of Light and Darkness, most especially as embodied in Wind the Hunter, the First Daughter. He rang his bell, then asked Rockdream, "Have you done any act which is unquestionably wrong, which you wish to renounce and atone?"

"No," said Rockdream.

There was silence for a long minute, then the second priest rang his bell, and asked, "Have you done any act which may be wrong, but which you had reason to do?"

Again Rockdream said no, but more hesitantly.

The first priest rang his bell after a shorter wait, and asked, "Do you want to talk about yourself and the young woman, a few nights ago, and earlier times?"

"We did nothing wrong," said Rockdream.

The first priest took a deep breath, then said, "Something is wrong. Is it a lie, or a misunderstanding?" He rang his bell again.

Rockdream shuddered. "She thinks I love her because I kiss her and touch her—and touch her. I do not know whether I love her or not, but we both enjoy—"

The first priest rang his bell. "Have you told her of your uncertainty?"

Rockdream hesitated. "—No."

"Then you must do so, before the next time you touch each other." He rang the bell again, and the sound seemed to travel up and down Rockdream's spine, making him relax.

"I agree to this," he said. He did feel better.

The second priest rang his bell, and asked, "Have you done any other acts which may be wrong, but which you had reason to do?"

"I painted my arrows red, so that I can recover them more easily."

The second priest coughed to stifle a laugh. "You were not forbidden to do so, and a warrior uses what strategy he or she can use. You have done well. Any other acts which may be wrong?"

"No."

The third priest rang his bell, and asked, "Have you had any thoughts or feelings which are unquestionably wrong?"

"I do not believe so," said Rockdream.

After a long silence, the fourth priest rang his bell, and asked, "Have you had any thoughts or feelings which may be wrong, which trouble your inner peace?"

"Yes," said Rockdream, "almost all of them. That is why I need this ceremony. I am afraid that I will fail my test. I am troubled by my love for Salmon, because we argue about everything—"

The first priest rang his bell. "These thoughts may indeed trouble your peace of mind, but there is no wrong in them." He looked steadily at Rockdream, and breathed slowly. "Do you deserve to be a warrior?" he asked.

Rockdream hesitated before saying, "Yes."

The first priest said, "You doubt that you are worthy of love and honor. You think you must be perfect, or else you are not good."

"The city depends on its warriors for its defense."

"And on its farmers and fishcatchers for food," said the first priest, "and on others for other things. But no human is perfect, and those who strive for perfection often become flawed in some serious way. All humans are worthy of love and honor."

"I suggest a reading," said the fourth priest.

"Past or future?" asked the second.

"Sometimes feelings like this come from the forgotten past."

"We must read what the Lord of Light and Darkness wills us to read," said the first priest.

"So be it," said the others.

And the priests all stared at Rockdream for what seemed a very long time, then the first priest spoke from his trance.

"There is light beyond the darkness. Always remember the goddess of love, who seems last and least of Sky and World's Sons and Daughters. Her yielding way makes her most powerful in the end."

"Are you reading my past or my future?" whispered Rockdream, and they all rang their bells together, and because each bell was of slightly different pitch, a rich high throbbing filled the room. The fourth priest bowed and left the room, while the others continued blending their bells.

A few minutes later, the fourth priest returned with a midpriest. The midpriest stood in front of Rockdream and gestured for him to stand, then the midpriest took his place in the fifth chair. Rockdream began to ask a question, and the midpriest gestured silence.

After a timeless time, the midpriest spoke, in a normal voice, saying, "The purification ceremony is completed." He touched Rockdream's forehead in blessing. "Father Starmoss will show you to your room."

At the door to this chamber, Rockdream asked Father Starmoss, who was the first priest, what he saw in his future.

"The future is choice," said Starmoss. "I saw yours—" he hesitated "—farther than I usually see, and I sent for my Overfather. Talking about a foreseen future is dangerous, Rockdream. If I told you I saw you passing your warrior's test, this might cause you to assume you will pass it, and you might fail through carelessness."

"Wondering what you saw that you cannot tell me might cause me to make wrong decisions also."

"You must listen to your own heart, and pray for guidance, and your decisions will be for the best. I saw a great confusion of events and possibilities, but the one scene I saw clearest was you killing a drakey in Spirit Swamp, with a longbow, not a crossbow, and you were with a wife and son."

"What did she look like?"

"Thin and rather small, with very curly light brown hair.

The boy was an infant. But these are only possibilities. You might choose to marry the young woman you are so concerned about now. Or you might befriend a woman who looks like my description, who is actually someone else than the person I saw."

"I will listen to my own heart, and pray for guidance. But thank you for telling me this."

Rockdream entered the room, which had a lamp burning, a small straw mattress covered with sheets and blanket, an altar with two statuettes and a bell, a basin filled with steaming water, with soap and toweling beside it, and a chamber pot. His pack, crossbow, and quiver were in the corner nearest the door.

After he bathed himself, he sat cross-legged on the bed, facing the altar. The statuette of Wind the Hunter was likely the same one he had with him in the meditation room, but now she seemed to be smiling. Beside her was her youngest sister, Lake the Lover, who was sculpted as though wearing a very filmy dress which showed every detail of her breasts and belly. Rockdream found himself imagining the goddess nude, and his body reacted, and he felt ashamed.

"There is no shame in wanting to sleep with the goddess of love," said a thought in his mind, and he found himself blowing out the lamp, and lying down between the smooth sheets.

4.

The great bell rang at midnight, though Rockdream did not hear it, and at this time the priests all retired to their chambers, and the priestesses awoke and left theirs. Before dawn, the bells rang again for the morning chant and prayer, and Rockdream woke, with the sense that he had dreamed something very important, but he could not remember any of it.

He used the chamber pot, and ate some cheese and dried apples, and pulled on his cloth underclothes, his leather pants and tunic.

A priestess knocked and asked, "Are you coming to the morning chant and prayer?"

"Yes. Should I bring my things?"

"Everyone brings their gear to the morning ceremony."

Rockdream shouldered his pack and quiver, and opened the

door. The priestess wore a heavy red robe; her hair was cropped short; her face looked stern. She directed him to the stairs to the sanctuary.

The morning ceremony differed little in form from the one the night before, but the priestesses chose different hymns and canticles, and worded their prayers differently, and it was morning, with the stained-glass windows brightening instead of darkening.

When it was over, he put on his pack and quiver, picked up his crossbow, and moved with the slow flood of people leaving the Church. Even though the crowd soon divided to walk different streets, there were still many walking with him all the way to the Market and through the wide gate and down the long ramp to the walled harbor, where riverboats and ships were anchored at the many docks.

Walking toward the riverboat section, he asked several sailors whether they knew of any merchant boats going to Upriver, or at least as far as Spirit Swamp.

"That looks like one, eh?" said one sailor woman with a foreign accent, pointing toward a riverboat being loaded by sailors, men and women, while a heavy man with carefully groomed red hair and beard, dressed in silk, spoke with the captain.

"Excuse me," Rockdream said.

"I am going all the way to Upriver, but I have no room," said the captain. "There will be a passenger boat leaving the 48th, which is the day after tomorrow."

"I will not need bunk space—" Rockdream began.

The captain laughed. "You could sleep on deck, where my sailors would trip over you every night. I am sorry, but no."

"What I mean is I am only going to Spirit Swamp."

"Even so, we will not be there till sometime tomorrow, or tomorrow night," said the captain.

"Are you a warrior?" asked the red-haired man.

"Trying to become one."

"So I guessed. I am Fairwind the Merchant, and this is Captain Terrapin."

"I am Rockdream the Squire."

"Take him with you," said Fairwind. "He will bring us good luck, I am certain of it. And if the merchants at the other end want to pay for the spices and silks with moonstones, rubies, or diamonds, so much the better, for these are worth almost twice what they think. No more sapphires though, unless you can trade them on Goblin Plain for good mammoth leather, or ivory. The cinnamon comes from Yellow River overseas, so it is the best, if anyone asks.''

"If Fairwind says to take you, I will take you," said Captain Terrapin. "My usual fare to Upriver is three singlestars, and five for a round trip. I guess one singlestar would be a fair price for a ride to Spirit Swamp."

"But how will I get back?" asked Rockdream.

"You can flag down another boat long before my return. Anyone will pick up a human in Spirit Swamp, even fishcatchers."

Rockdream took off his pack, took out four fourstars, and gave them to the captain.

Soon the boat was loaded, the anchor raised. The sailors took the oars and rudder; the captain beat the drums; and the boat, named the *Golden Turtle*, moved slowly into the open water of the harbor, and through the gap into the muddy main stream of the Turtle River. "Set sails!" yelled Captain Terrapin, and half the sailors left their oars to work the ropes, while the others continued rowing to keep the boat from drifting with the current, which in late spring was still relatively swift. Soon the *Golden Turtle* was moving upstream in a favorable wind, past the farmlands and orchards of Newport to the north, and the reeds and mudflats of the delta to the south.

"Rockdream!" said a young sailor man.

"Bloodroot?"

"Who else? I suppose I look different with my beard filled out. What brings you aboard—" he began to ask, then guessed the answer, and fell silent.

Bloodroot was a former squire who had failed his warrior's test two years before, and decided to become a merchant, saying that he would still be able to afford silk one day, and he would have a house of his own far more comfortable than even a tower lieutenant's quarters.

"I hope your luck is better than mine was," Bloodroot said. "But I do not miss the castle a bit, nor the city. This work is much more suitable to me than waiting for dragons who never come. It seems real."

Rockdream shrugged. "The women look nice enough."

"None of these like me that well. There was one who did, but she decided to become a mariner when old man Fairwind offered her work on the Middle Kingdom run. She wanted me to go along, but I refused.''

"I did not know our merchants sent ships west of the sea."

"When you own your own ships, you can send them anywhere you want. Of course, some of them will not come back. If you run into pirates; or worse, if the port you choose is newly occupied by a dragon, too bad."

"I thought they had less dragon trouble over there."

"Well, as of last summer's end, Cherry Blossom City was still occupied by the dragon Swordrot, despite all the efforts of the Queen's army to remove her. So much for Royalty keeping their countries free of dragons! And some say that Swordrot is not even as big or clever as Mugwort, let alone Redmoon or Riversong."

"Which kingdom is that in?"

"Godsfavor, most people name it in our tongue. Even translated, their names sound foreign."

"The place belies its name. Hey, how much does a sailor get paid to go to the Middle Kingdom?"

"Fairwind promised two pounds of gold this time."

"Bloody death! Why did you not do it?" asked Rockdream.

"It is a two-year trip. If you add up all the silver I make for each Upriver run, seven singlestars each time, it comes to at least a third as much, and here there is no risk."

Which was why Bloodroot was no warrior, and why he would likely never become a merchant: warriors and merchants both took risks. But Rockdream gave this thought no voice, and instead asked, "What is Upriver like?"

"It is a small city in a big forest, with mountains all around. The houses are all timber and thatch, and no one seems the least concerned about dragons."

"Have you seen the Upriver Inn?"

Bloodroot laughed. "There are three inns in Upriver, the Sleep and Spirits, the Green Oak, and I forget the third; but if you come from Newport, all three innkeepers have stories about how their inn used to be called the Upriver Inn, and if you pay extra, they will even rent you the very room where Wentletrap and Pip became lovers. Some joke! The real Upriver Inn was torn down thirty years ago, when they rebuilt the market.''

5.

In the following hours, Rockdream learned that sailing a riverboat was much more work than he had thought. The sailors had to be constantly alert, for the wind might change, or the river might bend, or a sandbar or a drifting log might appear, and they would have to act quickly.

Twice, the wind dropped to nothing, the captain beat the drums, and the sailors rowed to keep the boat moving; but as soon as the wind rose again, he would stop drumming. Upriver was three weeks' journey upstream from Newport, and there would be many times when the sailors would have to row. Terrapin was not a captain to drive his sailors hard for the sake of gaining a day or two. Three weeks upstream, one week to return, and he could make five or six profitable trips each season.

It was midafternoon when the *Golden Turtle* passed the ruins of the first Turtle River Keep, destroyed by Mugwort the Dragon more than a century ago, and never rebuilt. The Foggy Mountains, long forested ridges with scattered rocky peaks, were free of fog now and looming closer. Astern, some of the sailors trolled for fish.

Beyond the second and third keeps, the Turtle River passed through a broad gap in the mountain range, and beyond this, it followed a slow twisting course through the marshes and hummocks of Spirit Swamp. The sun was low behind them and the moon rising over the marshes when the wind stopped for a third time. They rowed until twilight, then Captain Terrapin ordered the anchor dropped.

"Where you want to go is a good twenty or thirty miles farther," he said to Rockdream. "In the cypress and swamp pines is where you find drakeys."

They cooked a meal on a large grill, of fish they had caught on the way. One of the sailors, a woman named Lightstraw who was about ten years older than Rockdream, wanted to lower a skiff and hunt for a turtle, but the other sailors just wanted to eat their fish and go to bed.

"Warrior!" she said to Rockdream. "Do you want to hunt a turtle? They are a real delicacy, and this is a perfect place to find them."

In the bright moonlight, the high marsh reeds looked pale

and mysterious. Thousands of tiny reedfrogs were calling their mates, and the chorus was a loud, throbbing drone.

"Have you a weapon for me?" he asked. "I have only two arrows for my drakey, and I cannot afford to lose either one."

"You need harpoons and clubs for a big turtle. Even crossbow arrows barely stick in their shells. You need to pull them in and bash their heads. They bite viciously too, more than you would think."

"I am sure I can do it," said Rockdream.

"Of course you can," said Lightstraw. "You are a warrior. I am just a sailor, but I have done it many times. I will be back in a moment."

To Captain Terrapin, she said, "The warrior will go with me."

"Good enough," he replied. It took two to hunt a turtle, but any two could do it.

So Lightstraw and Rockdream both took harpoons and axes. The harpoons were made much like large spears, but the steel points were jagged. Each was securely fast to a long line. Once the skiff was lowered, Lightstraw wrapped cloth around the oars so they would not creak, then began rowing toward the reeds.

Ahead, Rockdream saw a slowmoving bump in the water, and pointed. Lightstraw turned to look, and shook her head, whispering, "That is just a river lizard, not very tasty, and hard to catch up with in the water. What we want to see is broader and lumpier. If you take the oars, I will watch."

"All right. Why are we whispering?" he asked, hardly able to hear her over the frogs; but when his own voice made the nearest frogs suddenly stop, the river lizard disappeared underwater, and he understood.

"That is why," she whispered.

They changed seats, and Rockdream began rowing.

"Make it a smoother, slower motion, and your arms will last longer," she whispered.

"What do I aim for?"

"Whatever part of the turtle you can see. If you hit hard enough, and directly enough, the harpoon will break through the shell, and we pull it to the boat and club it to death."

For some time, they rowed through channels in the reeds, without seeing anything.

"Right there on the edge," she whispered, picking up her harpoon. On the bank of a hummock was a large rounded lump like a rock. She threw her harpoon, and Rockdream threw his. Both hit the shell with a loud thud and crack, and the turtle slipped underwater.

"Pull fast, but smoothly," she said. "We got it."

There was a tug on both lines, and the skiff began moving. The turtle broke the surface, about twenty feet away, and paddled right toward them, with the two harpoon shafts sticking out of its shell like the masts of a boat. "Hold the line! Grab your ax!" Lightstraw shouted. The turtle rammed the skiff. "Pull your line tight!" The turtle bumped them again, and Rockdream swung his ax. It stuck in the shell near the neck, and the turtle snapped at Rockdream's arms. Lightstraw swung her ax blunt end first and bashed the turtle's skull.

"I told you to club it, not split it!"

"I misunderstood," said Rockdream.

"You did well enough. We have to pull it to the hummock to load it." They each took an oar and poled the bottom. Soon the skiff was resting on mud, the turtle lying beside it.

"Watch the mud. Sometimes it swallows your legs," she said, but it seemed firm enough at first. "Blood! Your harpoon head went all the way in. No wonder it fought so fiercely! You are a strong one."

He gripped one edge of the shell while she gripped the other, and their feet began sinking into the mud. "What does this thing weigh?"

Lightstraw grunted. "Maybe three hundred pounds. We killed a big one."

With some struggle they got it aboard, and braced their arms against the skiff to pull their feet free of the mud, and climbed back in. "We did it!" she said, and after a moment's hesitation, they hugged each other. In the moonlight, her blond hair looked white.

"What are you thinking?" she asked.

"Nothing. You look kind of like an elf woman, with fluffy white hair, and—"

"You look kind of like Wentletrap must have looked as a young man. Hey! You want to share my bunk tonight, turtle partner?"

"I do not think—" Rockdream began.

"There is nothing to think about," she said; and maybe it was the full moon, maybe the excitement of winning the strug-

gle with the turtle, but in an instant, Rockdream changed his
mind and was sharing her eager kisses.

"Yes," he said.

"Good. Let us take this delicacy back to the cook, and go to
bed."

Rowing back to the *Golden Turtle* took little time, and soon,
the three sailors of the night watch were helping them pull the
skiff back up.

"This is the biggest one yet," they said, when they saw the
turtle.

In the hold, it was totally black, but Lightstraw knew her
way, and led Rockdream by hand. "We have to be really quiet
and slow, because it is so late, but that is fun too," she
whispered. They sat on the edge of a lower bunk, about three
feet wide and six feet long. "Hand me your clothes and I will
stow them."

When he handed her his tunic, pants, and underclothes, he
felt so excited he was trembling, knowing he was naked next to
a naked woman he hardly knew, and could not see. Warriors
took risks, and this was a risk he had refused, before now.

"Move, so I can turn down the bed," she whispered, running her hand down his smooth side.

In moments, their bodies were pressed together under the
blankets, their hands exploring unseen warm skin. Rockdream
was surprised by the wetness, when Lightstraw pushed him
inside. "Be very slow," she whispered, moving her hips gently.

It was so relaxing. How could anything in the world feel as
good as this kissing, caressing, streaming? He did not remember falling asleep, but remembered waking up in the darkness
next to her, and in moments they were making love again.

In the first glimmer of dawn, Lightstraw reached over to
close the curtain in front of the bunk, and Rockdream reached
up to touch her breasts.

"One more go," she said, "and this time we can be wilder."

She kissed him hard, twisting tongues, and squirmed her
body over his. She trembled and slammed her hips against his,
breathing hard and sweating, staring wildly into his eyes, squeez-
ing him tight while she shuddered and he streamed.

"Some sailor I am. We never even got drunk first," she
said, and laughed. Rockdream looked bewildered, but he smiled.
She kissed him more gently. "I am sorry. You are young, and
I could be more gentle. Was this your first time?"

"My third," he said, then added, "the other two were last night."

"I guessed so," she said with a laugh. "But I also guess there is someone you have almost done this with more than once, and you will likely see her long before you see me again. Try it out."

Rockdream nodded. He knew that Lightstraw did not really want to know about his complicated feelings toward Salmon.

Lightstraw pulled out her clothes, and his, from the cubbyhole behind the bunk, and put hers on, bloomers, undershirt, baggy sailor's pants, wool shirt. His clothes were fitted more tightly, and harder to put on inside the bunk. While he dressed, he thought about how their clothes marked and separated them, he to his tower, she to her boat. When they were fully dressed, the separation seemed complete, even though she held his hand while they walked through the hold to the ladder.

Some of the other sailors smiled, but none made any remarks. If real privacy did not exist aboard a riverboat, neither did certain kinds of gossip. The only thing about their night together which was ever discussed was the big, delicious turtle they killed, which everyone had for breakfast.

6.

At first there was no breeze that morning, and for several hours the sailors rowed. When the wind did rise, it was from the east, but they were able to make use of it by tacking back and forth, for the river was very wide. Even then, their progress was slow. But in late afternoon, the wind moved to the west, and now they moved steadily past the reeds and into the swamp itself, where dark twisted willows and cypress grew on mudflats, and swamp pine covered the hummocks.

"That big hummock up ahead we call Fire Island," said Captain Terrapin. "It is one of the few places along this part of the river where the ground gets dry before late summer, and the best place for a base camp."

"That sounds good," said Rockdream.

"I will take him ashore," said Lightstraw, and she did, when Captain Terrapin anchored the *Golden Turtle* close to the hummock. In a few minutes they were ashore, unloading. Lightstraw kissed Rockdream goodbye and rowed the skiff back to the riverboat, which was soon sailing out of sight.

Rockdream shouldered his pack, walked up to the center of Fire Island and found a large fire ring, doubtless the source of the hummock's name. Here he arranged his camp, and spent the next half hour gathering dead branches, as dry as he could find, for a fire. Now all he had to do was find a drakey and kill it.

The view behind the hummock was discouraging, a thick grove of willow and cypress in several inches of muddy water. Rockdream took a careful step, and found that the mud bore his weight, and the grease on his boots kept his feet dry. He put on his quiver with the two red arrows, picked up his crossbow, and set off. Soon the ground rose out of the water, and here the mud was awkwardly sticky.

He heard a strange-sounding scrawk and startled, but it was only a raven. A mosquito hummed in his ear, then went away, then came back. He swatted it, and immediately a frog splashed. A warrior must not respond recklessly to sudden noises and mosquitos, he admonished himself.

Whenever he came to an open place, he walked around the entire edge, to give himself a view of as much of the sky as possible. If he could find a large carcass, likely there would be several drakeys tearing it apart, with condors circling overhead waiting for leftovers. When he saw one condor soaring, for lack of a better guide he moved in that direction, and soon found himself back at the river, some distance upstream from his camp.

On a mudbank near the water's edge sprawled three river lizards, each about seven feet long, but they looked harmless and stupid, with legs absurdly short and flat froglike faces with small bulging eyes. Deciding to use one as bait to lure a drakey, Rockdream drew an arrow, cranked his crossbow partway, for this would be a close-range shot, and walked lightly up the bank.

Two of the river lizards grunted and slid into the water; Rockdream shot the third in the head. It opened its mouth and went limp, bleeding, and the other two turned back, and seized it by the tail and left hind leg to pull it into the water.

Rockdream ran to the carcass, shouting, and kicked at the snout of the river lizard biting the leg; it grunted but did not let go. Then he tried to seize the front legs and pull it up the bank, but it was heavy and its slimy skin was hard to grip, and the other two river lizards were strong. Finally, because he could not afford to lose one of his two arrows, he tried to pull the arrow from its head, but at that instant the live ones gave it a jerk, and freakishly the shaft snapped in two, though it was a steel arrow.

In desperation he took the broken arrow and stabbed the nearer one's eye. It let go and lunged at him with surprising speed, while the other one pulled the dead one into the water. Rockdream jumped to its blind side, pushed the broken arrow deeper into its skull, and it stopped moving.

He picked up its front end by the shoulders to drag it away from the water; it must have weighed nearly a hundred pounds. He heard a sudden screech, and looked up to see a drakey swooping toward him. Its head and neck were like a heron's, but larger, darker gray, and filled with sharp teeth; its wings were wide and leathery, supported by ribs; its front and hind legs, stretching toward him, each had four large claws; and its long tail ended in a small fin. Probably it weighed less than the river lizard, though it was longer, but in the air with wings spread and mouth agape, it looked huge.

Probably it was attracted by Rockdream's desperation and fear while he struggled with the river lizards; at close range it sensed that he was having bad luck, and swooped down screeching to drive him away from the carcass. This worked. In an instant, Rockdream was behind a tree, and the drakey tearing flesh from the river lizard's back.

Ordinarily, no human hunter would have an opportunity to shoot a preoccupied drakey less than thirty feet away, but this drakey perceived only Rockdream's turbulent fear, and was totally surprised by the arrow which pierced its stomach and flight bladder.

Surprised, but not immediately killed, and its wrenching pain gave power to rage. It jumped toward Rockdream, who sidestepped to use the tree for a shield. But it landed with a stumble, and vomited chunks of river lizard meat mixed with its own blood. It lay on its side, trying to grip the arrow's fins with its front claws, and managed to pull it out several inches, but this increased the bleeding and it vomited again.

The drakey thrashed around, then lay still, with its eyes wide open. Rockdream watched until he was certain it was dead; but though its eyes did not blink and it did not seem to be breathing, when he came close enough, the drakey whipped its neck around to bite him, and when he jumped back, the drakey jumped onto him.

If Rockdream had not been large and strong even at sixteen winters, the drakey would have killed him; but somehow he managed to grab its scaly neck just below the head with both hands, and squeezed with all his strength. The drakey tried to twist free, but Rockdream fell forward suddenly and his weight broke its neck. It was dead.

Rockdream picked up his crossbow and propped it against the tree, and stooped to pick up the carcass and balance it on his shoulder so it would not drag on the ground, then retrieved his crossbow and set off for Fire Island. It was a heavy, awkward load to carry so far, and when he finally reached camp and kindled the fire, it was twilight and the moon was rising high.

From his pack he took a knife and began skinning and butchering the drakey. He had deliberately not taken any knife along on his hunt, lest he use it as a weapon and break the rules of his test. He certainly would have used it when the drakey jumped on him; anyone would have done so.

He cut the meat into steaks and roasted these on a stick, then made a frame of sticks to stretch the wing leather. The flight bladder, pierced by an arrow, probably held no gas, but to be safe Rockdream cut it away from the rest of the entrails before throwing them on the fire, because the flight gas of drakeys and dragons burns explosively.

Finally he ate his meal. He had tasted drakey meat once before, but that had been salted, not fresh, and this had a strong flavor that seemed disagreeable at first; but after a few bites, he decided he liked it. He did not like the aftertaste which came when he ate a dried apple.

"I am Rockdream the Warrior," he said, facing the fire. "I thank the goddess Wind and her sister Lake, and any others of the Holy Family who may have helped me."

But even while he said this prayer, he wondered whether it meant anything, whether he might not have won this struggle by his own strength and wits. Perhaps Salmon was right about the Church, after all. But then Rockdream shuddered with fear, remembering the legend of Lovering, the warrior long before who became a king with the help of the gods, and what happened to him when he became so proud of his own gifts that he forgot they were gifts.

"Please forgive me if I think blasphemy," Rockdream said. "I am very tired." He unrolled his woolen bedding and went to sleep.

7.

The sun was already high when he woke, feeling every scratch and sore muscle from his struggles the day before. He shook his head to clear the cobwebs from his mind, and walked down to the river to fill his water pouch. Even after drinking, his mouth felt like it was stuffed with cotton. He did not feel like eating any more drakey meat just then, and instead chewed some dried apples, hard cheese, and some of the waybread Birdwade had baked for him.

This made him feel more like himself, and soon he was preparing a tanning grease for the wing leather from the drakey's brain, and smoking the meat to preserve it. All the while he watched the river for boats, but none came that day. He ate some of the smoked meat for his other two meals, and found it more to his liking. Perhaps his meal the night before had been undercooked.

That night the moon was perfectly round; it was nearly overhead when Rockdream was wakened by a long loud screech, followed by some grunts, splashes, and thumps, which seemed to be coming from the side of Fire Island away from the river. After what seemed a long time of quiet, the frogs began chirping again, and Rockdream drifted back to an uneasy sleep.

In the morning, the first thing he did was check the hummock for signs; he found fresh marks of swamp pigs, and farther away, prints of a large cat, probably a leopard, though perhaps a fangtooth. He pressed his lips together and shook his head, and offered a prayer to Wind the Hunter, thanking her for turning the leopard away from his camp.

It was midafternoon when a fishing boat came by; Rockdream yelled, waved his jacket, and shouted, "Newport warrior bound for Newport!" when the boat tacked close to Fire Island.

"We are hunting turtles, but on our way home!" shouted the captain, a husky-voiced stout woman named Sculpin. She ordered the skiff lowered, and soon Rockdream, his gear, his drakey meat and wing leather were aboard the boat, a short-masted, shallow-draft fishcatcher named the *Happy Gutter*, which might have been built in Wentletrap's time, if not earlier. It stank, not only from the eight clubbed but still living turtles stored in the hold, but from whatever had been caught and gutted there the season before.

The crew consisted of Sculpin's brother, Thrush, who brought

Rockdream aboard with the skiff, and two old men who looked as much like pirates as fishcatchers, who were called Green and Blotch, but Rockdream doubted that these were their real names.

"We want to get four more before going back," Captain Sculpin told Rockdream, when the *Happy Gutter* was once more under way.

"If we had this warrior yesterday, we could have caught ten more," Blotch grumbled.

"You keep your mouth shut," said Thrush, then mumbled some more words to the man.

From this exchange, Rockdream guessed that the *Happy Gutter* had been as far east as Goblin Plain, possibly violating some fishing rights agreements, and encountered some goblin warriors. "Has anyone threatened a citizen of Newport?" he asked the captain tactfully.

"We were catching turtles where we always catch turtles and the bloody goblins ran us off," said Captain Sculpin. "They said we took too many turtles, and soon there would be no more turtles left."

"I admit I am not familiar with fishing rights agreements, but if you like, I can discuss this incident with Baron Swordfern—"

"No—please," said Captain Sculpin. "I would rather not make trouble. Even a high priest has trouble telling when a goblin is lying, and if this came to an inquiry, I might be blacklisted at the port."

"If I was someone of power and position, I would offer you one-time amnesty in exchange for information," said Rockdream. "As it is—"

"He is obviously a squire taking his test," Thrush said to the captain. "Look at where we found him and what he has with him."

"Goodman Thrush, I am a warrior, for I have passed my test."

"And likely you believe what they taught you about how warriors behave," said Captain Sculpin. "Well, I have seen justice miss its mark more than once when fishcatchers were concerned. And even laws and treaties that seem completely fair to lords and ambassadors can make it hard for other folks to earn a living."

"Yet without those treaties with Goblin Plain, you might not be alive now to complain," said Rockdream.

"Now listen," said Sculpin, squinting her eyes and deepening her frown wrinkles. "I have fished and hunted turtles in those marshes along the Blue River below Goblin Plain more years than you have been alive, and I know them like you know your own bedroom. Not more than once or twice in all that time have I ever seen goblins hunting or fishing there; but now the Portmaster proclaims that I cannot go there anymore, and now the goblins point spears at Thrush and Blotch, and take the turtle they killed away from them, and force us to leave."

"This is Strong Bull's doing," said Blotch angrily. "Yes, you warriors hear his fine speeches about friendship between different peoples, but what he tells his own people is something else. Every year since he was made high chief, the goblins become more aggressive."

"I have heard this," said Rockdream. "However, Strong Bull is not lord of an organized city, but high chief of many scattered villages. He may have even less control over what his people do than Lord Herring has over where you choose to hunt turtles."

"Bah! It is all one policy," said Sculpin.

"You will get no good from talking to this one," said Green, who had been silent while trimming the sails.

"I am sorry," said Rockdream. "I did not mean to offend, and I do think you have an honest complaint. But I wonder, are there in fact fewer turtles in the river than there used to be?"

Captain Sculpin shrugged. "Maybe fewer than in Lord Wentletrap's time, but still more than enough for everybody."

However, when the *Happy Gutter* reached the marshes on the west side of Spirit Swamp, the region where Rockdream and Lightstraw had killed their turtle three days before, Captain Sculpin and her crew had trouble finding and killing even two more turtles, even though they spent the night there, and searched the reeds again the next morning.

Sculpin made excuses about the weather and turtle migrations, but plainly was more concerned than she pretended to be. When she suggested to the crew that next trip out they try for a big sturgeon, Blotch said there were not many sturgeons left in the Turtle River either, and Thrush suggested that they do day runs for small fish until the salmon started running.

"We can find a sturgeon," said the captain.

"There may be sturgeons in the Blue River, but I am not going up there again," said Thrush.

"We can make our plans tonight at the Tidewater Tavern, and talk to some of the other old river lizards and see what kind of luck they are having this season," said Captain Sculpin.

8.

It was twilight that day when Rockdream finally returned to the castle, after paying Captain Sculpin for the ride, and selling the smoked drakey meat at the Newport Market for more than his traveling expenses both ways. He was disappointed, but not surprised, to learn that his final hearing could not be arranged until late the following afternoon.

"I am probably a warrior," he told Fennel, the younger of his two roommates. "I fulfilled my quest. The rest is formality."

"So how did it go?"

"The drakey nearly killed me. I had to choke it with my bare hands. Do you want the whole story?"

Fennel thought Rockdream was treating him like a child, telling him exaggerations, and tried to scowl and swear like an angry warrior, though he knew his freckles and red eyebrows were against him. "Only if you tell me the bloody truth," he said.

"That is the bloody truth," replied Rockdream, who scowled like a warrior, and knew it. He told Fennel the story of his hunt, and when he got to the drakey's last struggles, he stood up and held his arms outstretched as if seizing its neck, and flexed his muscles. "Then I jumped on top of it and broke its neck!"

"That I believe," said Fennel. "You weigh enough to crush anything."

"It was dying, and played dead to get revenge on me."

"Just like a dragon," said Fennel.

"No," said Rockdream, shaking his head. "I hope I never get close to a dragon."

"But that is what warriors are really for."

"Rockdream, is that you?" asked Salmon's voice from the hallway. It had not taken her long to learn he was back.

"Is she still after you?" Fennel asked with mock disgust.

"You be quiet. This is not your concern," Rockdream said, stepping into the hall and closing the door behind him.

"I would like to sit with you alone for a while," Salmon said, and in the torchlight her large eyes and dark hair looked prettier than ever before.

"Yes," said Rockdream.

"Is something wrong? You are trembling," she said when she took his hand. "Are you afraid I will insist that you—" She smiled at him hesitantly when they turned a corner.

"Oh—," he said, and stopped there, pulled her into his arms, and kissed her lips and tongue.

"Not in the hallway," she said, pulling back. "I am a squire, not a common sailor or something."

Rockdream shuddered, thinking of Lightstraw, and thinking how Salmon had a talent for saying exactly the wrong thing, but Salmon misinterpreted his shudder as excitement and squeezed his hand. "Be patient. We can be in my room in less than a minute, and Swanfeather will be gone for a while."

While they walked through another corridor and up a stairway, Rockdream kept thinking about the promise he had made to Father Starmoss at the purification ceremony, and how he might try to tell Salmon about his uncertainties. "When I was a young boy, I wanted to become a priest," he began, at the door to her room.

"Bloody death, are you going to talk about that, now?" Salmon said with exasperation.

"No, please, listen. Even though my parents, who you know are both warriors at the western end of the North Wall, wanted me to become a warrior, and were very much against me becoming a priest. When I was seven I went to the Church by myself and asked for a first examination. I wanted, and I still want, so much, to feel the spirit of the One, and the Eight, and—"

Salmon pulled him into the room, closed the door, and sat him down beside her on one of the two beds. "What happens between a man and a woman is divine, Rockdream. You know that the goddess of love is one of the Eight." Her face looked serious, much older than her years.

"Yes," he said. "The priests gave me the first examination, and refused me. They said I would need the love of a wife and family. And in the purification ceremony, they gave me a statue of Lake the Lover to stand beside Wind the Hunter. But Salmon—" He was about to tell her that she was probably, or possibly, not the woman he would marry but his heartbeat became fast and heavy, and his throat went dry, and he could not say this, but instead said, "You never said anything about anything being divine before."

"Well, this is divine, and I love you, or at least I am trying to love you. Did you think I am a stranger to the goddesses and gods because I shun the Church? Do you know me at all after all this time?"

Rockdream sighed. "I am not good at talking about this."

"I know, and sometimes I get so frustrated. Do you want to be my lover, or not?"

"I—I think so."

"You think so. That is nice," she said with some sarcasm, but she moved her lips close to his, and he kissed her.

It felt good, but it also felt wrong, if not very wrong. "I promised I would tell you—"

"You promised who?"

"You never let me finish. I do want to make love with you, but I am not certain—whether I want to marry you or not."

"Bloody death, I know that," she said. "But I will never get a decent chance to convince you. The moment I start feeling warm and tingly and slippery down below, you say something that freezes me like ice. Who on this side of the sea made you promise something like that? Was it the freckled brat, or some backstabbing priest?"

Rockdream did not answer.

"I knew it!" said Salmon, looking at him with squinted eyes. "I knew it! What kind of honor is that? What did you tell him about you and me?"

"I just said I was confused, because he heard my thoughts and brought up the subject. I said I was confused, because I enjoy touching you, but I am not sure about anything; and he said I would feel better if I told you this."

"Touching me?" Salmon said, with her voice shrill and cracking. "Did you say that, or touching my breasts?"

"I said nothing about where I touched you, or even who you are."

"That hardly matters. He could see me in your thoughts." She swallowed twice, trying to keep her voice. "Well, I hope you feel better for telling me this," she said, shaking her head and blinking away tears. "I think you had better go."

Rockdream wanted to say he was sorry, but he felt his life separating from Salmon's like the distributaries of the Turtle River Delta, when he opened the door.

"The priests were wrong!" Salmon yelled at him. "You will

never have the love of a wife and family, because no woman will ever want you inside her.''

Rockdream walked slowly toward the stairway, then his own anger rose, and he turned and said coldly, ''You are wrong about that. I have already been inside a woman.''

''When? Who? I do not believe this! Rockdream, how could you? I waited so long. I never wanted anyone but you.'' She was sobbing.

Now he felt confused again, and very sorry, but helpless. ''Nothing I do with you is right,'' he said, and walked down the stairs, feeling each step become slightly easier than the one before. She did not follow him.

2

DANCING IN THE GARDEN

9.

Canticle's Tower, the second south of Eastgate, was little different from the one Rockdream had once lived in with his parents before training in the castle. On the ground floor were the guardpost, the kitchen, and servants' room; on the middle floor, the common room and four bedrooms; and on the top floor, six more bedrooms. Above this were the ramparts and roof, where day and night someone stood guard, watching the sky for dragons.

Fifteen warriors, including Rockdream, lived in this tower. The second youngest was several years his elder, and most were older than Canticle, the lieutenant. Ten of the warriors were married to each other, two to farmers, and one to a fishcatcher, and some of these couples had young children. Aside from Rockdream, only Canticle himself, and a woman of thirty summers named Fledgeling, were single.

Canticle was little interested in having a spouse or family, but rather dedicated himself to perfecting his warrior's skills. In a fencing contest, he could, in moments, disarm anyone in the tower, and he could repeatedly crank up and accurately fire a crossbow almost as fast as some warriors could fire a longbow.

He and Rockdream were standing on the ramparts of the wall after one such brief fencing match, and he said, "As the men and women of the Church are dedicated to saving human souls, so the men and women of the towers and castle should be dedicated to defending human lives and property. Others can raise families; I will defend them.''

Rockdream hesitated before replying, ''The war goddess Fire is but one of the Eight.''

Canticle laughed. ''You have a skill with weapons, and you are strong; you killed the drakey with your bare hands. With practice and dedication, you could become one of Newport's best, with a tower of your own.''

''The rewards of ambition are less than the rewards of a balanced life,'' Rockdream said.

''You can quote proverbs, but do you truly understand them?'' asked Canticle.

Rockdream licked his lips. ''Where can your own ambitions take you now? You are a tower lieutenant already, and Lord Herring has five children. He will not make you a baron, or give you a larger command.''

Canticle snorted, pulling his beard. ''Baron or baroness means no more than son or daughter of Lord Herring; it is no title of merit. Barons Oakspear and Swordfern are able warriors, and each in command of a wall; Baron Pelican and Baroness Lupine are competent warriors, but depend heavily on their lieutenants; and Baron Drill is no warrior at all, and has no command. I can advance in responsibility, trust, and power; as can you. Newport needs more warriors with ambition.''

''Ambitious warriors strive with each other for power.''

''Ambition may be tempered by responsibility, and by love for those you protect.''

''That seems true,'' admitted Rockdream.

''You have been here for more than a month, and it is time you stood the night dragonwatch. Tomorrow night the moon will rise bright not too many hours after dusk.''

''I would be honored,'' said Rockdream.

This was the hardest and most important of all guard duties, standing on the ramparts, watching the night sky for any movement that might mean an approaching dragon. Only twice in the seventy years since Wentletrap and Pip founded Newport had a dragon dared come within sight of its walls. The first, early in Lord Stock's reign, attacked and was shot out of the sky, and her skull was a trophy beside the much larger skull of Mugwort. The second, seven years later, passed over the city twice in the same month, but did not attack, and was not seen again. Under these circumstances, many dragons were imagined when no dragon flew, especially on foggy or stormy nights; but it was better to give a false alarm than to chance being unprepared for an attack.

Rockdream slept early that night, woke while it was still dark, and went to bed again before noon, to prepare for his duty. He stood watch for three nights in a row.

The first night began clear and starry, and warm, for this day was the first day of summer, the 80th of the year, and less than two weeks before the solstice. To the west and northwest, he looked over the blocks of brick homes with flickering windows and smoke from cookfires curling out their chimneys. To the east and southeast, outside the walls, were some few homes of timber and thatch, but mostly open farmland, fields and orchards. To the south was the river, and the flatland of the delta.

The stars were bright, but brightest was the double twilight planet, Lake and her companion Cloud, named after the goddess of love and the god of sorcery. Rockdream considered making a wish, and considered what he really wanted. Perhaps no more than to perform his duties well this night; but perhaps to meet the small thin woman with curly dark hair, who was seen as his wife by the priest at the purification ceremony.

Every few minutes he methodically scanned the sky. At first the only flying things he saw were bats, small and close, chasing moths. Later he saw an owl flying over a nearby field, hunting mice or rabbits.

The moon rose, at first a streak of light on the crest of the Foggy Mountains south of the river, and moments later a broad gibbous; and now the land was touched with silver light and deep shadow. He could see an offshore fogbank over the ocean creeping toward land, and also thin twists of fog beginning to congeal over the river. Lake and Cloud sank below the horizon, and the stars seemed dimmer.

Sometime after the Church's midnight bells, when the moon was near its highest over the delta, Rockdream saw a winged shape flying high. Soon it showed a blunt tail, which marked it as a large bird, eagle or condor. A dragon of the same apparent size would be much higher, and would seem to be moving much more slowly. He saw another, similar bird, or perhaps the same one returning, perhaps an hour later.

The fog spread and thickened over the delta, and joined with the sea's fog, which now foamed over the shorecliffs. In the bright moonlight it looked white and magical, but soon it smothered the castle and quickly spread over the city. Rockdream rang the lesser gong, for it was the rule for at least two warriors to stand guard during fog or storm; and soon an older man named Margin joined him on the rampart, just when dark nothingness swallowed the sky.

"This is a thick one, but dawn comes soon," he said, and soon indeed the fog turned a rich blue which brightened to gray, and the morning guard replaced Rockdream, who ate breakfast with the others in the common room before going to bed.

His second night was much like the first, except that the fog moved in much earlier, and he spent much of the night standing beside Margin.

"What good are we doing if we cannot even see fifty feet away?" Rockdream asked when the fog was particularly thick.

"The fog may thin for a moment somewhere, and somebody from one of the towers may see something, if there is anything to see; and also we do have ears. Anything that gives us even a slightly better chance of not being surprised is worth doing. That is what they say now, anyway. When I was your age, we were less vigilant, but that was before the dragon Riversong destroyed Moonport."

"On a night like this, that is frightening to contemplate."

"Sudden fear can be another clue, or would be if we both felt it," said Margin. "Some dragons put despair in your heart just before they swoop to kill. Lord Stock's female tried to do that. But those who had their sense of duty shot at her anyway, even though they were certain they would miss, and she went down. You have seen her skull. I was just a boy then, but my father was one of those who shot her."

"Yes, you strengthen my heart," said Rockdream.

The night passed without incident; and on Rockdream's third night the sky was clear except for a few high clouds, and he stood dragonwatch alone the full night.

10.

At midmorning on the day of the summer solstice, Rockdream walked into Birdwade's parents' bakery, for the first time in several weeks.

"Oh, look who is here! Hello, stranger!" said Birdwade's mother, Orchid.

"It has not been so long," said Rockdream.

"For the young man who used to come most every day for pastries, it has been long. Do not tell me that the cook of Canticle's Tower is better than the cooks of the Castle."

"Indeed she is, but do not spread word of it," Rockdream said in a low voice.

Orchid smiled. "Well, what would you like today?"

"Mother, is that Rockdream?" called a voice from the kitchen. "Ask him to wait a minute, would you?"

"Now do not be neglecting your work for gossip with your friends," said Orchid, but she winked at Rockdream.

"Everything smells so good in here, I cannot make up my mind," he said.

Birdwade came out, sweaty and disheveled, but smiling. "The loaves are in the oven."

"At least clean yourself up first," said Orchid. "Rockdream has not even made his order yet, and looks to be in no great hurry."

"I will wait," he said.

"The butter cookies are very good today," Birdwade said before returning to the kitchen. When she came back out, her face was clean, her hair brushed, and Rockdream was eating a butter cookie. "My husband churned the butter himself; it is especially rich," she said.

"It is good to see you again," said Rockdream.

"And even better to taste my cooking, I guess," she said smiling. "Which dance are you going to tonight? I hope Canticle does not expect you to stand guard or something."

"I was thinking of going to the Rose Garden, which is nearest the tower."

"So that if you meet someone interesting, she will likely live in your part of the city?" Birdwade asked, with a wink like her mother's.

Someone came into the bakery, wearing a plain brown dress, and asked Orchid whether Birdwade was there.

"Oh, Coral!" Birdwade said laughing. "My back was turned."

Coral was a little more than five feet tall, with curly brown hair lighter than Birdwade's, and amber-colored eyes, and she looked at first like a twelve-year-old girl. "I brought the ginger roots you asked for," she said, and reached into a large, slightly tattered, leather pouch. When she sat down at the table,

Rockdream could see that her brown dress was worn thin, and also she had no shoes or sandals but wrapped her feet in rags. He guessed that she was a servant, making delivery for a merchant or an unusually wealthy farmer.

Birdwade took one of the roots and sniffed it, then broke off a tiny piece and tasted it. "Oh, these are excellent," she said, then said to Rockdream, "We will be having some very fine gingerbread soon, well worth crossing the city to sample."

He said to Coral, awkwardly, "My name is Rockdream."

"Oh, I am sorry," Birdwade said, looking from one friend to the other. "I was so excited about the ginger, I did not think to introduce you; but now you know each other's names."

Coral smiled shyly but said nothing.

"Have I seen you before?" Rockdream asked.

She then looked directly into his eyes, with no trace of shyness or fear, and now she seemed to be a grown woman, and a quite beautiful one, and certainly no one's servant. "Yes," she said quietly. "You have seen me before."

Neither Rockdream nor Birdwade could think of anything to say.

Coral laughed softly. "Is it so very odd to have a question answered? Please continue the conversation. Your next question might be 'Can I see you again?' or it might be something quite different."

"Can I see you again?" asked Rockdream.

"This is the solstice; and tonight we could dance," said Coral.

"How about the Rose Garden?"

"Wonderful!" Coral said with a suddenly animated voice. "That is my favorite! But for now, I do have another errand to run; so Birdwade, if we could weigh these—"

"Yes," she said, and they both got up and walked to the counter, weighed the roots, and Birdwade passed Coral some copper pennies. Orchid seemed to give them no notice whatsoever, which Rockdream thought was odd, and most unlike her. Then Coral gave Birdwade a little bow and left the shop, and Birdwade sat back down with Rockdream.

"I know this is not my concern, but I never thought you would be interested in the likes of Coral," she said.

"I do not know that I am," said Rockdream.

"No? Well, she certainly got interested in *you* quite suddenly, which is just as surprising. You may have seen her before, but I know one thing; it was not in the Church. Do you want to have the same arguments you had with Salmon all over again?"

Rockdream sighed. "I think all I want right now is to have a good time dancing tonight."

Birdwade smiled and said, "You will."

11.

The Rose Garden was one of the four great gardens of Newport. The original city built by Lord Wentletrap had two such gardens, the Rhododendron Garden and the Wisteria Garden, plus the smaller oval of Castle Park; and when the city was enlarged during Lord Stock's reign, two new gardens were set aside, the Rose Garden and the Lilac Garden.

Near the center of the Rose Garden was a marble fountain with a large spray that filled a deep, very clear pool, in which swam several big ornamental goldfish. Surrounding this was a grove of rose trees planted by Lady Blackberry, which were now grown twenty or thirty feet high, and bore many red roses as large as small plates, and of marvelous fragrance.

There were also eight circles of lawn surrounded by cherry trees or flowering hedges, and in five of these were marble statues of members of the Holy Family, by Spiral the Sculptor, who tragically died before she could complete the set. So perfect was her work that Lord Stock and Lady Blackberry refused to even consider hiring another sculptor to carve the other three figures.

The summer solstice celebrations began in each park about an hour before sunset, when musicians began playing their flutes and lyres, harps and viols, and others followed them into the parks, and began dancing, in couples, groups, or by themselves, to delicate improvisations, traditional tunes, and new compositions.

When Rockdream came to the Rose Garden, it was almost dusk, and hundreds of people were dancing. Soon he was dancing too, as part of a group figure around Spiral's statue of Thunder the King, to the music of two lyres, a harp, and a viol. During this dance the western sky reddened, and other people began hanging glowing lanterns in the rose and cherry trees.

Fledgeling from the tower joined that dance, and afterwards

Rockdream danced two songs with her, one with the same ensemble, and one following a wandering flutist on a path toward the fountain. She thanked him for dancing with her, then joined a circle dance around the fountain. He began wandering from place to place, looking for Coral.

Yes, he had to admit, she was on his mind. But he did not encounter her right away, and in fact it was much later, when he was dancing an interweaving double circle to a chorus of flutes, near the statue of Cloud the Wizard, when he first saw her, in the women's circle, moving toward him. When it was her turn to grasp his hand and be his partner, she twirled herself completely out of the circles, and he followed her, holding her hands and twirling round and round, while the flutes played a lively counterpoint.

The music stopped; and she was standing on tiptoes in his arms, looking up at him. She felt airy, light, ethereal, more like a bird than a woman.

A harpist joined the flutists, who played softer to blend with her strings. If Coral was dancing like a bird, Rockdream was moving like one of the great cats, heavy-footed for certain, because he was a large, solid man, but with a grace of his own.

"A cat and a bird," Coral said when the music stopped.

"You put the words to it well," said Rockdream.

"We can talk later. For now, let us dance."

And so they did, for so many dances that Rockdream lost count, until long after the Church's midnight bells, which no one in the Rose Garden heard over the music.

"A very magic night," Coral said, when there were noticeably fewer musicians and dancers in the park. "But even birds must rest at times. Come sit and talk with me?"

"I would love to," said Rockdream.

She chose a spot under one of the rose trees, and after feeling the trunk for thorns, leaned back against it. Rockdream sat beside her, and she took his hand and began caressing the fingers. She was sweaty, but she also smelled of perfume, which might be odd for one apparently so poor, but Rockdream did not think of this.

"Who are you?" Coral asked him. "I think I know who you really are well enough, but, where do you live? What do you do?"

"I live in Canticle's Tower, and I am a warrior."

She squeezed his hand tight, and for an instant her whole body tensed.

"Are you cold?" asked Rockdream, putting his arm around her back, and she turned her head to press her lips against his, and moved so that she sat on his lap, with her hands under his hair, caressing the back of his neck, while their lips and tongues melted together.

"Dear one, this may not be easy," she said, stroking his lightly bearded cheeks, then reaching back with one hand to wipe the tears from her eyes.

"What is wrong?" he asked.

She broke into sobbing, then looked into his eyes and said, "What is wrong is that we belong together, and yet I fear we cannot be together."

Rockdream looked into her eyes, as well as he could see her by the light of distant lanterns, and hesitantly said, "I think—I was told I will—I will marry you, by a priest who read my future."

Coral shuddered. "This is too much, too soon. A priest read your future, and told you about it? That is very unusual. What did he say?"

"He described you, and said that he saw us both, with a young son, hunting a drakey in Spirit Swamp. He warned me against becoming attracted to someone just because she fit his description, but—you also seem to be very attracted to me."

"Of course I am. Our spirits are close friends. And that vision seems possible to me. But did he say anything more that you remember?"

Rockdream paused in thought. "While he was in trance—I do not remember clearly but—he told me to always remember the goddess of love, that she was the most powerful—I have never heard a priest say that before."

"It may be that she is most powerful for you. Come, let us have a look at her," Coral said, springing to her feet and taking Rockdream's hand.

He walked with her a few steps, but then said, "That is one of the statues which were never made."

"The statue may not exist, but the lawn is dedicated to her," Coral said, and they walked to that place. There, only one musician was still playing her lyre, and only three couples were dancing. "Shall we dance one last dance before we continue?" Coral asked, and Rockdream took her hand and they did a reflection dance, in which each person's movements mirrored and slightly changed the other's. When the music stopped, they were standing in each other's arms, near a cherry tree at the edge of the circle.

"Your priest gives me hope," Coral said. "Was there anything else he said about his vision?"

Rockdream sighed. "It seemed important enough to him that he called in a midpriest, but the midpriest said nothing at all. Oh yes—the priest did say that he saw farther into my future than he could usually see."

"Which would be why he called the midpriest, I guess," said Coral.

"He said one thing that puzzled me, I remember now. 'There is light beyond the darkness.' "

"I wonder what that means. It sounds hopeful."

"I am no good at guessing riddles," said Rockdream.

"This one may be important to both of us, for if we do come together, we may watch his prophecy coming true."

"I hardly know you, but already I feel something like love," said Rockdream. "I think I would like to—come together with you."

Coral sighed. "I do not doubt you. My own heart is pleading with me to give voice to my love for you, but—" She reached up to wipe tears from her eyes.

Rockdream stroked her curly hair. "But what?" he asked gently. "You can tell me."

Coral kissed him, and her fear moved through calmness to excitement, and she pressed herself close to him. "I can tell you," she said at last, and took a deep breath. "You are a warrior, and I am a witch."

"Oh," Rockdream said, and nothing more for several awkward moments, but continued to hold her close.

Coral said, "When Pip the Elf became Wentletrap's lover, she said that she would always be a riddle to him, because they were so different. The same is true of us. Do not try to hide how shocked you are. And yes, I know you love me, also."

"You hear my thoughts."

"At this moment, you are very open to me," she said softly. "I know you very well, in some ways. We were married, long ago, when we were both other people, and maybe more than once. I never thought I would marry in this life. I thought my mother betrayed the way of being a witch by marrying my father, a farmer. Most witches never marry, but mate whoever they choose, whenever they choose. That is what I have done—but no more. Now I understand. I remember now, what a true love is.''

"Now it is my turn to say this is too much, too soon," said Rockdream. "I wanted to be a priest when I was younger, and—''

"You heard all the stories about Bracken the Wizard, and Auroch the Witch, and others of the same sort. That was a long time ago, and besides, they were dragonbound.''

"Exactly. Which is why I—''

Coral sighed with exasperation. "Everyone who is dragonbound is called wizard or witch, which is unfair to those of us who develop our art in honorable ways. You, you are so honorable who stand on the walls watching for a dragon which may come once in forty years; but I, I who just this day may have saved a baby's life, am an exile in my own city, forbidden to live inside the walls, forbidden to even set foot in your castle. And I am no more likely to chant the spell that calls a dragonling out of the sea than any priestess, or even you yourself.''

"Coral, can you give me just a few minutes more to sort out my thoughts?''

"I am sorry," she said. "Of course. I am too sensitive.''

The thought came to Rockdream that Salmon had never allowed him time to consider a response carefully, nor did most of his friends.

"Your work is very important to you," he said.

"Yes.''

"And mine is important to me. I nearly died to become a warrior. The drakey that was my warrior's test pretended to be dead, and jumped on me when my arrows were spent, and I had to kill it by breaking its neck with my bare hands.''

Coral shuddered. "I have been close to live drakeys. Your deed impresses me.''

"I have served in Canticle's Tower for only a month and a half, but already I have stood dragonwatch at night, even on foggy nights.''

"I did not mean to scorn your duties," Coral said hastily.

"Canticle thinks I might someday command a tower of my own, where—we could not live together, but I do not think I want to be a tower lieutenant. My work is important to me, but it is not my whole life. But I must live in the tower for at least a year, to learn all that I must, and afterwards, while I am on duty.''

"Rockdream, I love you," said Coral, and this time she kissed him without tears. "You can come see me sometimes, can you not, for a whole night or a whole day? We can talk about everything, and you can tell me your drakey story and I will tell you mine. And we can make the most wonderful love—"

"We can keep this sort of secret for a while, can we not?"

"No one can keep secrets better than a witch," she whispered, and giggled. "Come home with me?"

Rockdream hesitated. "If the Eastgate guard sees us walk out together at this hour, it will not be much of a secret."

"Well, would you rather climb up to the ramparts of the wall and let yourself down with a rope? Or else go to the harbor and swim up the river? I think if anyone by chance saw you doing something absurd trying to be secretive, they would wonder and talk a lot more. Besides, how many people saw us dance together all night? This is a moment of passion. We can be secretive later."

Rockdream laughed, and walked hand-in-hand with her out of the park and through the nearly deserted streets.

12.

The main bars of Eastgate were lowered, but the narrow gate was open, and brightly lit with lanterns. A guard turned to face them when she heard footsteps. "By what code will I know your return?" she asked.

"Birdwade bakes better butter cookies," Coral said. "Not that either of us is likely to return before dawn."

The guard laughed and said, "Coral's codes cannot be quoted quickly. Good night to you also, master merchant."

Rockdream bowed hesitantly, and walked with Coral into the starlit darkness. "Bloody death, I know that woman. Why did she take me for a merchant?"

"You look wealthy, you were not striding like a warrior, and I tried weaving a glimmer into my tongue-twisting gate code, and it worked!"

"A glimmer, like the one Pip the Elf used to make herself appear human?"

"People see what they expect to see, more often than what truly is. You thought I was a servant, for example."

Looming over them now were apples and pear trees planted not long after the city's founding, and beyond these were fenced fields of grain, and open grazing land. They turned off the road onto a cart-trail which Coral called Apple Road, where there were many orchards. The trail moved east through more open fields, where stars shown brilliant in a clear, moonless sky.

"Look at the Sky River. Is it not beautiful?" Coral said. "The elves say that it is many stars, too faint and far away to see."

"It does look like that," Rockdream said.

A meteor streaked across the Sky River, like a spark thrown from a fire. "They also say that meteors are hot rocks in the sky, but this is harder to believe."

"Who even knows for certain what stars are?"

"Other suns, like our own, but farther away."

"And each a Father Sky, with his own Holy Family?" asked Rockdream.

"The sun and moving stars are just named after the Holy Family," said Coral. "Other people have other names for them."

"But look," Rockdream said, "there is Fire, the war goddess, red and bright toward the south. Can you not feel her strength, her very being, when you look at that star?"

"Yes, her being is there, but also in statues made of her, and in the swordsmith's forge, the dragon's breath, and other things that are named Fire, and other things that are not named Fire. But that moving star is a world, a world like this one. Or maybe it is not like this one."

"I have never heard such things from any storyteller."

"I read it in a book called *Wisdom of the Elves,* by Hornbeam the Wizard, who talked to Pip extensively and wrote down many things that she never said to anyone else. There is a copy in the Church, or should be, but I do not think many people know that. I read one of the other two copies. It tells all about how to make a glimmer, how to do dreamsendings, how to remember previous lives. My mother does not think witches should do anything but heal, but I think—"

"Yes?"

"I think sorcery is like a weapon, and you can do many things with it. You could use your crossbow against a dragon, but you could also use it to hunt, or to guard. Or you could use it to steal or kill, which of course you would not do. Me, I could use sorcery to heal sickness, but I could also use it to send messages or see things. Or I could use it to make people sick or frightened, or summon dragonlings. But I would not be a black witch any more than you would be a bandit, because I have honor. Honor is important to people who work with dangerous tools. We are very much alike.''

"Awhile ago, you said we were very different."

"That is also true. You are big and I am small; you are a man and I am a woman; you wear silk and I—"

"I would rather think about the similarities," interrupted Rockdream.

"Maybe we are turning the differences into similarities," said Coral.

They followed the cart-trail through another orchard to a small forest, where a foot trail led to a cottage, dark and quiet, except for the mewing of a housecat.

"Oh, Finite!" said Coral, stooping to pet something unseen. "How are the mice this shortest of nights?"

She held aside a piece of coarse cloth that served for a door and guided Rockdream inside. All he could see at first was the dying embers of a cookfire in the hearth, but then she fumbled for a candle, and touched the wick to a glowing coal to light it.

The room was lined with shelves and cupboards filled with boxes and jars of every description, and even a number of books. Such wealth as Coral's parents had was here, and not in the cottage itself, which was made of rough boards, with a dirt floor, and the hearth had no chimney, just a vent in the roof.

"We must be quiet. My parents are asleep,'' she whispered, and pulled aside the curtain which divided the cottage, motioning him to come with her. Finite, an undersized female black cat, came also.

Rockdream was relieved to see that a second curtain divided the back of the cottage into two private rooms. On one of Coral's two outer walls were more shelves with boxes and jars, and also folded clothes and blankets. Against the other wall was the bed, just a thick layer of straw covered with blankets, but it looked comfortable enough.

Coral dribbled wax onto a flat stone and stuck the candle there, then sat on the bed and pulled the rags off her feet. Rockdream took off his shoes and sat beside her. She turned, so that her legs were on the bed, and hugged him, rocking slowly from side to side, in rhythm with her breath; and without thinking about it, he found himself breathing the same rhythm. They turned their heads to kiss, slowly and gently, and continued swaying together for timeless time.

"You ready to blow out the candle?" she whispered, reaching to turn down the cover, and moving Finite out of the way.

In the sudden blackness he heard the cat purring, and after a moment of rustling, Coral was back in his arms, and his first caress told him she was naked, smooth and warm. He fumbled with the fastenings of his silk shirt and trousers, and pulled off his underclothes. Her small hand stroked his skin. He breathed the scent of her neck and breasts while he kissed, and when he entered, the movement was as slow and soft as the breathing, the swaying.

"I love you," he said, and his words deepened the joy.

"And I love you," she replied. "Ah. Ooh! Do that again, yes."

He did, and found a thought, not of Salmon or Lightstraw, but of the drakey. The depth of meaning of this was the same, but this was life, not death; love, not struggle; and for a moment it seemed he was sliding into the goddess of love herself. Lake, dearest Lake, last daughter, indeed she was strongest.

Coral's body convulsed suddenly, then she covered his face and mouth with kisses, and he streamed fluid. "I do not know what you were thinking just now, but it was truly beautiful," she whispered.

He moved slowly to a gentle stop. "The goddess is here."

"Yes, dear love, we will sleep in her arms tonight. May we walk together in our dreams."

They kissed once more, and then the sound of Finite, purring at the foot of the bed, took them both to sleep.

3

THE CHOICE

13.

All that summer, fall, and winter, Rockdream lived a double
life, dividing his time between his duties in the tower and his
developing love with Coral at her parents' cottage.

Her father, Cliffbrake the Farmer, was much older than her
mother, and had a back injury that stopped him from doing any
heavy work, but if he could no longer grow wheat or raise
cattle, he was skilled at growing difficult herbs and spices, and
spent most of each day in his garden.

Her mother, Moonwort the Witch, was often in the house,
cooking either a delicious stew or a pungent preparation, and
sometimes she would order everyone out of the house, so that
she could chant with the wholeness of herself. Equally often
she was gone, gathering wild herbs or seeing a patient in the
city.

Coral herself always had something new and interesting to
talk about each time Rockdream came to see her, usually
nothing directly connected with her work, but rather some
oddity of the forest that she had seen or heard about, such as
the mating habits of snails or lizards, or which kinds of trees
grow back from stumps, or how to tell a bluffersnake from a
viper. In this, she was testing her lover to learn his prejudices,
but he did not know this at the time.

In the tower, Rockdream stood dragonwatch and doorguard
more often than anyone else, and worked hard to improve his

swordplay and archery. Canticle assumed first that this meant Rockdream was taking to heart his advice about ambition, but it was not so.

"I have no desire to be a tower lieutenant," Rockdream said. "I want to be a good warrior, nothing more."

"Bah! You are already that," Canticle said. "But your example is inspiring some of the others to better work, and that is the heart of leadership."

"I am not a leader," said Rockdream.

"You think you are not good enough, or else you fear it will be too burdensome."

Rockdream did not respond. No matter what he said, Canticle would argue.

"That man does not respect who I am," Rockdream told Coral a few days later at her cottage.

"Does he talk the same way to the others?" she asked.

"I—I do not know. He only talks that way when we are alone."

"There must be someone else in the tower you can talk to about this," Coral said.

In Rockdream's silence, Moonwort, who was slicing potatoes for the stew, said, "You warriors are trained to fear nothing but disapproval. That is the enemy you now fear to fight. You keep your lover secret to keep your position in the tower, but lose your position in the tower because you do not trust anyone there."

Rockdream stood up and walked outside.

"Mother!"

"He is your lover."

Coral glared at her mother, and ran outside after him. "Can I walk with you?" she asked.

He took her offered hand, and they walked through the autumn woods. Each breeze carried away more yellow maple and brown oak leaves, but many of the trees were evergreen, the laurel and winter oak, the fir and cedar. On the ground, mushrooms were sprouting, quickened by the season's first heavy rains.

"They are right," Rockdream said. "I would make a good tower lieutenant, and keeping myself distant from the other warriors is hurting me."

"Perhaps much less than other choices might hurt," Coral

said. "Please do not let your heart be changed now. It would be a very hard hurt to heal, for both of us."

"I know that."

"Mother does not understand or believe what I know about us; and as for Canticle, the more you tell me about him, the less I like him. What does he care, whether you become a tower lieutenant or not? It is no concern of his, none at all, yet he pressures you. He is keeping harder secrets than yours, and his plans feel twisted and ugly to me, though I cannot yet sense what they are."

"Can you hear his thoughts, any of his thoughts, at this distance?" Rockdream asked with disbelief.

"Through the rope he has attached to you," Coral said, and touched Rockdream's lower back. "Your skin is usually colder there where it touches you."

"Are you saying—that Canticle is a wizard, trying to control me with this spell?"

Coral laughed. "No, not at all. I mean yes, he is trying to control you, but he is not a wizard. I thought I told you about ropes."

"You never talk about spells."

"True, but I thought I did tell you about ropes. I guess they are spells of a sort, but they are a magic which everyone does, without being aware of doing it. Everyone is attached to the people who are important to them by ropes, which I can see with my trance-eye. You and I have a bright strong rope connecting our hearts, and, um, other parts of our bodies also."

Now they came to the edge of the forest, and at the end of Apple Road, where a rolling pasture with groups of cattle and sheep stretched toward the foothills of the Foggy Mountains.

"I might be able to do something about Canticle's rope," Coral said. "Would you like me to try?"

"I do not want to be attached to him at all."

"That is impossible, while he is your lieutenant, but maybe the rope can be changed. As it is, this rope is dishonorable."

"What do we do?"

"Pick a place where you can sit comfortably for a while," she said, and Rockdream sat on a flat, dry rock, facing the sun, which was already low in the southwest. She told him to close his eyes, and kneeled beside him, her left hand on his back, her right on his stomach.

"Now you can feel the warmth of the sun, and perhaps you can imagine this light swirling all around you, making an egg of golden light. You can pretend this egg of sunlight is a shield, protecting you."

"From what?" Rockdream asked.

"From anything going wrong with my magic."

"But—"

"What you can imagine is real, in a way. There, now I have told you something about spells. Feel the egg of sunlight as a shield while I chant, and do not speak again unless I ask you to."

Coral's hands were still on his back and stomach, and they were becoming warmer, so warm that he could feel the heat through his leather tunic. When he stopped pondering how what he imagined could be real, and started imagining the egg of sunlight, he did feel different, more relaxed.

Coral was swaying and chanting softly, words about her roots being deep in the Nameless Mother, over and over. Her voice became louder, then fell to a whisper.

She spoke. "Canticle, if Rockdream is a worthy warrior, you must respect his freedom of choice."

After a long silence, she said, "What duty do you believe Rockdream must do?"

She paused again, as if waiting for an answer. "Then you must tell Rockdream everything about it, so that he can make his choice."

She began chanting again, and after a while touched Rockdream's forehead lightly, then the top of his head. "You can open your eyes now," she said, and kissed him. "How do you feel?"

"Better, I guess, but also—suspicious? What did you do?"

"I talked to Canticle's spirit. His waking mind will not be aware of our conversation, but his spirit will influence him to change his connection to you. The rope is much smaller and brighter than it was, and has moved to your right side."

"Coral, you cast a spell on him!"

"I only talked to him!" Coral protested. "I tried to reason with him. He did not like or trust me, but I appealed to his highest good. I did nothing to compel him to obey— You are not listening to me! I tried to help you and now you condemn me for something I did not do.

"And what have you said to my spirit when I was unaware?"

Coral's face was frozen between anger and grief, and she began to cry, wondering how the man she loved could suddenly become a stranger. "Only that I love you, and I am so glad for the time we have together, and I wish we could have more, and right now I am saying I wish you understood and respected me."

Rockdream winced. "I—oh, Coral, I am sorry! Please forgive me. You were trying to help me."

She stared at him for a long moment before her face relaxed. "It is hard for me, when someone I try to help or heal thinks dark things about me, when he or she feels real change and does not understand how this could happen. But maybe it is a sign that things will be different when you get back to the tower."

14.

For several months after that, Canticle said nothing more to Rockdream about becoming a tower lieutenant, or about ambition, and the young warrior became more relaxed, more able to speak his mind and heart to his companions in the tower.

It was deep winter, ten days after the solstice and raining hard, and Rockdream was eating a meal, sitting near the warriors Fledgeling and Vein, and the fishcatcher Frogsong, who was Vein's wife, and their son, Hyssop, who was about ten years old.

"Can anyone guess how long this rain will last?" Rockdream asked.

"Oh, I would say until the spring equinox, and maybe a month longer," said Frogsong. "But at least I do not have to go out in it. Is it your turn to stand dragonwatch next?"

"Soon enough," said Rockdream. Actually he was thinking about the long cold walk to Coral's cottage, which lately seemed farther away from the city each time he went there.

"See what you are in for if you become a warrior?" Frogsong asked Hyssop. "Rain and sleet falling on you all night long, while all the fishcatchers are sleeping snugly in their beds."

"But Mom, by the time I grow up, there will not be any fish left in the river."

"Nonsense! Who told you that?"

"Everyone knows it is true," said Hyssop. "And look what happened to the *Happy Gutter*."

"No one knows what happened to the *Happy Gutter*, Hyssop."

"That was the boat which brought me back from my warrior's test," said Rockdream. "Has it disappeared?"

"The goblins sunk it," said Hyssop. "The timbers and bones are rotting in the river."

"How do you know that?" Vein asked his son.

"Everyone knows it. I talk to people at the docks. That captain with the white beard. They all ask when will the warriors do something. When I become a warrior, I will do something."

"This disturbs me," said Rockdream. "The *Happy Gutter* was threatened by goblin warriors for hunting turtles, but they were planning to go back up the Blue River to get a sturgeon. I guess they thought the goblins would not attack if they stayed away from shore."

Frogsong said, "The *Happy Gutter* did not disappear until after Midsummer, which was quite a few trips later. I would not say Captain Sculpin was any friend of mine, but I knew her well enough to know that she fished where she bloody well pleased, treaty or no treaty."

"We should report this," said Fledgeling.

Vein said, "There is no proof that the goblins did attack, and the castle already knows about the threats, and the boat's disappearance."

"The bigger boats, the merchants and passengers, have hired guards," said Frogsong. "Everyone else has been warned not to go up the Blue River."

"Because the goblins sank the *Happy Gutter*," said Hyssop.

"We do not know that for certain, but it is wise to take precautions," said Frogsong.

Some people down the table were talking about the spring equinox tournament, and conversation around Rockdream drifted to that topic.

A few days later, Canticle asked Rockdream into his room for a private talk. "I understand you are concerned about the sinking of the *Happy Gutter*," he said.

"I am disturbed by its disappearance," Rockdream replied, choosing his words carefully.

"You should have told us that you knew who had been threatened."

"I know that now, but it was a matter of honor, and mistakes are often obvious only when it is too late to correct them."

"Hum. Yes," said Canticle. "You did what was right, even if it was wrong. Blood! Strong Bull wants war, and sooner or later he will get it."

"I would guess that he has as much trouble controlling his warriors as we have controlling our fishcatchers," said Rockdream. "Goblin camps often fight each other over hunting or fishing territories, and—"

"You think we should make allowances because goblins are crude and savage?"

"I did not say that."

"Bandits are crude and savage also, but you know what we would do to any bandits who killed four Newport citizens!"

"Goblins are not bandits, and we cannot judge them by human standards," Rockdream protested.

"How many goblins have you actually talked with?" asked Canticle. "None? I am not surprised. I have talked with Strong Bull himself, and in my heart I know he is an enemy. If he had his way, he would slaughter us all, or send us back across the sea."

"What does Lord Herring think of him?"

Canticle snorted. "The only enemies our lord seems able to recognize are those with great ribbed wings who breathe fire. I wonder what he thinks will happen if a dragon ever does destroy Newport. Where will the survivors go? Surely not to the mountains south of the delta, or to Riversong's lair in Moonport, or to Spirit Swamp! And if we ever are forced to conquer Goblin Plain, it would be better for us if Strong Bull thought we were a strong people. But Lord Herring's policy seems to be to let him have whatever he wants."

"No wonder Strong Bull treats you as an enemy, if this is how you are thinking!" said Rockdream.

"I prefer to think that no dragon will ever conquer Newport, but do you see the possible weakness of our position?"

"The best solution to that would be to kill Riversong," Rockdream said, and immediately regretted his words.

"Are you a wild man like Wentletrap, with an elvish witch wife to help your impossible plan succeed?" Canticle asked mockingly.

"No."

"Then, since no one else seems to want to try to kill Riversong either, you must admit it is important for us to impress Goblin Plain with our strength."

Rockdream thought carefully before saying, "I admit only that we have a fishing rights dispute, caused by a shortage of turtles and larger fish. The other things you say feel ugly to me, and I cannot make them my concern."

"Then you may go," Canticle said coldly.

15.

It was raining hard outside Coral's cottage, and the roof leaked in one place over Coral's bed, dripping into a pot hanging between two rafters, with a plunk, plunk, plunk, that kept Rockdream awake. Suddenly Coral was shuddering and crying, clinging close.

"Nightmare?" he whispered.

"Those things you were telling me that Canticle said—I dreamed them," she said in a low voice. "I dreamed he was trying to conquer Goblin Plain, but most of his army were not real warriors, and—it seemed so real—the goblins killed almost everybody. I was there, and I saw your—your body, lying with a host of others, beside the river in an open grassy place."

"It was only a dream," said Rockdream.

"I guess it was unlikely," she said, calming herself. She drifted back to sleep in his arms, and he listened to the plunk, plunk, plunk, for what seemed like hours. But he must have eventually fallen asleep, for he woke up to daylight, Coral's kisses, and the murmur of her parents talking about something in the main room.

"Yes, right now," she whispered, rubbing her body against him. "I need you this morning."

He was dazed from a poor night's sleep, but surrendered gladly to the pleasure, and matched, as well as he could, Coral's eager caresses. But his mind was blurred and wandering, and she suddenly stopped moving, and asked, "Where are you?"

"What do you mean? Here with you, I think."

"I feel disconnected from you," she said.

Rockdream sighed and shook his head slowly. "Must my mind be naked? I did not sleep well because of the dripping, and you woke me up, wanting me, and here I am. What do you want?"

"I think—" Coral said, and hesitated. "I think you should

transfer to another tower, as far away from Canticle as possible, and—"

"Do I have to think about that right now? My mind is filled with rattling stones."

"Please do not raise your voice—"

Rockdream made a mock-angry face at her.

"If you married me, we could live in our own house, where—"

In this moment of irritation, Rockdream was not sure he wanted to live with her. Having to deal with Canticle's pressure was bad enough, but now Coral was pressuring him also.

"You are not listening to me!" she said.

"Can we please talk about this when I am feeling better, or at least when I am wide awake?"

"Oh, I—" Coral hesitated, then lowered her voice. "I am sorry. It was that dream. That man! I do not even know him, and he has a rope attached to me. I do not even know him, and I—I hate him."

"He need not be your concern," said Rockdream.

"I know that, and yet he is, somehow, or I would not have dreamed—" She stopped, and lowered her voice to a whisper. "When a witch startles herself awake from a nightmare, she has to trust her feelings about it, and I feel in the deepest heart of me that you are in real danger, and that the light beyond the darkness in the priest's foretelling will only shine for you if you marry me—" She suddenly flinched, as if he had struck her.

"Coral, what is it?"

She looked with fear into his eyes. "These visions of the future, the priest's and my own, and others that people have told me in whispers, all fit together, but I cannot say aloud what it means, not even to you. Dear Rockdream, can you listen to my thoughts? Please, close your eyes, and see the first thing that you see."

Rockdream closed his eyes, but he did not see, and did not understand.

"Coral!" said Moonwort sharply. "What are you doing in there?"

"What do you think, Mother?" she said sarcastically.

Suddenly her hands were all over Rockdream's body, her hips rocking his penetration back to life. "This is not her concern at all," she whispered.

Without understanding how his mood had changed, Rockdream

wanted to love and love and love this small, beautiful, yes, beautiful woman, whose face was surrounded by waves of brown curls, who understood and loved him better than anyone else possibly could, and who was destined to be his wife. His whole being was with each movement of his hands and lips, and his streaming into her seemed longer than ever before.

"Keep moving, just a bit more," Coral whispered, and he did, and she shuddered with joy. She dressed, and left him lying under the tangle of bedding.

He woke up some time later to the sound of renewed rain dripping into the pot above the bed, and strange medicinal smells, and the low voices of Coral and Moonwort talking.

"He made you so excited that you saw dragons?"

"Mother!"

"You were thinking so loudly that I thought you were casting a spell."

"Certainly not."

"Then what were you doing? Tell me the truth."

Coral dropped her voice, and from the few words that Rockdream could hear, she seemed to be talking about the nightmare, and the foretellings.

"You could be killed for that!" Moonwort whispered.

"Mother, be realistic. I could lose my right to practice witchcraft."

"Why would you want to see such things? Knowing the time and manner of anyone's death is no comfort, but rather an agony. Whether you are right or wrong, you will worry, and the worry will grow in your mind. We are not living in this world for that, but to comfort and heal each other."

"But if I think I see a way through to the light—"

"You think, and you feel, but you do not know," said Moonwort.

"I know enough not to tell anyone but you what I think."

"I appreciate that, but it would be better not to tell even me."

"Mother, I am frightened."

"Of course you are! It is better not to see such things."

They said nothing more about this, but talked about the medicine they were making. Rockdream puzzled what he had heard, and finally decided that Coral had foreseen that Newport would not only be attacked but destroyed by a dragon. Such foretellings were illegal, because the emotions they caused, which a dragon could sense, would encourage a dragon to attack, even as the emotions Rockdream felt while struggling to kill a river lizard encouraged his drakey to attack. But was Coral truly foreseeing, or merely frightened by what Canticle believed? The possibilities circled round and round Rockdream's mind while he dressed.

He was lacing his boots when he heard someone enter the cottage, a young woman who was very upset, to judge from her voice.

"Come, sit by our fire and warm yourself," said Moonwort. "You must be soaked to the skin."

"Phew!" said the woman. "Begging your pardon, good women, but your brew—"

Moonwort cackled, but Coral said, "I am certain that it smells just as bad to me. How may we help you?"

"Are you Coral the Witch? I am a friend of Birdwade the Baker, and she recommended you. My husband, Bloodroot the Sailor, is very ill, and I—" The woman's words were broken by sobbing.

Rockdream was so concerned about Bloodroot that he pulled aside the curtain without thinking, and there, sitting on a stool between Coral and Moonwort, was Salmon.

"Rockdream!" she said. "I—I do not—this is—" She broke into hysterical laughter. "This is too unbelievable! Blood, it feels good to laugh again! Begging your pardon, but I have not laughed in many days, and if you knew what he used to be like— This is funny."

"I suppose so," Rockdream said dryly. "But I would appreciate you keeping this joke a secret."

"Why, because you might get in trouble with the likes of Canticle for being a witch's lover? Listen, get a job as a boat guard. I have been doing this ever since I passed my warrior's test. The pay is good, everyone respects you, and you only work in the summer."

"That sounds like a wonderful idea," said Coral.

Rockdream sighed. "My duty is to serve the people of Newport."

"By doing what other warriors think is important?" asked Salmon. "Rockdream, people are getting killed out there on the river. Anyone who can accurately fire a crossbow can stand dragonwatch, but our merchant boats need guards with good judgment, like you, and what they mostly get is hotheads who are eager to fight goblins. Well, you will do what you will do.''

She sighed, and turned to Coral. ''My husband is very sick. He is bedridden, with a hot fever, and he vomits half the time, and feels a constant ache in his lower back.''

''What does his water look like?'' asked Coral. ''Is it dark?''

''Not especially.''

''How long has he been like this?''

''About five days, and I thought he was getting better, but this morning he was worse.''

Coral asked more questions, and started packing bundles of dried herbs. ''This may take awhile,'' she told Rockdream. ''I probably will not come home tonight, so you may as well go back to the city. I know that we have too many things to talk about to say goodbye, but we must. I am sorry.''

''Just do what you can for Bloodroot.''

''Are you not coming with us?'' Salmon asked.

''If you want me to, I will,'' he said, and the three young humans walked to the city together, and gave their names to the Eastgate guard: Salmon the Warrior, Rockdream the Warrior, and Coral the Witch.

16.

Salmon and Bloodroot lived in an apartment on Turtle Street, not far from the Tidewater Tavern. The stone walls were whitewashed, but on this rainy day it was dark inside, for the windows were small. What Rockdream noticed first was the smell of sweat.

Bloodroot lay on a stuffed feather mattress, covered with blankets and furs. His mother, the warrior Bayberry, sat on a wooden chair beside the bed.

''I brought a witch,'' said Salmon. ''This is Coral, and you probably know Rockdream.''

''Rockdream,'' said Bloodroot in a weak voice.

''Are you all right?'' asked Rockdream.

''Of course not!'' Bloodroot said, and coughed. ''Would I send for a—'' He coughed again.

''Be calm,'' said Coral, moving to take Bayberry's seat. ''I am Coral, and I have come to help you heal.''

''You look so young,'' Bloodroot said with a cracked whisper.

''So do you, much too young to be so weak,'' she replied.

"I need to ask you some questions which may embarrass you, though there is no blame in anything your body does against your will."

"I can control myself," said Bloodroot. "I can use the chamber pot."

"Good," said Coral. "Very good. And is there anything different than usual about—"

"My problem is my stomach. It will not keep anything, and my back hurts, and everything feels cold, and Salmon says my whole body feels hot."

"How about your throat? I notice you have trouble talking."

"It feels tight, as if someone was choking me."

She continued questioning him for some time about his symptoms, then pressed her fingers into various parts of his hand and arm and asked what places were painful. Then she asked Salmon to bring an oil lamp close to the bed, and took out a polished round clear crystal, and looked through it into his eyes.

"This must be painful, and you may not believe that you will recover," she said, and put a subtle emphasis on the words, "believe that you will recover," by saying them more slowly than her usual rhythm of speech. "—but I will make you a special soothing brew." She turned to Salmon and Bayberry. "Hang a pot on the hearth and start some water boiling."

"The priestess gave me several brews and teas, and I could not keep any of them down."

"Did you feel a burning in your stomach?"

"No, but about an hour later—"

"I know something you can do with yourself to stop that. Can you take a deep breath? Good. Now, holding that deep breath, breathe in and out shallowly."

After doing this for a few moments, Bloodroot burped.

"You can breathe normally now," said Coral. "But every time you feel like vomiting, I want you to take a deep breath and breathe the way you just did, until your stomach calms. I am going to make your brew now."

Coral sat down at the table in the main room, and chanted softly while unpacking her herbs. Salmon and Bayberry watched with curiosity while she spread a very small square of cloth on her lap, and sprinkled certain amounts of dried leaves, twisted roots, and slivers of bark from some of the bundles on the table onto the cloth. Salmon noticed that somehow she knew in advance just which bundles the witch would choose, but she said nothing about this intuition at the time.

Coral took out a needle and thread, and stitched the herbs into a small bag, put the bag in a bowl, and ladeled some of the boiling water.

"Why do you not just use a straining cloth?" Salmon asked.

"This is cleaner, and you can get a stronger brew," Coral replied.

In the bedroom, Rockdream was talking to Bloodroot about things they did when they were both squires at the castle.

"I miss those days also," Salmon said, "but now that we are all friends again, these days will be even better." She looked at Coral with suddenly fearful eyes, and silently mouthed, "I hope."

Coral made a silent prayer to Cloud, the god of sorcery, for confidence, and nodded her head yes.

When she judged the brew was strong enough, and not too hot to drink, she brought it to Bloodroot.

"It smells odd," he said.

"It will probably taste even odder. Drink it slowly."

With some difficulty, Bloodroot sat up and sipped the contents of the bowl. "Not as bad as I thought it would be."

It took him several minutes to finish the bowl, then he lay back down, and Coral had him practice the breathing exercise once more. Then she began chanting and moved her hands in patterns several inches above Bloodroot's covers, mostly over his torso and neck. She did this for what seemed like a long time until he fell asleep. Rockdream and Bayberry went back to the hearth, and began to make a stew for dinner, but Salmon stayed and watched the entire ritual.

"That is so amazing, the blue light that comes from your fingers," Salmon whispered. "The priestess did nothing like that."

"You saw the light?" asked Coral.

"Of course I saw it. Why should I not?"

"I do not think Rockdream or Bayberry saw anything of the sort. Most people would not. Do you ever find yourself hearing other people's thoughts?"

"No. Sometimes I can guess what Bloodroot will say before he says it, but that is not the same thing."

Coral nodded slowly. "Yes, it is."

"I could become a witch," said Salmon.

Coral gave her a sudden hard look. "You are a warrior!" she whispered.

"Yes, but I do not work for the city."

"You would not even be able to live in the city."

"That law must be changed," said Salmon. "It is absurd to have to go all the way to the gate and beyond just to find a healer who is competent. It was the Church that made Lord Stock pass the law, because they are jealous of anyone with real power."

Coral sighed. "I should admit that even before that law, most witches and wizards lived outside the walls, because that is where the herbs grow, and because, um, the more sensitive you become, the more privacy you need."

"That would not be true for me, because I love being with other people. As for the herbs, do not farmers live in the city and ride out to their fields? Witches could do the same."

"I think we should appoint you Lord Herring's legal advisor," Coral said, and both women laughed. "But I will have to stay here tonight, and I wonder, could Rockdream stay with me?"

"Of course. I want us all to become friends."

"I would like that very much," said Coral, and she felt for a moment tears swelling in her eyes.

"How is he?" asked Rockdream. "The stew is ready to eat whenever you want it."

"He will be fine," said Coral, "but it may take him awhile. Right now, he is asleep."

They sat at the table and ate the stew, after offering prayers for Bloodroot's recovery. Bayberry then left, and Rockdream and Coral slept together in front of the hearth. Bloodroot slept through the night, and the next day his fever was broken, and he was able to eat small meals.

17.

After a long talk with Salmon and Coral about the possibilities of being a riverboat guard, Rockdream returned to the tower. He spent most of the next day doing target practice with Fledgeling, Vein, and Margin, who were all eager to compete in the spring tournament, still two months away. Rockdream had never before seen old Margin enthusiastic about anything.

The day after that, Canticle returned from a conference at the castle, and apologized to Rockdream for getting angry, and admitted that it might be better to cultivate friendship with the goblins. He had just spoken to one of their other leaders, an older man named Drakey, whose title was High Shaman. Drakey was a perceptive, reasonable, and honorable person in Canticle's opinion, and his influence over Strong Bull was great.

By the time Rockdream next saw Coral, he was not certain he wanted to leave the tower. He had trained for six years to become a Newport warrior, and he could not lightly give this up. Also, if the new conferences restored true peace between Newport and Goblin Plain, boat guards might not be needed.

Coral was most interested about the High Shaman, Drakey, who she said was reputed to be one of the wisest and most powerful wizards east of the sea, but Rockdream only knew that he was someone Canticle had spoken with.

On the third full moon of winter, which was the 334th day of that year, the 194th year of humans east of the sea, a large public meeting was held in Newport Castle's great hall, in which Lord Herring and Redthorn the Portmaster carefully explained to Newport's fishcatchers the terms of the new fishing rights agreement with Goblin Plain, something which had not been done with the previous year's agreement.

Both humans and goblins would be allowed to take turtles and sturgeons from the Blue River in Spirit Swamp, but both peoples would only be allowed to take a limited number of these each year, even in the Turtle River all the way to the sea, which was Newport's territory, and the Blue River all the way to the Silver Mountains, which was Goblin Plain.

There was some grumbling among the fishcatchers that the limits meant that even fewer turtles could be taken, but the seriousness of the turtle shortage was understood by nearly everyone. The limits would be enforced by human warriors at the harbor and the market, and if need be on the river.

Some of the merchants did decide not to hire riverboat guards for the next year's shipping season, but Fairwind, Salmon's employer and one of the city's wealthiest merchants, sent messengers to all his guards, telling them he wished to keep them. In most countries across the sea, all merchant riverboats were guarded, especially those which passed from one country to another, and Fairwind considered this prudent, even if there was complete peace with Goblin Plain, and even though no bandits had attacked a Newport riverboat since the days of Bluebeard the Swamp Fox.

18.

In the last month of winter, a bad storm came to Newport, with high winds and sleet turning to snow. At Canticle's Tower, Margin and Notch stood the night dragonwatch, and afterwards Margin became sick.

"It is backstabbing folly to stand dragonwatch in weather so bad no dragon can fly," he said in his bed to Canticle.

"You should have built a bloody fire on the rampart."

"With what? Oil? It was pouring buckets out there last night."

Rockdream took Margin's place at dragonwatch the next night. He wore wool clothes under his leather tunic and pants, and oiled his leather well to keep dry. It was snowing and windy when he took his post, but Fledgeling, who he relieved, had already built a good fire. By midnight, the snow was piled several inches deep on the rampart, but then it stopped and the sky cleared. The moon had already set, so the stars were brilliant. Rockdream now saw fires atop the city walls near many of the other towers, where other warriors stood dragonwatch. He thought of Coral, who was expecting him, but knew that she would understand. The whole night, he saw nothing flying in the sky, not even an owl.

The next day, Margin had a high fever and a headache, and Canticle sent a messenger to the Church requesting a healer.

"If I die from this, I want it carved on my stone that I died protecting Newport from dragons," Margin told Canticle.

"You are in no danger of dying," said Father Chainfern, the healing priest.

"That was what they told my wife."

The priest looked the old warrior in the eye for a moment, then said, "I understand your bitterness, but it is bad for the spirit. Would you like a purification ceremony?"

"I would like something to stop my bloody head from pounding."

"I am sorry," Chainfern said, and rubbed the sides and back of Margin's head. "Where does it hurt?"

"All over, and my stomach feels uneasy also."

"I will prepare you a brew."

And again Rockdream stood dragonwatch. It was even colder this night, well below freezing, but at least there was no wind, and most of the snow had melted in the afternoon sun. The gibbous moon set about two hours after the midnight bells, leaving the Sky River gleaming pale behind the bright stars.

The next day, when Margin began vomiting Father Chainfern's medicines, Rockdream suggested to Margin that he knew someone who might be able to heal his sickness.

"A wizard?" Margin asked with a cracking voice. "I do not know—" He coughed. "—oh, blood, why not?" He coughed again.

"She helped a friend of mine who had the same sickness," Rockdream said. "If you are interested, I will try to get Canticle's permission for her to enter the tower."

"Yes," Margin said weakly.

To Rockdream's embarrassment, Canticle made this a topic of conversation with Father Chainfern, and to Rockdream's surprise, the priest did not object to the idea, and was even interested in watching this witch at work, to learn what he could, but Rockdream did not think Coral would accept this.

Canticle gave Rockdream use of one of the tower's message horses, which much shortened the time of his trip to Coral's cottage. But only her father, Cliffbrake, was there, and he was not sure when either Coral or Moonwort would be back.

"Many people got sick in the storm," he explained. "That was a bad one, though they say that Rockport and Coveport get worse storms than that several times each winter. Makes you glad to live farther south, does it not? Storms like that make my bones ache. I will give them both your message. Coral may be home tonight, or maybe not."

Rockdream rode back to the tower, explained the situation, and went to sleep. In the middle of the night his dreams were broken by a knock on his bedroom door.

"Who is it?"

The door opened and closed. "Coral," she said. "I am supposed to be under personal guard of one of the warriors tonight, so naturally I chose you." She found him in the dark and kissed him. "Rockdream, he may be a hard one to heal, because he is not sure he truly wants to live. He is bitter about his wife's death, but I hope—" She was caressing Rockdream's hand and forearm. "We can talk about Margin later. Let me get undressed."

"Coral, we cannot do this here."

"Why in the world not? I have to be in here with you, so that you can watch me, and no one else is watching, so let us take advantage of an opportunity. Mmm, you have a soft bed. It swallows me."

Rockdream sat up to look out the window, but it was so dark that he could hardly see the window. "Has the moon set already? Dawn will be coming soon."

"No, no, the midnight bells just rang. It is cloudy."

Rockdream's worries melted into the joy of hands, lips, tongues, and slow wet movements. "I love you so much," he said when they were done, "so very much."

"And I love you, so very, very, very much," she said, and kissed him goodnight.

19.

The spring tournament was held in Newport Castle's outer courtyard, on the first three days of spring, and the beginning of the new year, the 195th year of humans east of the sea. Several thousand people crowded the edge of the courtyard, and perhaps another thousand watched from the ramparts. The judges were the champions from the past four spring tournaments. Canticle was one of the fencing judges.

The first day was mostly fencing events, and the second day mostly archery, which included this year a surprise demonstration of goblin spear-throwing by two human warriors who had mastered the technique. Rockdream entered the archery contests, and won his first four matches, which was more than he thought he would win, but then he lost twice in a row and was out of the tournament.

The third day was playoffs, climaxing in a battle with a live drakey by the champion archer, a woman named Bronzeberry, and the champion fencer, a man named Edge.

It was an unusually exciting contest, because the drakey, instead of trying to fly away as fast as possible when released from its cage, swooped to attack Bronzeberry before she could crank up her crossbow, and rose out of reach when Edge rushed in with his sword. The drakey repeated this maneuver twice before Bronzeberry was able to fire an arrow, and she missed. No other warrior was allowed to attack the drakey unless Lord Herring so commanded, which he would do immediately if the drakey attacked anyone else, but this drakey was behaving as though it understood the rules and was playing to win.

But Bronzeberry's second steel arrow, by skill or luck, pierced the drakey's heart and flight bladder, and it suddenly crashed to the ground dead. Before the judges could declare their decision, Bronzeberry said in a clear voice, "I share this victory with Edge, for had he not defended me with his sword, I would not have made the killing shot," and the crowd cheered her honor.

20.

One morning, about five weeks after the tournament, Rockdream woke up in his tower room with a strong impulse to tell Canticle about Coral. He knew that if he married her, he would have to move out of the tower, but he felt confident that there would be a way for him to continue serving as a warrior there. He remembered saying to Coral when they first became lovers that he wanted to spend a year living in the tower, and it was just short of a year since his warrior's test. Canticle knew Coral, from her healing work with Margin, and seemed to respect her.

Canticle gave Rockdream a private hearing after the noon meal, and after Rockdream carefully and honestly explained the dilemma he had been trying to live with, Canticle said, "We have a security problem, which I ignored, probably unwisely, as long as I did not know for certain about you and the witch. When that woman healed Margin, she did not quite do anything illegal, but she used some very powerful forces. She called up the spirit of his dead wife, and—" Canticle hesitated, pulling his black beard. "Well, bloody death, it worked! Margin not only recovered his health, but he is something like the person he used to be, and I am grateful for that. I do believe that Newport needs its witches and wizards. However, and this is a big however, humans with abilities like that do attract the attention of dragons."

"Coral would not become dragonbound," said Rockdream.

"I will not argue with that," said Canticle. "I am more

concerned about her attracting the attention of a full-grown dragon.''

"What do you mean?''

"Let me put it this way,'' Canticle explained, "if you walked into a room crowded with humans, and some were whispering, and some were talking normally, and some were shouting, which ones would you most easily hear?''

"The ones who were shouting,'' said Rockdream.

"That is the problem. When a dragon flies over the city, trying to hear human thoughts, the priests and priestesses are whispering, because their minds are very disciplined, and most of us are talking normally, but the wizards and witches are singing and shouting. Now you, while you work in this tower, whether or not you live here, know a lot about our defenses, and what you know, the witch will know also, whether or not you tell her, and what the witch knows, a dragon may easily learn. I must ask you to either give her up, or else leave the tower altogether.''

Canticle's brown eyes no longer looked fierce, penetrating, or inscrutable, but rather filled with sympathy, perhaps even love.

Rockdream slouched in his seat, staring down at his hands, feeling the tears swell in his eyes. "I hoped—'' he said quietly, "that there would be some other choice.''

"I am sorry,'' said Canticle.

"Can I have—some time to make this decision?''

"A week should be enough,'' said Canticle. "For that time, you are relieved of all your duties. Should you decide to stay, I will trust your honor that you will stop being the witch's lover. Should you decide to leave, you may have an additional day to move out.''

Rockdream felt a lump in his throat like a fist. "I understand,'' was all he could say.

He left Canticle's room, saw Fledgeling talking to Vein and Margin in the common room, and tried to explain the situation to them.

Fledgeling said, "There is no blame in whatever you decide. The wisdom you need is in your own heart.''

"I wish I could believe that.''

Margin looked at Rockdream with an exaggerated scowl, and said, "If you have the chance to marry Coral, and you do not, you are the worst backstabbed fool I have ever known.''

Rockdream looked at the gray-bearded old warrior with surprise, took a deep breath, and felt his throat relax. "That was what I needed to hear," he said.

"Truly?" asked Vein.

"I need to talk to Coral, and I need to find new employment, which may not be easy."

"Bah," said Margin. "Somebody always has something they want guarded."

"Maybe you can still work for the city," said Fledgeling. "You might consider the new river patrol, which has nothing to do with dragon defense."

"I do not want to sound too discouraging, but I think they already have all the warriors they need for that," said Vein.

"I want to try talking to some merchants today," Rockdream said. "Thank you so much."

"We will miss you," said Vein.

Rockdream went to his room, changed into his best silk shirt and trousers, and a few minutes later, he was walking the streets from Canticle's Tower toward Marketgate in the Old Wall, thinking about merchants and guardwork, and wondering how his parents would react to this. If they had any objections, it was not their concern, he decided. He felt very strange, as if somehow all this had happened to him before, as if this moment of walking Rose Street on a sunny spring day was very important, for reasons he could not even imagine.

"Rockdream! Hello!"

It was Coral, walking around the corner from Marketgate.

"I am so glad—I need to talk to you," he said.

"I was just going to the Rose Garden. Do you have time to go there?"

"I think it is the perfect place."

"You certainly are colorful today," Coral said, touching the bright blue silk of his sleeve while they walked. "What is the occasion?"

"Wait until we reach the park."

Coral could tell that Rockdream felt awkward about something, but did not hear his thoughts.

The Rose Garden was brilliant and fragrant, with the irises, snapdragons, winecups, and nasturtiums all blossoming, as well as many of the rose trees and bushes. There were quite a few other humans in the park, taking time out from their work to enjoy the flowers, or else coming with barrels and carts to collect water from the fountain's overflow.

"I talked to Canticle today," Rockdream said.

"What did he say to you this time?"

"I told him about you—and me."

Coral stopped walking and clenched her eyes, as if she felt Rockdream's pain. He felt the lump in his throat again, and did not know how to say what he needed to say.

"Coral, I know what you are, but I love you even so."

She looked at him carefully, and said quietly, "You must love me because I am myself, not despite it."

"I do, I do," he said, and walked to the fountain, cupped his hands, and drank, which she did also. "What I mean is, no matter what anyone else thinks, it makes no difference. My words are coming out all wrong."

She took his hand and sat down beside him on one of the benches. "I think I know what you are trying to say, but I want you to say it."

"Coral, I want to marry you."

She took a deep breath and looked into his eyes. "Yes," she said, and shuddered twice. "Yes, yes, you know how much I want this, how much this is meant to be. We can do it right away if you would like. Would you? I know the ritual."

"It seems a strange way to do it, but yes."

"We can use the fountain for holy water. This park is dedicated to the goddesses and gods." They walked back to the fountain, where they stood facing each other.

"Let us imagine an egg of sunlight surrounding both of us, and let us imagine that anyone who happens by will take no special notice of us. Now, we breathe together, and look into each other's eyes, and each sees the part of the other that is human, and the part that is divine."

"Yes," said Rockdream.

"We remember always that we are each both of these things, and we remember always that we love each other."

"Yes."

"Then I call to witness the Nameless Mother of All, and Sky the Father, and their Three Daughters, Wind the Hunter, Fire the Warrior, and Lake the Lover, and their Three Sons, Thunder the King, Cloud the Wizard, and Mountain the Priest, to hear me say that we who stand here together, Coral the Witch and Rockdream the Warrior, are now wife and husband."

She wet her fingers in the fountain pool and touched them to his forehead. ''Now you do the same to me,'' she whispered, and he did. ''Now we kiss—and now we go home and make love.''

Rockdream said, ''I do have one concern—a big concern. Canticle has given me only about a week to leave the tower, and I need to find work.''

''I know some of the merchants, Fairwind, Speartail, Driftwood, though Driftwood does not like witches or wizards very much, and I sort of know Forecastle.''

''You know them?'' Rockdream asked with surprise.

''Well, if I want to pay anything like a reasonable price for ginseng or weirdroot or cinnamon, I must buy in bulk from the merchants themselves. Actually, my mother and I are part of a small group of witches and wizards who pool their funds to buy these goods.''

''That seems wise.''

''But could we talk to the merchants tomorrow? This day is too special.''

They heard the clip-clop and creaking wheels of a horse and cart, and saw two men and a woman unload six empty barrels to fill with water from the overflow.

''Yes, let us go home,'' said Rockdream.

21.

The next morning, they walked back to the city together. For this occasion, Coral wore her new green muslin dress and the drakey-leather sandals that Rockdream had given her. He again wore his best silks.

The office of Fairwind the Merchant was on the ground floor of a warehouse on the corner of Market and Salmon Streets, which like all buildings in that part of town, had walls of large stones and a lead roof. He was sitting in a green velvet chair, in a room hung with tapestries, and was looking at a large map spread on a cherry-wood table. The young man standing beside him, Ironweed the Bookkeeper, was talking to him about the duties, port fees, and tax laws of various seaports up the coast.

After Rockdream and Coral explained their situation, Fairwind told them he was sorry, but he already had all the riverboat guards he was likely to need this year, but he did offer Rockdream a most well-paying job, four pounds of gold in fact, if he wanted to guard a ship bound for the Middle Kingdom. This would mean a voyage of at least two years, and perhaps one chance in four that he would not return at all; but on the other hand, four pounds of gold was enough to build a comfortable cottage and live quite well without working at all for at least four years after that, maybe longer.

But if this seemed too risky, Fairwind could offer him guardwork on a smaller ship leaving in just two days for Midcoast, Coveport, and Swordwall, the venture he had just been discussing with Ironweed. This was a voyage of only four or five months, and relatively safe, unless Riversong began attacking ships again, which he had not done in the past six years.

"What do you think?" Rockdream asked Coral.

"I think we should consider this very carefully and come back tomorrow, if that is all right with you," she said to Fairwind.

The merchant agreed to this, and Rockdream and Coral left his office. Outside, the sun was moving toward noon.

"That was a disappointment," Coral said. "I do not feel good about you taking either of those jobs."

Rockdream said, "I feel uneasy knowing that dragon guns are his ships' main defense. Dragon guns! Warriors stopped using them on land seventy years ago. Fairwind's argument that a ship is a small target for a dragon to attack may be right, and maybe a dragon does have to fly in close range of the dragon guns to destroy a ship, but even so, they are awkward weapons to fire accurately, even on solid ground, let alone bolted to a ship riding the swells."

"I am glad you agree with me," said Coral.

"A year ago, I thought Bloodroot was faint-hearted for refusing this risk, but now I understand. Who shall we try next?"

"Speartail's office is right across the street."

Speartail was favorably impressed by Rockdream's size and strength, and remembered watching his archery matches in the last tournament. He questioned him about his warrior's test and experience, his special skills, and most particularly his feelings about the fishing rights dispute with Goblin Plain.

He said, "I have one captain, my wife's sister, Daffodil, who refuses to sail through Goblin Plain until I hire at least two guards for her boat, and I let most of my guards go after the new treaty. But you will have to talk to her about this, and I warn you that Captain Daffodil does not like goblins, or witches, so you might want to tell her less than you told me."

"She sounds like a difficult person to work with," Rockdream said.

"Your arrow hit the heart of the target," said Speartail, "but you will not find any truly good guard jobs on riverboats right now. One incident could change that, but I hope there will be no incidents."

"So do I," said Rockdream. "Where would I find Captain Daffodil?"

"She should be at the docks, readying her boat, but if she is not there, try the Tidewater Tavern."

But when they reached the harbor, the portmaster's assistant told them that Captain Daffodil had hoisted anchor and sailed out of the harbor early that morning.

Speartail was infuriated that she would sail without sending an immediate message and having the bookkeeper tally the cargo. He told Rockdream and Coral he would talk to them later, because right now he had to find out, as best he could, exactly what Daffodil was doing.

Coral and Rockdream had lunch at the Tidewater Tavern—lobster with buttered sourbread, which was delicious, but cheap, because lobsters were common and easy to catch.

That afternoon, after getting no offers from three other merchants, they became discouraged. "At the very worst, I could buy a horse and become a hunter," Rockdream said.

"Let us go to the park and pray," said Coral. "When human effort fails, sometimes it is because we do not recognize or understand the gifts the goddesses and gods offer us."

"That sounds good. A year ago, I would have gone to the Church and asked for a purification ceremony."

"Do you feel impure?"

"Not exactly, but the Church does teach that confusion is a sign of impurity."

They walked through the stone streets of the city, and the shaded paths of the Rose Garden, until they came to the statue of Fire the Warrior, which was Spiral the Sculptor's last work.

It showed the goddess as a young woman with two long braids, dressed in tunic, trousers, and boots, with sheathed sword. By omitting the round shield slung over her back that was traditional in this pose, Spiral was able to emphasize such subtle details as the flex of muscles beneath her tunic sleeves, and the very slight counterpoise of her hips and shoulders, which made her seem very lifelike.

Just seeing the Second Daughter standing on the pedestal was inspiring to Rockdream, who bowed and sat cross-legged on the grass in front of her, and closed his eyes to quiet his mind. In this quiet, he felt the special joy that comes with the full living and appreciation of each moment, and he knew he was doing exactly what was best for him to do. But this realization puzzled him, and in trying to understand he again felt confused.

Coral, who was seated beside him, began singing a series of long, soft notes, which somehow reminded him of purification bells, then stopped, and he was aware of the quiet sounds, bird calls, wind in the cherry trees, people talking in the distance. "I feel happy," Coral said. "I think we can go home. I think the goddess will help you."

When they came to Eastgate, the main gate was open, and filled with a long procession of farmers on horseback returning from their fields. Coral and Rockdream walked through the lesser gate, where a guard stopped them and asked their names.

"I have two messages for Rockdream the Warrior," he said. "Lieutenant Canticle wants to see you at your soonest convenience, and Lieutenant Coaljay wants to see you right away."

Rockdream started to ask who Coaljay was, then realized she must be the lieutenant of Eastgate.

The guard said, "Go back through the gate, to the door in the north tower, and the doorguard will let you in," and to Coral, "I am sorry, but you cannot go inside the tower."

"I am used to that. I can wait," she said.

Rockdream cut across the stream of farmers walking their horses toward the Eastlands Cooperative Stable, and came to a narrow door, barred with steel.

"Rockdream the Warrior to see Lieutenant Coaljay, as directed," he called, hoping his voice could be heard over the clamor of hooves.

The guard who opened the door was a brown-haired woman of about thirty summers, who he had seen many times at the gate. "I am Maplewing," she said. "Welcome to Eastgate. Coaljay will explain your duties to you. I think she is in the common room, but if not, anyone will direct you to her."

Rockdream offered a silent prayer of thanks to the Warrior Goddess, for surely she inspired Canticle to arrange this, and he walked upstairs to the common room, where several warriors were seated at one of the tables, sampling, of all things, freshly baked cinnamon rolls.

"Rockdream the Warrior to see Lieutenant Coaljay," he said.

"Come, have a roll with us," said Coaljay, a strong stout woman of about forty-five summers, with white strands in her coarse black hair. She was the one warrior at the table who Rockdream had not seen before.

Coaljay was clearly a very different kind of leader than Canticle, who always discussed everything in private, for she began explaining Rockdream's duties to him right there at the table, and some of the others offered observations and suggestions.

"You will be strictly a gate guard," Coaljay said, "which I know is a demotion from a warrior who stands dragonwatch, but this demotion implies no dishonor, but is merely a security precaution. In the unlikely event of attack, of course you will fight with us."

"Then I am, in the way that matters most to me, still a warrior of Newport," said Rockdream. "I am honored."

"You are honorable, and also skilled," said Coaljay, "and in my opinion, so is your wife."

4

GIFT OF LIFE

22.

It was a day before Market day, and not many days before the Fall Equinox of the 197th year, and farmers with loaded carts and wagons passed through Eastgate into the city all day long, and into the evening. Harvest season was every gate guard's least favorite time of duty. Every now and then, a castle bookkeeper or tax collector would discover something that needed explaining, and then a line of carts and wagons would pile up behind while the farmer in question explained whatever it was, and often as not someone else would start grumbling and cursing. But the gate guards had to act cheerful and friendly, but firm, and as soon as possible get the procession moving again.

This was Rockdream's third harvest season at Eastgate. Some of the guards claimed that traffic was moving more smoothly this year, now that they no longer were looking for smuggled turtle meat, but Rockdream did not notice any real difference.

Finally the hour came when he was off duty. He walked around to the south tower stable, struck a sparker, and lit the lamp. This stable was small, and five of its six stalls held Eastgate's young, fast messenger's horses. The sixth held Rockdream's old gelding, Plowpuller, which he had bought from the farmer Spineball last year. It was unusual for a Newport warrior to own a horse, but it was also unusual for one to live in a cottage nearly two miles from the city. He led

Plowpuller to the stable door, blew out the lamp, mounted, and rode around to the gate.

"See you tomorrow," said Maplewing, who was standing night guard at the narrow gate.

"Not me," he replied. "My next duty is doorguard, the day after tomorrow."

"Lucky you," she said.

He rode through the overcast, moonless night, over fields and into the dark but familiar forest. Ahead he saw a light glowing, a lamp in the window of the cottage he and Coral had built together just a few hundred feet beyond her parents' cottage. He tied old Plowpuller to the winter oak and walked to the door.

Coral was seated at the workbench with a large book, pen and ink, and several piles of cut parchments. "Just give me a moment to finish this line," she said, then put down her pen and stood up to give Rockdream a welcome kiss.

"How can you write so tiny?" he asked, looking at her work. "Are you copying this whole book?"

"Yes, and I want my copy to be a manageable size. This is Hornbeam's *Wisdom,* which I am renting from Treeworm."

"Renting?" asked Rockdream.

"This is priceless knowledge. Do not be concerned about the cost. I am making two copies, and when I sell the second, I will make a tidy profit."

That was Coral. She thought nothing of wearing mended clothing, and used to wrap her feet in rags before Rockdream gave her sandals and boots, but she would spend large amounts of silver for a few weeks of borrowing another wizard's book.

"I suppose you know what you are doing," he said.

"Of course I do. I have wanted my own copy of this book ever since I was twelve. There is so much in it. Did you know there was a time when a third of this continent was covered with ice a half-mile thick?"

"Wait a moment. Is this the book that told you about the stars being suns?"

Rockdream looked at the page Coral was copying, a passage about pooks, the little furry people of the forest:

> Pooks live in close harmony with the effective powers. They have no names, and when they dance they are without selves. Every detail of each other and of their

surroundings is close and vivid, and they can hear thoughts as clearly as dragons do. This way they avoid being seen.

He stopped reading and said, "This seems as hard to understand as the pooks themselves are said to be."

"The elvish idiom takes getting used to, but I can connect what it says to my own experience. Being without a self means partly to empty your mind of thoughts, as I do in my healing work. In this condition, it is easier to be in close harmony with the Holy Family, which are human effective powers. So when pooks dance to empty their minds of thoughts, their perceptions are sharpened, and they hear thoughts as clearly as dragons. Their dances are very powerful. But think about that first night when we danced together in the Rose Garden. That was almost the same thing. We were in close harmony with the goddess of love, and I could hear your thoughts very clearly."

Rockdream sighed and slumped onto the stool. "Right now I do not feel in close harmony with anything. When I close my eyes, I see farmers with carts to be inspected."

Coral laughed and tousled his hair. "—and all complaining that their pumpkins will rot by the time they get through the gate."

Rockdream laughed. "Something of the sort."

Coral stood next to him and kissed him slowly, and in that kiss, he left behind the farmers at the city gate for a big-eyed curly-haired witch who was very much in love with him. Soon they blew out the lamp and snuggled together naked under the blankets and furs. Their lovemaking was long and slow, and his contractions sent a stream deep into her body.

"I want to have a child," she said.

"All right," said Rockdream.

"If you want to have a child," she added.

"Yes, I do."

Coral leaned over, rustled through her clothing, and pressed a small leather pouch into Rockdream's hand. "This is my pouch of freedomwort root, for you to hold until I conceive and give birth to our child. Will you accept this?"

"I will," he said, and his heart was pounding to emphasize how much he wanted this.

"Put it in your deepest pocket and carry it always, for luck," she whispered.

23.

But when Coral's mother, Moonwort, learned of her resolve, she tried to dissuade her. "I should have said something when you first brought him home, and I should have said something when you married him. He is so much larger than you, and your hips are narrow even for your size. The baby may be too large to come out."

"Oh, that is ridiculous, Mother. Look at Hook the Blacksmith and Sparkle the Weaver. He is bigger than Rockdream, or at least stouter, and she is no larger than me, and they have four children. And of all the births I helped, with you or alone, the only hard ones were both big, broad-hipped mothers."

"A baby tangled in the cord and a breech-birth are different problems."

"Rockdream and I are meant to have a child, just as we were meant to be married. I have talked to the child's spirit. I can close my eyes and feel him in my arms, suckling."

"Wishful thinking," Moonwort said. "Sometimes such visions are false, and can lead you to your death."

"Mother, I know what is real!"

"Do you now?" Moonwort asked sarcastically. "In the spirit world, *nothing* is real, not until it manifests in this world. I could close my eyes and see Newport smashed to pieces by rocks falling from the sky, and have dreams about buildings tumbling down, and think about it all until it seems real to me, but is it real?"

Coral shuddered.

Moonwort laughed. "I did not expect you to react that way, but it proves my point. You were just now frightened by a vision that was no real vision at all, but something I just made up, and if—"

"You underestimate your own power," Coral said.

"Pooh! You let me finish! If you can be frightened by something unreal, you can also have false confidence in something unreal, such as a vision of yourself nursing a child. I suppose nothing about nursing a child seems unlikely to you, but how can you trust your judgment about which future visions are likely, if you believe Newport can be destroyed by an impossible meteor fall?"

"I know that nothing like that has ever happened, but something about falling rocks seems real—"

"Bah! You just never grew up, and I wonder whether you ever will. But when I think about it, when I was in my own twentieth summer, I knew all the secrets of the universe, and my mother was at least as stupid as a river lizard, but five years later, it seemed as though she was quite smart, and I was the ignorant one."

"Oh, then that explains everything," Coral said. "If you lost that much wisdom between your twentieth and twenty-fifth summers, you must be incredibly stupid now." She broke out laughing and hugged her mother.

"Make certain you have at least two witches to midwife you," Moonwort said. "When you were a girl, I told you that you had no brothers or sisters because we could not afford to feed them well, with your father's back the way it is, and that was true, but also, I nearly died bringing you into the world, and with you and your father both needing me, I could not try to have another child."

"I never guessed," said Coral. "You should have told me then. I really did want a brother, but I would have understood. But you did live, and so did I, and we are both doing quite well twenty years later, so I trust I can do as well."

"A child can be quite a distraction from your studies—oh, very well, when you make up your mind, you are as stubborn as I am. Will you consider the extra midwife?"

"I will see how it goes," Coral said.

24.

Coral sat behind Rockdream on old Plowpuller while they rode the Coast Road, north of the Newport wall. They were going to Treeworm the Wizard's cottage, to return his copy of *Wisdom of the Elves.*

"I told him about you when I rented the book," Coral said. "He wants to meet you. He was my teacher. I lived with him for most of my twelfth summer. Before I met you, when I thought I was going to be a traditional witch and never marry, I even considered him as a possible father for my child."

Treeworm lived alone, in a cottage beside a stream near the sea, some sixteen miles north of Newport. He was seldom called upon as a healer, for few people would travel so far, when other wizards and witches lived much nearer the city. Even those who sought him out sometimes failed to find him,

for his stream looked much like many others, his cottage was
difficult to see from a distance, and that part of the coast was
often covered with dense fog. Some said the fog in the area
became denser when Treeworm wished to be left alone.

"But I can always find his cottage," Coral said.

When Plowpuller forded the fifth stream beyond the end of
the road, the fog was thickening. The hills and forests melted
into silver, and the sound of the sea became muffled.

"With the sea on one side and the hills on the other, I guess
we cannot become completely lost," said Rockdream. "His
cottage is on this side of the Elk River, is it not?"

"I know where we are," said Coral. "The next stream will
be much wider, but shallow enough to ford, and then comes the
dry stream, which may have water, and then Treeworm's stream."

Where they crossed the wide stream, Rockdream saw great
elk tracks, and in the meadow beyond they saw several she-
elk and one huge stag, all grazing placidly as cows or sheep.
The stag raised his head, displaying his magnificent antlers,
and stared at the newcomers. Plowpuller stopped short, but
Rockdream urged him forward and patted his neck to reassure
him.

"Just keep walking and ignore them," he told the horse.
"They will not bother us if we do not bother them."

Plowpuller snorted and quickened his pace, but slowed down
when the stag lowered his head to graze. They passed several
other groups of great elk along the next few miles of meadow,
and Plowpuller gradually got used to them.

Treeworm's cottage was cleverly placed so that it was hard
to notice until you came quite close, though it was out in the
open. Windswept cypress brush concealed the angles of the
walls, and the thatch roof mimicked the grassy mounds. But up
close, the cottage looked similar to Rockdream and Coral's
own home, a rectangular room with a porch in front.

"Welcome, Coral, and I presume, Rockdream," said a man's
friendly voice. "Set your horse free to graze in the meadow,
and come inside."

While Rockdream and Coral dismounted and unloaded the
packs, Rockdream said, "We probably should tie him up. If
he wanders off—"

"Oh, that would do you no good here," said Treeworm,
opening the door. "Let me have a few words with him, and he
will not run off." Treeworm looked like a wizard from an old

story, or at least from several generations ago. He wore sweeping dark robes, with voluminous sleeves with mystic symbols embroidered on the hems, and he had a long white beard and bushy eyebrows.

"Hello!" Coral said, and stood on tiptoes to hug him and give him a brief kiss on the lips. "I would like you to meet my true love and husband, Rockdream the Warrior."

To Rockdream's surprise, Treeworm hugged him also.

"Now let me talk to your horse," he said, and patted Plowpuller's nose. He sang something softly in a foreign language, mixed with a few sounds like snorts and nickers, and the words "stay near." The horse whinnied loudly and tossed his head, then Treeworm took off his harness and set him free. "He should obey the command 'stay near' after this," he said. "Now let us go in and be comfortable."

He went back inside. They followed, and set their packs by the door. Rockdream was surprised to see how much the inside of Treeworm's cottage looked like his own. There was the same workbench, shelves, and bed, though the shelves had many times more books, and the floor was covered with carpets rather than reed mats.

"I copied the design," Coral said with a smile. She and Rockdream took off their coats and boots, and sat facing Treeworm near the hearth, like children facing a storyteller.

"I presume you brought back my book," he said.

Coral removed the large volume from her pack and set it on the workbench. "Where did you learn to speak Elvish?"

"Right here in this cottage," Treeworm replied. "Not that I can say anything very complex in Laughing Water Song, which is what that particular Elvish language calls itself, near enough, but I do know enough to talk to animals with it. They always seem to understand people better than we understand them, but they understand this language most readily, because it makes compromises with their own natural sounds."

"But *who* taught you to speak Laughing Water Song?" Coral asked.

"The pooks, of course," said Treeworm.

"I never heard them speak anything but our own language," said Coral.

"You never asked us to speak anything else," said a high-pitched voice like a very small child.

Rockdream turned to see what looked like a furry doll seated on a high shelf. "Is that a real pook?" he asked.

The doll giggled and waved his legs. "Is that a real warrior?" he asked.

From across the room came another giggle, a female pook sitting on the bed. Then a third pook popped out from behind some large jars on the floor.

"Why do you not laugh?" the first pook asked Rockdream. "Are we not funny?"

"He would rather watch for dragons than watch for farmers with carts," said the third pook.

"That seems stupid," said the pook woman. "A dragon might burn him up and eat him. Farmers only do that to their animals."

"He and his friends would then try to kill the dragon with their crossbows."

"They really would."

"We should take his thoughts more gently," said the woman. "He is startled and does not know what to think."

Treeworm said, "Rockdream is not used to your games and you might make him sad. Forgive them, Rockdream. They have never been close to a warrior before, and they are curious."

"We know what warriors are," the first pook said, and climbed down from the high shelf to the workbench. "We just want to help him."

Coral explained, "They are speaking aloud your thoughts and reactions as colored by their own wisdom."

"But I was not thinking about my work before they brought it up," said Rockdream.

"The broad but hidden thoughts that affect your whole life are their favorites."

"We do not like thoughts of battling with dragons at all," protested the third pook.

"Not at all," agreed the first.

"You want to have a baby," said the woman. "That is a nice thought. The baby wants to have you, and your body is ready."

"Oh, come here and hug me," said Coral. "I have not seen any little people for six years, and that is far too long."

The pooks hesitated, then scampered past Treeworm to climb onto Coral's lap, and all snuggled together with her, and after another hesitation, Treeworm and Rockdream joined the hug.

"Will we all dance together?" asked one of the pook men.

"Yes! Three little ones and three big ones!"

"Stretch the old wizard's stiff muscles!"

"All right," said Treeworm.

"We would be honored," said Coral.

They went outside, where Plowpuller was grazing in the meadow, but instead of dancing there, as Rockdream expected, they followed the stream to the sea. Near Newport, the shore beneath the cliffs was mudflat and marsh, but here was a nice sandy beach. Beneath the fog, the sea looked silvery and luminous.

"Dance the fog and mist!" said one pook, and they began languidly moving their shoulders and hips while skipping slowly in random directions. Coral was first to join them, then Treeworm, who moved quite gracefully for such an old human, and finally Rockdream joined the dance. He felt awkward, dancing with people little more than a third his height, even as slowly as they were all moving. The patterns of the dance were subtle, and there was no music but the sounds of the waves.

Gradually the dance formed a circle, which expanded and contracted. The pooks moved toward the center of the circle, chanting "oooh!" and backed away, chanting "ahhh!" and the humans joined this. Rockdream felt this as the rhythm of the waves at first, then as the rhythm of breathing, then as the rhythm of lovemaking, which led him to think of Coral and the child, which led him to consider conception, birth, life, death and afterlife as one grand pulsation, and part of something vast. Each life was unique, but it was unique the way the patterns of foam in a particular wave were unique, a variation within a much grander theme.

Then the dance changed again, back to the slow undulations and irregular circling, and what was cause and what was effect Rockdream did not know, but while they all moved slower and slower, the fog thinned overhead, and when they stopped, the sun was shining. The pooks jumped up and down and laughed.

25.

When Rockdream and Coral returned home, long after dark, they made a small fire to warm the leftover stew, had some of this for dinner, and went to bed. They remembered the pook woman's words about Coral's body being ready, and the count

of days since her last bleeding agreed with this, but they were
so tired that they fell asleep during the first movements of
lovemaking.

In the middle of the night, Coral was awakened from her
dream by a voice like a child's voice or a pook's, calling her
name. She opened her eyes to the darkness, and asked, ''Is
anyone there?'' in a low voice, but heard no sound except
Rockdream's light snores. She felt the presence of her child's
spirit trying to speak with her, and focused her attention on her
breathing.

She was not quite in trance, not quite asleep, when she felt
Rockdream's hands pulling her close. Their lips and tongues
mingled, and her hands pulled away the blanket rumpled between them, and caressed his smooth skin.

When his hand touched her breast, she realized that she was
feeling the sensations of lovemaking through both of their
bodies, the hand on the breast, and the breast in the hand, and
she felt the third presence, a little sparkle floating in the room.
The double sensation of being penetrated and being engulfed
aroused her to frenzy, and flooded her heart with love.

Rockdream felt this also, a rising river of emotion deeper
and broader than anything he had felt before, too much love for
his body or hers to contain, and he was streaming, streaming.

''I am sorry,'' he began to say, for he knew it was too soon
for Coral's pleasure, but she touched herself until she shuddered, then kissed him.

''Do not be sorry,'' she said. ''We did it, I think. Your
stream means more than my shudder, right now. The spark is
inside me, taking the gift of life from both of us. It feels that
way; it truly does.''

26.

Not many weeks after Coral's next bleeding was due and did
not come, she began to wake up with headaches and nausea. ''I
am not entirely enjoying being pregnant,'' she told Rockdream,
and made a comic grimace that was all too real.

''Is there nothing you can do for yourself?''

''I am already doing the breathwork and relaxation that I would
recommend to another woman with this pain. Not every pregnant
woman goes through this, but it is common enough and no sign of
sickness. Strong herbs and teas might not be good for the baby.''

But even when Coral was not suffering from these complaints, her desire to make love was less than ever before, and though Rockdream tried to understand, and took care of his own urges when she was uninterested, he was irritated, and she knew it.

"We have never been together so much of the time," she said. "Usually I work more in the winter, when you work less, and the opposite in the summer, but now we are both home, and we need more things to share."

"What do you suggest?"

"Might music be of interest to us both?" she asked, and pulled a lyre off one of the shelves, and handed it to Rockdream. It was made of a wood he did not recognize, carved with a pattern of leaves, and strung with gut, rather than wire.

"When did you get this?" he asked. "It looks foreign."

"So it is. I got it yesterday from Loon the Minstrel, who comes from the Four Lakes Kingdom, though the lyre comes from either Vineland or Yellow River, I think. One of the southern countries west of the sea. She talked so much about her travels that I got confused. Anyway, she is married to a Newport mariner named Feathergrass, who is Bloodroot's friend. She had a throat inflammation, and an important recital at the castle tonight for Lord Herring himself, and she wanted to trade this lyre for a big batch of medicines."

"Can you teach me how to play it? I know next to nothing."

"So do I, but it is easy. Loon gave me my first lesson yesterday, and listen to this—" Coral played several simple arpeggio patterns, not without mistakes, but the sound was nice. "Do you see what I am doing? Each pattern has three strings, and I skip one or two strings between the ones I pluck, then I change the pattern to another three strings."

"I think I can do that," Rockdream said, and though it was harder than it looked, he began to get the feel of it.

He and Coral spent many rainy days sitting beside the hearth, practicing the patterns and fitting them to simple songs and chanted poetry. Rockdream sang heroic ballads, and Coral worked out arrangements for some of the sacred chants she used in her healing work.

"I have never heard anyone use a lyre with those chants," Rockdream said, "but it does sound good."

"I think the lyre helps me focus the power," Coral said. "I did something like this before, in a previous life, a long time ago and west of the sea. I was playing a harp, and chanting spells in another language. Perhaps someday I will remember those chants. They were very effective. I think there was a plague— ''

Coral was silent for a moment, then her face brightened to a smile and she passed the lyre to Rockdream, who began to sing a well-known ballad:

Windsong the Mariner cried in the prison,
for the life of her husband, the warrior Redmyth,
who was leader of the Legion of Honor,
who was put to death by King Woad's command.

"Give me my ship," she said to the King.
"Give me the others you hold in this prison.
We will all leave, and end the rebellion.
We will take exile, and never return."

"I think that would be unwise," said the King.
"I have the power and you are my captive.
Why should I release you to exile
when you will return to avenge your husband?"

"You understand neither my husband nor me,
if you think I will break my promise to you,
and whoever I lead will be bound by my word.
We will take exile and never return."

"And where would you go?" King Woad demanded.
"North or south, and how far away?
What other country would suffer your folly?
What king or queen would allow your dissent?"

"Not north or south, but east I will sail,
to a new land to build a new city,
where people can live with honor, instead
of dying or rotting in prison with honor."

King Woad told Windsong that he would consider,
and left her alone in the cold prison cell.
Her followers knew that she would have been killed,
and stormed the prison the next day at dawn.

Rockdream broke off, and said, "I do not remember the next part, about the riots in the city and the seizing of the ships.

Battle between humans and other humans is so repulsive, so much against everything that the Legion of Honor stood for. But they were pressed, and there is no dishonor in fighting for your own lives and freedom. But the song makes it sound like a glorious deed, and it was not.''

"What would you have done in Windsong's place?" Coral asked.

"I do not know. I am glad to live in a time and place where I need not make such a hard decision."

"May that continue to be so!" said Coral, but when she took the lyre, she chanted part of the Canticle of Fortune:

> The circle of fortune turns,
> and all things pass.
> Night becomes dawn,
> day becomes dusk.
> Winter becomes spring,
> summer becomes fall.
>
> Wealth and poverty come and go.
> Joy and despair come and go.
> Strength and weakness come and go.
> Love and loneliness come and go.
> Health and sickness come and go.
> Peace and battle come and go.
> Birth and life and death come and go.
>
> What is built, may be destroyed,
> and what is destroyed, may be rebuilt.
> What is learned, may be forgotten,
> and what is unknown, may be discovered.

Rockdream said, "I used to dislike that chant, but now it reminds me of the pooks, and their dance of the waves, when I saw my whole life as just one pattern of foam, part of a much greater pattern."

Coral said, "Sometimes making hard decisions is part of the pattern."

27.

Rockdream swung the ax high, and brought it down on the round of winter oak. Usually his third blow made the first split. It was a cold clear afternoon half a week before Midwinter's

Day, and a market day. Coral had resumed her usual amount of healing work since her morning pains had stopped, and this day she was selling salves and medicines in the Newport Market. Rockdream did not expect her to return until hours after dusk, but there she was already, riding home on old Plowpuller.

"How did it go?" he asked, after swinging his ax to make one more split.

"I sold everything. Looks like you did a lot, also."

"Enough to keep us warm for another two weeks, maybe. There is a stew simmering on the hearth, all ready to eat."

Coral dismounted carefully, untied the pack, and reached inside for a cloth-wrapped bundle. "I bought some cinnamon rolls from Birdwade. Did you know that her daughter, Ripple, is walking already?"

"Let us go inside and warm the rolls on the hearthstone."

They did this, and while they were eating them, Coral said, "I have an important decision to make, which involves you also. I saw Salmon again today. She wants to become my apprentice."

"Do you want her to be your apprentice?"

"I think so. She has an odd wisdom that is all her own, and she can see things with her trance-eye without training. She would make a good witch, and I can use the help." Coral patted her belly. "Sometimes when I stand up too long, I get dizzy, and there are potions I need to brew that are not healthful for a pregnant woman to smell. Also, I have dreamed of working with her."

"But she is a warrior."

"I no longer think that is reason to refuse her. She does not work for the city, and there is no law against a warrior also being a witch, even if it is against custom."

"Those sound like arguments Salmon would offer," Rockdream said.

"There is another problem with Salmon becoming my apprentice. She would be practicing witchcraft and legally required to live outside the city walls, which probably means that she and Bloodroot would move in with us." Coral looked around the cottage as if trying to imagine it filled with more people and possessions, and sighed. "It would be complicated."

Rockdream ladled a portion of stew into a bowl, passed it to Coral, and filled another bowl for himself. "If this is that important to you, I will agree," he said, "but only if they can find or build their own cottage next summer. I was Bloodroot's roommate when we were both squires, and that was fine, but living with Salmon might be hard for me."

"She troubled you years ago because she wanted you to be her lover and you refused, but that has all changed," Coral said.

And so, on the new moon three days after Midwinter's Day, Coral formally accepted Salmon as her apprentice, and on the next sunny day, Bloodroot and Salmon rented a cart from farmer Spineball, hitched it to old Plowpuller, and with some difficulty (they twice became mired in the muddy wagon ruts of Apple Road), they moved their furniture, tapestries, and personal belongings into Rockdream and Coral's cottage.

The furniture was nothing special, but the tapestries, which Salmon and Coral hung from the rafters to screen off private bedrooms, were imported from Jade Forest, west of the sea. These were not the priceless silk tapestries that one master weaver would spend a year designing and making, but merely simplified copies done in wool, but even so, they were stunning examples of the ornate style.

To Coral's mother, Moonwort, they were material affectations that had no place in the cottage of a witch, and when Salmon argued that they belonged to her husband, and were not Moonwort's concern, she and Moonwort took a dislike to each other. To Coral, the abstract patterns of these tapestries resembled the fabric of the spirit world itself, but she did not tell her mother this.

Rockdream found living with Salmon much easier than he had feared, for her summers of working as a boat guard had given her the friendly manners of a sailor who knows that the private affairs of the others aboard ship are not her concern. She was only feisty when someone else was offensive, as Moonwort had been about the tapestries.

Most of Salmon's study that winter was of herbs and potions, but each time Coral did a healing with energy threads, Salmon practiced watching the patterns of light with her trance-eye, and afterwards Coral would explain exactly what she had done.

"Sometimes I see a separate pattern of threads and light around your belly, sort of like that," Salmon said, pointing to one of the tapestries. "It is usually faint."

"The baby has a mind and spirit of his own," said Coral. "Sometimes he dreams."

28.

Rockdream seldom visited his parents, and even more seldom did he tell them anything about his life, for they both had a way of offering him advice that made him feel less competent to make his own decisions. He had never told them about his difficulties with lieutenant Canticle, and had not told them about his transfer to Eastgate and his marriage to Coral until several weeks after the fact, and he had slammed the door on their reaction. He had been married to her for almost three years, and they still had not managed to meet her. So, was it even their concern that she was pregnant? Rockdream sighed. He should have told them sooner, but it was so hard to tell them anything.

He was already standing in front of the door to their tower, and he still did not know what he would say to them.

"Rockdream the Warrior, to see the warriors Bane and Scallop," he told the guard.

"Go on in," she said. "They are probably in their room."

He walked up the spiral stairs to the common room, where two warriors were playing a board game. His parents' room was one of the doors. He knocked.

"Come in," said Scallop's voice. "Oh, Rockdream! We have not seen you for so long."

"Hello, son," said Bane. "Take a seat. Tell us how it goes at Eastgate."

"Well, some herders finally killed Old One Ear."

"I presume this is a wolf?" asked Scallop.

"Old One Ear was a fangcat, and he killed an unbelievable number of cows, steers, and even bulls. The herders trailed him all the way up into the foothills, during the heavy rain, which made the ground soft enough to clearly show his prints, while making their own scent and sound obscure. Their strategy impressed me, and also the skill needed to shoot accurately in such a storm. They brought back his carcass. Old One Ear was the biggest fangcat I ever saw, and I praised their deed, which was much harder than my own warrior's test."

"Hunting well with a longbow is not a warrior's deed," said Bane.

Rockdream argued, "Why not? If we kill a dragon with crossbows to protect our city, and they kill a fangcat with longbows to protect their herd, the deeds are different in magnitude, but not in kind.''

"You always were generous with your compliments," said Bane, "but compliments lead to complacency, which we cannot afford, not with dragons like Riversong in the world.''

"I disagree.''

"You would. You are a perfect example. Your warrior's test was an amazing achievement. Your mother and I were very proud, and we told you so, and what have you done since then? We thought you were tower lieutenant material, but you married a witch and became a gate guard, and even your performance in the spring tournaments is no more than adequate.''

"I am a far better archer now than I was when I killed the drakey!" Rockdream said indignantly. "Had I been so good then, I certainly would not have needed to strangle it with my bare hands. And you would not belittle my wife if you knew her. Both Canticle and Coaljay know and respect her.''

"I still think you should have married that nice young warrior," said Scallop.

Rockdream felt a momentary flash of anger, then laughed out loud. "You mean Salmon?" he asked.

"What is so funny about that?" asked Scallop.

What was so funny was that Salmon was now his wife's apprentice, and was probably at this moment preparing poltices from every ingredient on the Church's List of Proscribed Herbs, and the temptation to tell his parents this was strong, but he thought that Salmon might not like him discussing her concerns with them.

Instead, he said, "I have been happily married to Coral for three years, and I cannot believe you still think I made a bad choice. In fact, she and I are expecting a child next year, in the month after Midsummer's Day.''

"That is good news, I guess," said Scallop. "I would be concerned for the child's safety, so far outside the city walls and in the middle of a forest.'

"We have never been bothered by anything bigger than a raccoon," said Rockdream. "That forest is completely surrounded by farm and pasture land.''

"What kind of upbringing do you plan to give your child?" asked Bane. "How will he or she fit into the city?''

"Coral and I intend to raise our child to be as honorable, wise, and loving as we possibly can.''

"Make sure the child has a good occupation," said Bane. "Send him or her to the castle to be a squire, or—"

"Or maybe we will apprentice him or her to Coral to learn healing and sorcery," said Rockdream. "It really is a bit soon to make these decisions."

Bane scowled, but Scallop said, "We should come to visit you and Coral."

"Do you still have the map I made for you?"

"I think we might have misplaced it," said Scallop.

"That is no problem," said Bane. "We just go out the East Road about two miles, then turn right onto Apple Road, which is a rutted cart trail."

"No," said Rockdream. "Apple Road is close to the gate, near those big apple and pear trees. It is the third road to the right, and it is the only one which heads east rather than south. You follow Apple Road for two miles, till you come to a forest, and ours is the second cottage. If I am not on duty at Eastgate, I am probably home."

That evening, Coral asked him, "Do you really think they are going to come this time?"

"Possibly, but I would not hold my breath. Maybe after the baby is born."

"I hope I am here when they come," said Salmon. "That would be funny."

"I almost told them, but I thought you might think it was not their concern."

"I am proud to be learning witchcraft, and my own parents support my decision. They remember how Coral saved Bloodroot's life. My apprenticeship is no secret."

5

THE GOBLINS

29.

From the shelter of the deep stone arch of the lesser gate, Rockdream watched the sheets of rain pound the pebble surface of the East Road. Two people approached on foot, and at first he assumed they were more herders returning to the city after being relieved by their partners, and he started another imaginary argument with his father about herders being the warriors of their herds, which he stopped when he saw that they were not herders at all, but goblin warriors, armed with spears and spear-throwers.

He tugged a cord that rang a bell in the common room, and by the time the goblins reached the gate, two other Eastgate guards joined him. The goblins were both short by human standards, but powerfully muscled, or so Rockdream guessed from the way they walked, and from the size of their hands and soft shoes, for their bodies were hidden by their fur robes. One was very old, to judge from the wrinkles on his face, but his voice was as strong and clear as a young man's.

"I am Drakey, High Shaman of Goblin Plain," he said.

"I am Rockdream, guard of Eastgate, and I am deeply honored to meet you." This was the man who helped negotiate the turtle rights agreement between Lord Herring and High Chief Strong Bull, and Coral called him a wise and powerful wizard.

"I am Beartooth, chief of a camp of strong warriors," said the other goblin.

It was not usual for gate guards to introduce themselves as
Rockdream had just done, but the other two warriors, Pinchgrip
and Dusk, followed his lead.

"We have come to see Herring, Lord of Newport," said
Drakey. "He does not expect us, but he will say that we are
welcome. We come in peace. My dreams tell me to talk with
him. Beartooth is my partner in this."

"One of us will guide you," said Rockdream.

"You may do it," said Pinchgrip. "I will relieve you here."

Rockdream handed Pinchgrip the pike, and walked up Castle
Street with the two goblin leaders. The heavy rain was not at
all conducive to conversation, and goblins, especially the leaders, were known to dislike trivial talk, but Rockdream took a
chance, and tried to speak with them.

"I have spoken with very few goblins in my life, but I have
always believed that friendship between all people is best."

"That is good," said Drakey. "Do not be ill at ease with us.
If you want to talk, we will talk. We are here to deepen
understanding between goblins and humans."

"You can hear thoughts as well as my wife does, which is
good, for I am sometimes awkward with words."

"Is your wife a witch?" asked Drakey.

"Yes. She has told me stories about you."

After walking half a block farther, Drakey said, "I am the
High Shaman, which means I lead the circle of shamans who
decide matters of spiritual importance for all of Goblin Plain.
How do we choose a high chief? Why are all the turtles and
sturgeons disappearing from the rivers? These are problems we
have solved since I was chosen high shaman. How can we
make a stronger peace between Goblin Plain and Newport?
That is why we have come now. Some shamans say, 'Sit the
peace circle,' but too many peace circles between goblins and
humans have been broken. I say we are not ready for a peace
circle until we fully understand each other. A peace circle is
like a marriage. You do not do the marriage ceremony unless
you are certain you want to be married all your lives. You do
not sit the peace circle unless you are certain you want to live
in peace all your lives."

"And some of my people, and some of your people, are not
certain of this, though they should be," said Rockdream.

"Ah," said Beartooth.

Even in a storm like this, when water ran deep in the gutters, there were humans afoot on Castle Street doing errands, and when they saw the two goblins with Rockdream, they stared, or veered aside to avoid them, or smiled and waved.

Drakey said, "Goblins and humans have both lived on this land for many generations. You count the years as nearly two hundred. But still we are strangers to be stared at when we come to your city. This must be changed."

"It is the same when humans come to my camp," said Beartooth.

"Truly?" asked Rockdream. "I thought that humans came to Goblin Plain fairly often."

"They pass through," said Beartooth. "They do gift exchanges. They argue about gift exchanges, which to us is dishonorable. Humans say that whoever argues best in the trade, makes the best deal. Among goblins, men do men's work, and women do women's work, unless they are chiefs or shamans or shamanesses. One married couple can be a whole camp, can do everything they need to do to live. Among humans, it is different. Each person does just a few things, and must trade with others to get what they need to live. Because of this, gift exchange is vital to you, as it is not to us. But your way of doing it seems mean-spirited. That is hard for me to understand."

Rockdream gestured to the large building with fluted columns on the next block. "This is the Farmers' and Hunters' Market, one of the three large markets. When it is open, the humans inside do argue a lot. The buyer wants a lower price, and the seller wants a higher price, and they compromise to agree. I would not call that dishonorable, but perhaps it is mean-spirited. I will have to think about it."

They saw the warriors standing dragonwatch on the ramparts of the Old Wall, and walked through Churchgate, which like all gates in the Old Wall was unguarded except in times of emergency. Looming above them on the right was the Church of the First Son, and straight ahead were the tall towers of Newport Castle.

"We are halfway there," said Drakey. "Tell us something about your own life and deeds."

"I guess my most notable deed was my warrior's test, when I was given just two crossbow arrows to kill a drakey in Spirit Swamp. When it played dead and jumped on me, I broke its neck with my bare hands before it could bite me."

"Ah," said Beartooth. "Among our people, a deed like that would mark you as a warrior who might become a chief."

"I am considered a good warrior, but I cannot be promoted, because I am married to a witch."

"It is good for a chief to be married to a shamaness," Beartooth said firmly.

"Humans have two kinds of shamanesses," Drakey explained. "Priestesses are the respected ones. They are forbidden to marry or lie with men. Witches are the less respected ones. They can marry, or even lovemake promiscuously, but they must live outside the city walls. The two kinds of human shaman, the priest and the wizard, have the same distinctions."

"But why?" asked Beartooth.

Rockdream said, "The main work of priests and priestesses is chanting, prayer, and meditation. When they heal, they use safe herbs and limited magic. The main work of wizards and witches is healing, and they sometimes use dangerous herbs and potent spells."

Drakey said to Beartooth, "Humans see spirits differently than we do, but I might say this. The spirit beasts of the priests and priestesses are tame, like cattle and horses. The spirit beasts of the wizards and witches are wild and free, like aurochs and quagga.

"That is strange," said Beartooth.

Rockdream was still trying to understand Drakey's explanation when they passed Castle Park, the grassy island with a huge cypress tree and a fountain, just in front of the castle gates.

"I want to meet your wife," Drakey told Rockdream. "I will come to your home, before we return to Goblin Plain."

They announced themselves to the castle gate guards, one of whom led the goblin leaders inside, and Rockdream returned to Eastgate.

30.

Coral was overjoyed to hear of the high shaman's proposed visit, but a week passed, and another week, while Rockdream was practicing his crossbow for the Spring Tournament with other warriors at the Eastgate target range, and Salmon was learning to see the glimmer of light around each living thing, and Bloodroot, having nothing else to do, was learning to play Coral's lyre, but still Drakey did not come or send a message.

"If Drakey said he will come, he will come," Coral said one evening in response to Rockdream's doubts, but even while she said this, she herself was uncertain.

But that night she dreamed about Drakey not only coming to the cottage, but actually asking her and Rockdream to come to Goblin Plain. She told the others at breakfast that she thought this was a dreamsending.

"How can that be, when Drakey has never met you, and may not even know your name or what you look like?" Rockdream asked.

"Drakey is very wise, and the wise can learn whatever they need to know," said Coral.

Salmon and Bloodroot, who knew Drakey's reputation from their journeys through Goblin Plain aboard the *Golden Turtle,* both agreed with this.

At this moment, someone knocked on the door. "Lieutenant Coaljay of Eastgate to see the warrior Rockdream and the witch Coral," she said.

Rockdream rose to open the door, wondering why Coaljay had come all the way out here, when he would be on duty at Eastgate in a few hours.

"I will be quick and to the point," she said, coming inside and taking off her coat. When she saw Bloodroot and Salmon, she asked who they were, then decided that her news did not need to be kept secret from them. "I have a new duty for Rockdream, for the next month or so, and for Coral also," she said. "How soon is the baby due?"

"Not until late in the summer," Coral said, "and I have had no problems that would keep me from traveling."

"Then you know about Drakey's exchange plans. He said he spoke to Rockdream about this."

"Not exactly," Rockdream said.

"Then I will explain. Specifically, we want to strengthen the peace between Newport and Goblin Plain, by encouraging more contact between our two peoples. But this must be done cautiously at first, with people of balanced judgment, because humans and goblins all too often misunderstand each other's ways as dishonorable. Drakey wants you and Coral to come with him to Goblin Plain for a few weeks, to live with him and experience the ways of his people, and to answer their questions about humans."

"I will speak well for the honor of our city and its people," Rockdream said.

"Then you do accept? I must make it clear that you are not a diplomat. You are not going there to negotiate any official agreements between Newport and Goblin Plain. Make certain that your private opinions are not misconstrued as Lord Herring's policies, and be prepared to give a full report of your experiences when you return. Drakey has chosen you both, in preference to anyone else, because he has dreamed about you. I think this is a most strange way to make such a choice, but I think his choice is good. Lord Herring is more skeptical."

"They accept," said a man outside. "Now, the mysterious old goblin will come in." He removed his fur robe and set it beside Coaljay's coat. Underneath, he wore a vest and breeches of finer fur, which left his arms and legs bare, and on his feet were soft shoes. His weathered brown skin covered strong muscles for a man whose hair and eyebrows were turning white. At first, his direct stare made Coral uneasy, but soon she saw the compassion, sadness, and great wisdom expressed by his deep amber eyes and wrinkled face. "Your name is something that grows in the sea, farther south," he told her.

"Coral," she replied.

"My people have spoken your language since my father's father's time, but we do not know the words for certain things we have not seen."

"There are some corals on this part of the coast, away from the delta," she said. "The cup-sized fleshflowers that live in the rock pools are a kind of coral."

"Ah," said Drakey. "They are painful to touch."

"Some of them are," Coral agreed.

Drakey looked at Rockdream. "Have you ever paddled a canoe?"

"I have rowed a skiff."

"You are going by canoe, with the river swollen and swift?" asked Bloodroot incredulously.

"I looked at the river last night," Drakey said. "It has subsided since the last rain. No new rain will come for several days, and no mountain snows will melt for another month. Once we reach Spirit Swamp, flooding will not matter. We can paddle through the backwater. If a bad storm comes, we can wait on a hummock. There are advantages to using a boat small enough to carry. But to take best advantage of the weather, we must leave today."

Coral said, "That might be no problem for Rockdream, with Coaljay here to reschedule his duties, but I have clients whose needs I must consider. There is one old fishcatcher with an infected broken leg who must be seen every day, and a woman whose baby I promised to midwife. But I think that my mother and Salmon could handle those."

"You expect me to work with Moonwort?" asked Salmon.

"If the two of you are both going to be at my child's birth next summer, you should practice working together."

"But what if Sorrel's baby does not come before—"

"If Fairwind sends the *Golden Turtle* to Upriver before the birth, go ahead and work as a boat guard, and my mother will handle it, but I think the birth will come in no more than two weeks. But let us not talk to Mother until I am packed and leaving, or else I will have to listen to hours of her arguments about how frail I am."

Bloodroot said, "You may not be frail, but this will be a long uncomfortable trip, which could be made with ease aboard any riverboat a month from now."

Drakey said, "I prayed for a dream. The dream was clear. I will follow the instructions."

"I trust to your wisdom," said Coral.

31.

Drakey found the canoe where he and Beartooth had hidden it, beneath a clump of bronzeberry bushes in a grove of winter oak, near the riverbanks about four miles east of the cottage. Beartooth was not returning with them, but staying for a month as a guest at Lieutenant Bloodstone's Tower in the North Wall.

The canoe was about sixteen feet long, framed with cedar, and skinned with leather. After Rockdream helped him pull it out, Drakey inspected every inch of it carefully to make certain there was no damage.

"Should it smell like that?" asked Rockdream.

"Ah, you are not used to the smell of mammoth grease melted with pine pitch," Drakey said. "It stinks, but it is the best sealant. I think the canoe is fine. Let us carry it down the bank and see if I am right."

Here beneath the leafless willows was a pool, shielded from the current by a mound of mud deposited around a fallen tree still rooted to the bank. Rockdream pushed the canoe into the water and Drakey climbed in. After a few minutes, he said, "Not even a tiny leak," and they loaded their packs into the canoe. "To go upstream, we want the bow light," he said, so Coral sat on the front seat, Drakey on the middle, and Rockdream on the seat nearest the stern.

For many hours they paddled against the current, two at a time while one rested, until they reached the head of the delta, where the current became stronger, and all three had to paddle together to make progress. They stopped twice to eat meals of hard cheese, waybread, and dried fruit. In the evening, they found a sandbank to sleep on that was comfortably dry, and made a fire. Rockdream fell asleep while Drakey and Coral were talking about the stars.

On the second day, they passed the ruined Turtle River Keeps, and Drakey wondered why the humans had not rebuilt them.

"I wonder why they were built in the first place," said Coral. "The stone crumbles into sand, and the sandy soil is no good for most crops."

"I hate to admit it," Rockdream said, "but their main purpose was to keep goblins from coming farther down the river."

"Ah," said Drakey. "The keeps were built for Turtleport's wars, and Newport keeps peace with us."

A few hours upstream from the third keep, they stopped and made camp. While gathering wood for the fire, Rockdream startled a hare, which bounded away in zigzag leaps, and he sighed, for it would be long gone by the time he could string his longbow.

"If you want fresh food, we can fish tomorrow in the swamp," said Drakey. "Hares are hard to catch, even for a wolf or a lynx."

They reached the western marshes of Spirit Swamp at noon the next day, and now made much better time, paddling through the shallows where the water was almost still. But now there was no dry land, only sodden mudflats, and they had to eat their meals aboard the canoe, and use the chamber pot that Coral had thought to bring. The humans began to wonder where they would sleep.

"When we reach the trees, there will be hummocks," Drakey assured them, but at sunset few trees and no hummocks were in sight, and the water was so wide that they might easily miss seeing one in the dark.

"We will see the one we are meant to see," said Drakey.

"We have no other choice," said Rockdream.

"I hope the carp are still fresh when we get there," said Coral.

For what seemed like half the night, Rockdream and Drakey took turns paddling through the dark still water. By the time they began to see significant numbers of trees on their side of the river, Coral was asleep, slumped forward on her seat. Finally they found a hummock that rose several feet above water level, and stopped.

Drakey touched Coral's shoulder to wake her; she was stiff and clumsy from sleeping cold sitting up, and Rockdream half carried her to the center of the mound, an open place in a grove of old trees where the ground was damp but not sodden. Next he and Drakey brought up the packs, and Coral was by then enough awake to help them carry the canoe to the campsite. "You do not want to risk losing your canoe in Spirit Swamp," said Drakey.

Making a fire in the dark with wet driftwood was hard, but Drakey finally kindled one with pitch pine twigs he had thought to collect at the last campsite. The fire grew quickly, and by its light, Rockdream recognized the hummock as Fire Island, the same place he had camped four years before, when he killed the drakey for his warrior's test.

"We should check for river lizards," he said.

"If you want to check, check, but I have never seen river lizards in the winter," said Drakey.

"Where do they go?" asked Coral.

"No one cares," said Drakey.

They cooked the carp on sticks and ate them, and by this time the ground was somewhat dried by the fire, and they spread their furs and blankets and went to sleep.

Rockdream woke long after dawn, to the sound of Drakey and Coral discussing the weather. He was saying he expected rain that afternoon, lasting at least several hours, but no more than a day, and he was explaining exactly what patterns of cloud and wind led him to expect this.

"—but it is more a feeling than anything else. When you

have talked much with the spirits, you get true feelings, and you know the feelings are true."

Rockdream sat up, and saw that they were both wrapped in furs, and drying their other clothing over the fire.

"We both took baths," said Coral. "I think the best place is over there. The water is cold, but not as muddy as it looks. It made me feel much better."

Rockdream did not much like the idea of a cold bath on a cold morning, but his body smelled, and the fire was hot, so he walked through the trees to the place Coral indicated, where he saw an eight-foot-long river lizard sprawled on the sunny mudbank. He walked quietly back to the fire.

"Drakey, I have something to show you," he said.

When the old goblin man saw the river lizard, he said, "There is always something new, but I never expected a river lizard in winter, even if there are more and more every summer. Bah!" He kicked the overgrown salamander's blunt snout. "Away with you! Come back and sun yourself after we leave."

The river lizard grunted and tried to move, but torpidly stumbled over its own feet. Finally it managed to flop back into the water, where it swam slowly away.

"Just punch or kick its snout if it comes back," Drakey said, and left Rockdream to his bath.

This day's journey was relatively short, and ended at another hummock, just when the rain Drakey predicted began falling. He showed them how to build a goblin traveler's tent with bent sticks covered with some of the sleeping furs, skin side out. They made a small fire at the open end, and all three snuggled together fully dressed, between the humans' woolen blankets, and slept.

It was still raining when they broke camp in the morning, and it continued through most of that day's journey, but stopped late in the afternoon. They made a big fire to dry their things, and slept outside. In the middle of the night, Coral pressed herself as close to Rockdream as her swollen belly would allow, and began to kiss him. He took down his pants and she her bloomers and they made love, tangled in their clothes, blankets, and furs.

The journey through Spirit Swamp continued, through a cloudy day, a partly sunny day, and a day when it rained hard and long. The river was already so broad and flooded that this rain did not noticeably quicken the current or raise the water level. The wind blowing in gusts from the west helped move them upstream, and they paddled through the shallows where it did not whip up waves.

Before building a traveler's tent that evening, they kindled a large fire to warm themselves, with dry sticks saved from an earlier campsite. The sight of hard rain sizzling and sputtering on flame and ashes reminded Rockdream of the winter when he stood dragonwatch on the ramparts of Canticle's Tower.

Coral said, "Bloodroot was right about this being a long, uncomfortable journey. But I do not mind, in fact, I am glad to be standing by this fire in the rain, with my husband and my new friend. I feel stronger and healthier than I have felt any-time since my pregnancy began."

Drakey said, "Among goblins, for a person to call another person friend is a very serious thing."

"I meant no offense," said Coral, "but is that not what you wanted, to make us both your friends? Why else travel with us for all these days, in a canoe, in this rain? I thought that was your dream, to make humans and goblins friends with each other. You are a person I trust and admire. We have spent much time together, and shown each other kindness. Is this not friendship?"

"Beartooth is my friend," said Drakey. "He is like a brother or a son to me. His friends are my friends. His family is my family. His enemies are my enemies. Am I like that to you?"

When Coral did not reply, Rockdream said, "Friendship is between one person and another, and must not become a web of alliance and opposition. As a squire I was taught to make my own judgment about each person. A friend's foe need not be my own."

Drakey said, "Strong Bull was my friend. When we choose the high chief, the winner of the contest may kill any of the losers who might threaten his authority. The two men Strong Bull killed were also my friends. I thought we chose the wrong high chief. But Strong Bull has been a good high chief. My mistake was to befriend men who were each other's enemies."

"I would put the fault on a custom which encourages people to be enemies," said Coral.

"Our ways are different," the shaman said. "Some goblins say the human way is soft, but I disagree. You are not soft people. Many goblins would not paddle a canoe through the flooded swamp. I say your way is not soft, but compassionate.

This is a strength in the spirit world, and also in the solid world. We are starting a friendship. Perhaps someday you will be my friends, as Beartooth is my friend.''

When they crawled out of the traveler's tent the next morning, the rain had stopped, and a brilliant mist was dissolving in the sunlight. After some hours of paddling, they reached the mouth of the Blue River, a clearer water with noticeable current, and now they paddled two at a time or all three together.

The second day after the rain, the river was a rich coppery green, and they caught several brown trout, a welcome change from carp and whiskerfish. That evening, they even saw three turtles swimming through the braided waters of the shallows.

"A time will come when we can hunt them again, maybe in five or ten years," Drakey said.

32.

On the next day they came at last to Goblin Plain, a wide grassland with scattered oak and scrub trees, and willows by the edge of a river with well-defined banks and a current strong enough to give them aching arms. Some of the oaks were winter oaks, which never shed all their leaves, but most of the trees were bare. The grass was bright green, ankle high, and already speckled with the yellows and blues of spring blossoms, for it was indeed spring, and the second day of the new year, the 198th year of humans east of the sea, but Rockdream had not yet counted up the days, or thought about the tournament he was missing.

Not far beyond the junction of the Goblin River and the Blue was the first goblin camp. They beached the canoe near several others, and while they climbed out, two guards approached, goblin men armed with spears and throwers.

"Ah, Drakey!" said one. "Welcome to Beadback's Camp. Who are these?"

"These are my guests, Rockdream the Warrior, and his wife, Coral the Witch, humans of Newport."

"We mean no disrespect, high shaman, but the warriors of Beadback's Camp do not welcome humans," said the other guard.

"These humans are not like the ones you know," Drakey said. "The sun sets soon. Will you refuse a night's lodging to three weary travelers, one a pregnant woman? If so, you are more mean-spirited than any human merchant.''

"Bah!" said the second guard.

"Come to the cookfires, and we will see," said the first.

Beadback's Camp at first looked like a haphazard cluster of conical tents, some small and portable, some almost as large as cottages, all made of poles covered with leather, many with plumes of smoke. The big smoke, a smell of mammoth meat, came from the center, where the humans saw that the tents were placed in two concentric circles around an open court-yard, with three cookfires and work areas covered by awnings in the center. Through a gap in the circles they could see the camp's totem pole, carved with the faces of six different spirit beasts.

Perhaps seventy or eighty goblins, men, women, and children, were gathered in the center, standing or sitting, conversing or eating. All turned to stare at Drakey and the humans, while the two guards spoke with a big man who was probably Chief Beadback.

A young goblin woman wearing a sleeveless leather dress with a short skirt offered Rockdream and Coral a plate-shaped basket with steaming grain and smoked slices of meat, and said, "Be careful of your fingers. It is hot."

"Thank you," said Coral.

"Should we get spoons?" Rockdream whispered.

"It does seem messy, but let us try it their way," Coral said, and after a tentative touch, she scooped a small bit of hot grain onto her fingers and put it into her mouth. "It is good."

"I would say it needs seasoning."

They sampled the meat, and found it flavorful, if tough to chew.

When Beadback came with Drakey to talk to the humans, he denounced everything he considered mean-spirited about their society, including the greed of merchants and fishcatchers, the use of domestic animals for food and transport, and the thick stone walls around the city that sealed out the world. Beadback reminded Rockdream of Lieutenant Canticle, who would make assertions just to provoke an argument, and he phrased his replies and explanations as carefully as he could.

Coral was less patient. At one point, she said, "I feel as though we are in a wolves' den, and the leader is baring his teeth and growling, while the rest of the pack watches intently to see how we will respond.''

Beadback howled and stamped his feet. ''Yes, I am a son of the Great Mother Wolf, and I growl when strangers come.''

The humans spent the night in Beadback's tent, and learned to their surprise that the young woman who had served them dinner was Beadback's wife. She was curious about the woven wool blankets and clothing, but Beadback said this was unnecessary work, that fur left on the skin was warmer still, and after that she asked the humans no more questions about their things.

The more Coral thought about this interaction, the more it disturbed her, and the next day, while she and Rockdream were walking with Drakey toward Beartooth's Camp, she commented, ''Beadback did not even have to tell her not to talk with us. His hint was enough to frighten her into stifling her curiosity. It is wrong for one person to try to control another's thoughts.''

''Among goblins, the wife obeys the husband,'' Drakey said. ''But she has chosen him to be her husband, and she can leave him if she finds him overbearing.''

''Obedience is for children, not for grown women,'' said Coral.

Rockdream said, ''When I make old Plowpuller obey me, I am taking his spirit, according to your people. If I made Coral obey me, would I not be taking her spirit?''

''Yes, that is just what Beadback did. He took his wife's spirit,'' said Coral.

Drakey made no immediate response to this, but after a few minutes, he said, ''You will like Beartooth's wife, Cicada. She is a strong woman like you.''

He also said, ''Both of you have many questions, about how goblins live, about how your own people live, about what is true and right. You give me a new question. Do I dislike the human way because it is wrong, or because it shows that my own way might be wrong? You make me wonder what is good and bad about both ways of life. You make me want a new vision.''

''Asking many questions is the heart of witchcraft,'' Coral said. ''It seems so natural to me that I am always surprised when other people blindly accept old customs and ideas.''

''I felt that way when I was young,'' Drakey said. ''Now I am less certain that I know better than anyone else, whether I question old customs or accept them.''

33.

The grassland they crossed was rich with animals: several kinds of fast-running antelope, each with differently shaped horns; a herd of quagga grazing in the distance; a circle of condors and ravens above a pair of fangtooth cats dismembering a carcass; and a lone valley mammoth bull, stripping leaves from a winter oak.

Beartooth's Camp was slightly larger than Beadback's, with a taller totem pole with eight spirit beasts. The guards welcomed Drakey and the humans, and led them to the center, where again it was the evening meal. Cicada herself served them each a basket-plate of grain, flatbread, and slices of auroch meat. She was a stout muscular woman of about thirty summers, and a shamaness skilled in healing who was very interested in comparing knowledge with a human witch.

She introduced them to Screaming Spear, who was acting chief in Beartooth's absence, and his daughter, Glowfly, who was her apprentice, and her own sons, Stronghorn and Fang, still boys, and some of the other warriors and women.

"Why are goblin warriors all men?" Coral asked.

Screaming Spear said, "Men are stronger. It is natural for men to hunt and fight, and for women to gather grain and care for children. I have seen human warrior women, but I do not understand why any woman would want to be a warrior."

"Why not?" asked Coral.

"Women give birth," said Cicada. "How can we also give death?"

"I have never killed anything bigger than a chicken, but I can kill," said Coral, "and I obviously can give birth."

"Killing a ground bird and killing a person are not the same," said Screaming Spear.

"I do not think there are many warriors alive in Newport now who have ever killed a person," said Rockdream.

"I have killed three men in battle," said Screaming Spear. "That was many years ago, before Beartooth was chief, even before I was chief. This camp fought a battle with another camp. The reasons seem foolish now. A woman left her husband and they said we held her captive. They killed a mammoth too close to our camp. Before Strong Bull was chosen high chief, there were too many battles between camps."

"Even one such battle was too many," said Drakey.

By the time most of the goblins finished eating, the sun was setting and the gibbous moon was bright and high in the east. Glowfly said that she would tell a story, especially for the camp's human guests, and everyone who wanted to hear should form a circle around the main fire. When this was done, she began:

> Hear my chant of a goblin people
> who lived north of the Turtle River's mouth,
> where waves of the sea struck sandy beaches,
> where mussels and abalones grew on the rocks,
> where herds of great elk grazed the meadow,
> where silver unicorns browsed the forest,
> where salmon swam up the sparkling streams.

Glowfly described in great detail the small camps and tents of these goblins, how the men hunted elk and caught fish, and how the women gathered shellfish, nuts, berries, and herbs.

In one of these camps at one time lived a shamaness named Raven, who was wife of the chief.

> One morning, Raven told her husband,
> "I dreamed I was picking herbs in the forest.
> I came back to camp, but it was burned down.
> All the people were horrible ghosts.
> Their faces and bodies were burned to the bones.
> The dragon is death! The dragon is death!
> They were chanting this.
> I ran away, up into the forest.
> I heard them follow but did not look back.
> I came to a secret place of power.
> I prayed to my totem, Great Father Otter.
> He told me to turn and look.
> I saw all the people healthy and whole.
> I asked him what this meant.
> He warned me that a dragon is coming,
> and everyone must flee to the forest."

The people of Raven's husband's camp heeded this advice, and moved their camp that very day, away from the lush meadows and herds of elk, to the secret power place hidden in the forested foothills. They also sent two messengers, both men who had relatives in the camps a few miles north and south, to spread the warning to these camps. Both men rejoined Raven's people two days later, for she had told them where to come.

> All that summer, all that winter,
> they camped in that secret power place.
> They all had dreams of their spirit beasts.
> Some days they were warned to make no fire.
> Sometimes the air was smoky from fires
> the dragon kindled, miles from their camp.
> Sometimes the hunters killed a deer,
> but most of the food was gathered by women,
> berries and nuts and tubers and herbs.
> Sometimes they even ate termites and grubs.
> The women all chewed freedomwort.
> Nobody wanted any babies then.

Finally they sent a scout to see how it was on the coast. He saw campfire smoke, where the next camp north used to be, and walked there. He saw no fresh signs of great elk. The goblins at that camp told him that the dragon killed and ate all the great elk it could find, and also the people of two camps who had not listened to Raven's warning. But there was plentiful food, small game and fish and shells. When the scout returned to Raven's husband's camp, they moved back to the sea.

> Their descendants still lived on that land
> after Windsong's humans made Turtleport.
> Some of their chiefs sat the great peace circle.
> They gave that land to the humans.
> Some of them came to Goblin Plain,
> and joined the people who lived here already.
> They brought the story of Raven with them.

Glowfly's audience stamped their feet, slapped their knees, and howled, which was the goblin way of applauding.

"I was deeply moved," Coral said. "I feel as though I want to be a woman like Raven, who knows the truth when she hears it. Your people have a better way of coping with dragons than mine do. But how could this lesson be applied to human cities? It could not. Ten thousand people cannot hide in a forest a few miles away when a dragon comes. Maybe humans should not live in cities.''

"Coral, these people were starving in the forest and eating grubs,'' said Rockdream. "They were not even truly safe from the dragon. It could have heard their thoughts and found them.''

"Goblin thoughts are not so easy to hear,'' said Drakey. "They were in the place where Raven's dream told them to go. She dreamed they were safe there, and they were safe.''

34.

That night they slept in Screaming Spear's tent. His wife, Antelope, and his two sons, Brown Fox and Big Toad, aged twelve and eight, also lived there. Glowfly lived in her husband's tent.

Antelope woke Coral at dawn to ask whether she wanted to help the women prepare breakfast. They were frying loaves of flatbread and strips of meat with melted fat, on hot grills made of tiles and bricks. Though Coral carefully watched how the goblin women spun and stretched the loaves of flatbread, her own attempts were laughable, and the loaf she tried to flip with the bone tongs broke in half. She ended up tending the fires, carefully so as not to crack the tiles, and frying the meat.

After breakfast, about half the warriors left camp with Drakey, to hunt the lone mammoth that he and the humans had seen the day before. Rockdream wanted to go with them, but Screaming Spear said, "Before you try to hunt a mammoth, you must learn to throw a spear.'' This was true. Rockdream had once harpooned a turtle, but goblin spear-throwers had much greater range.

"I will teach you,'' said Brown Fox confidently.

"No. I will teach him. A man must learn from a man.''

"May I watch, Father?''

"It would be better for you to get your brother and some of the other boys together to hunt some small animals or catch some fish. I have a feeling the warriors may not get that mammoth.''

"All right,'' said Brown Fox.

Screaming Spear took Rockdream to a place away from camp. For practice, they used blunt poles with the weight and balance of real spears, and for a target, they used the mound of a groundchuck hole. The goblin demonstrated how to hold the practice pole in the carved groove of the spear-thrower, which deepened toward the pole's butt end. He stood in the simplest throwing position, snapped the spear-thrower forward, and the pole struck the target. "The spear-thrower makes your arm longer, so that you can throw farther, and with more force," he said.

Rockdream picked up the pole and laid it in the spear-thrower as Screaming Spear had done, but when he snapped the spear-thrower forward, the pole flipped end over end.

"Too much swing and not enough push in your release," the goblin said. "Get the pole and try again."

This time it only wobbled in flight, but it still struck nowhere near the target. Rockdream tried again and again. One time it spun horizontally, and Screaming Spear said this was because he twisted his throw slightly to one side. Each time that Rockdream thought he was getting the feel of it, the pole would wobble or flip or land nowhere near the target. His arms became sore.

"You did well for someone just beginning," said Screaming Spear. "More practice is the only way to gain control."

But Rockdream had a feeling for weapons. He knew he was best with the longbow, and gaining mastery with the crossbow, but his skill with the sword would always be indifferent no matter how much he practiced, and the same was likely true of his skill with the spear-thrower.

That evening the warriors returned from their hunt empty-handed, but no one seemed particularly concerned. There was still quite a bit of auroch meat, and the boys had caught some fish. But the portions of meat on each person's plate were smaller, and when the next day's hunt brought back no fresh meat, Cicada said, "Tomorrow is the first full moon of spring. If whoever goes out tomorrow does not come back with something before noon, we will have to feast on grain and fish, or maybe even stew, before we dance."

Screaming Spear, Sees Far, Gray Lizard, and the other best hunters rose to this challenge, and went out to hunt before dawn. They killed a quagga stallion, and though they did not quite return before noon, the women had plenty of time to prepare a memorable feast.

At sunset, Drakey began the Spring Moon Ceremony with a prayer to the four directions: to the west, where the sun was setting, to the east, where the moon was rising, to the north, where the winter was retreating, and to the south, where the summer was approaching.

Glowfly told a spirit beast story, about how Great Mother Wolf, and her husband, the high chief of wolves, and all their chiefs and warriors, drove the winter away, a long time ago when snow and ice tried to cover all the world.

This story was prelude to a dance, and when Glowfly struck her drum, Cicada, Antelope, and two other women beat their drums, and everyone got up to dance the Wolf Dance, even Coral and Rockdream. This was the most important dance of the Spring Moon. On years when it was cold and rainy, the goblins would put power from their own totems into the dance, to help the spirit wolves drive the winter away. On years when the weather was good, as it was now, they danced in celebration of the wolves' success.

They also danced a Moon Dance, and the men danced a Hunting Dance, to bring the animals closer to the river.

35.

The next day, after the morning meal was done, Coral sat down by herself, near the totem pole on the edge of camp. This pole was a cedar log from the Emerald Hills, floated down the Goblin River and up the Blue, and rolled to the campsite, where it was carved with eight spirit-beast heads, Wolf, Raven, Fangcat, Condor, Bear, Otter, Elk, and Weasel. These were done in the symbolic style, which emphasized essence over appearance.

Coral was beginning to relax into trance when Glowfly sat beside her and asked what she was doing.

"When I ask you questions about spirit beasts, you say I must learn for myself. I am trying to learn for myself."

"By sitting in front of the totem pole?"

"If I went to the Rose Garden, and sat in front of the Statue of Cloud the Wizard, and entered trance, he would talk to me," said Coral.

"To speak with a god is a fearsome thing," said Glowfly. "A god is like a high chief, who tells you what you must do. A spirit beast is more like a wise and clever friend."

"If I can talk to a god in front of a god statue, why can I not talk to a spirit beast in front of a spirit beast statue?"

"Because a god is out there." Glowfly spread her arms

wide. "A spirit beast out there is no different from any other god. But a totem is in here." She tapped her heart. "My own Father Otter is in here."

"Then I must not have a spirit beast," said Coral, "for I have looked deeply inside my heart many times, and I have never seen anything like that."

"Some goblins say that humans have no spirit beasts. I think they are wrong. I think if you look, not just deeply, but all the way down to the center of the world of your heart, you will find your spirit beast there."

"All right," said Coral, "when I enter trance, I will go there."

"This totem pole is a symbol to intimidate the enemies of this camp. You might want to choose a different kind of power place for your meditation. Come, and I will show you my own favorite place. Perhaps it will also be a good place for you."

Glowfly and Coral walked away from camp for almost a mile, to the hugest and most beautiful redbark tree the human woman had ever seen. It stood by itself atop a low hill. From a trunk more than ten feet wide, it split into four large branches, each branching many times, to make a broad, domed crown, lush and green, for redbark trees never shed all their leaves.

"Any place which can grow a tree like this one is a place of strong power," said Coral. "I have seen firs and pines grow bigger than this in the Foggy Mountain foothills, but for a redbark to grow so big, where there are few trees of any kind, is amazing to me."

Coral sat facing south, with her back against the smooth bark, next to a big buttressing root, and closed her eyes to enter trance, to make a journey to the center of the world of her heart. She began the wordless chant to the Nameless Mother, and felt her own roots go deep into the ground, beside the roots of the great tree.

She entered the world of her heart through a doorway, and found a lushly furnished bedroom, with a lace-canopied feather-bed, and Rockdream, nude and eager to make love. Part of her wanted to do this, but part of her wanted to continue the search, so she imagined these two parts of herself separating, one self a sensuous naked woman, to smother her husband with kisses and feel his penetrations, and the other self a serious student of witchcraft, who opened a door, marked *to the center*.

Here was a crying baby who needed to be nursed and

cleaned, who sometimes changed into a small boy calling her
Mommy and wanting to show her something, or wanting her to
tell him a story. She heard Moonwort saying, "I warned you
that a child would distract you from your studies," and she
replied, "Oh, nonsense, Mother!" and split herself in two
again, one self a light-hearted and patient woman to mother
the boy, and the other self a serious student of witchcraft, who
opened another door, marked *to the center*.

Here was a little girl, Coral herself at age six, who was very
frightened of dragons, dream dragons that swooped out of the
fog to burn and kill. "What if they become real? What if the
dreams come true?" the girl was saying.

"Those dreams are not prophecies, but a frightened young
girl's reaction to Riversong's conquest of Moonport."

"What about the battle dream?" asked the girl, and the fog
cleared to reveal a battlefield, with Rockdream's bloody body
among many other human and goblin bodies.

"That dream is no prophecy either, but a frightened young
woman's reaction to the turtle crisis."

"Are you sure?" asked the girl.

Part of Coral wanted to stay and comfort this child, and part
of her wanted to continue the search, so she split herself in two
again, one self a strong and rational woman, to drive the
child's nightmares away, and the other self a serious student of
witchcraft, who opened a very large, strong door, marked *to
the center*.

Here was Moonwort floating in a vague nothingness. "This
is the chaos," she said. "Your work as a witch is to organize
these points into strands of light which heal."

Here was her life's work, but another part of her was looking, looking—

"For a spirit beast?" asked Moonwort. "What use is that?"

Coral did not know the answer, but she split herself in two
again, one self a serious student of witchcraft to continue her
life's work, and the other self a vague shadowy woman, who
opened the next door, marked *to the center*.

"Not much of you left, is there?" called Moonwort's voice.

Something is left. I am a soul, a soul who has worn many
bodies before wearing the body of Coral. I have joy, compassion, love. Sometimes I am a woman, sometimes I am a man. I
think, I feel, I change. I twist chaos into strings of light to heal.
I see time from the timeless place, and bring peace, to displace

pain and fear. I am a mother, with a baby growing in my belly. I am wife, to a man who needs my love and help, and I also need his love and help.

Who am I? What am I? Why do I exist?

I twist chaos into strings of light to make myself.

To heal myself.

This was all that Coral could remember, afterwards. When she opened her eyes, she saw Glowfly sitting very still, looking up into the redbark tree. Coral turned her head, and saw, perched on a branch, a full-grown male speckled condor, looking back at her with big yellow eyes on either side of a sharp yellow beak.

"There is your totem," Glowfly said in a low voice. "Sometimes the spirit brings the real animal."

At the sound of Glowfly's words, the condor turned his red, featherless head to look at her, then turned back to Coral.

"Yes," Coral said to the bird. "I know I have a spirit much like you in my heart."

The condor shifted his right claw, and adjusted a wing, then jumped into flight, a vast stroke of brown and white wings, under the branches, and up into the sky.

36.

A few days later, Coral watched Cicada and Glowfly heal a young girl who had a stuffed nose, headache, and fever. The tea they made for her to drink was similar to what Coral would have given her; but the leather patches soaked in bowls of hot and cold water, which they put on her forehead, chest, and thighs, and the white smoke, fanned with feathers from a smoldering bundle of reeds, were new techniques to her.

With her trance-eye, Coral could see patterns of light in the bowls of water and the smoke, almost as if the shamanesses first put their magic into the water and smoke, then used these to heal, rather than using the magic directly, as Coral would have done. Cicada explained later that they did this so the sickness could not strike back at them, if their magic was not strong enough to defeat it.

Coral also went on herb-gathering walks with the two women. They knew many of the same plants she knew, but not all, and they knew some she did not know.

She felt a kinship with Cicada and Glowfly that transcended

race and culture. Cicada was at heart a healer, skilled especially with bad wounds, broken bones, and fevers. Glowfly shared with Coral a curiosity about everything in the world, and they exchanged stories about the habits of birds and snails.

In the meantime, Rockdream had given up trying to learn spear-throwing, and took his longbow to go hunting with the men, arguing that it was a weapon more than potent enough for aurochs and quaggas. Two days of unsuccessful hunts lost many of his arrows, but he made himself several arrows with bone points to replace these, one day when Gray Lizard and Sees Far were teaching the boys of the camp how to make bone-tipped spears.

As Gray Lizard said, "Steel points are better because they are stronger and sharper. Bone points are better because we can make them ourselves."

A few days later, the first human riverboat of the year, the *Golden Turtle* of Newport, bound for Upriver, stopped at Beartooth's Camp, to return Chief Beartooth from Newport, and trade with his people. Salmon and Bloodroot were among those who came ashore to help carry the goods into camp for Captain Terrapin, mostly because they wanted to see Coral and Rockdream.

Of these goods, the two bronze cauldrons and the bronze grill already belonged to Beartooth. This was part of a gift exchange between him and Tower Lieutenant Bloodstone, who would receive from him a pair of mammoth tusks at least four feet long, sometime in the next two years. A small number of steel spearpoints were given to Beartooth, as toll for passing through his camp's hunting territory. The rest of these, and the steel knives and other goods, were offered for trade.

Immediately a problem arose, for the market value of moonstones had dropped considerably since the previous summer, and the goblin men who wanted to trade these for knives or spearpoints accused the humans of being mean-spirited. Captain Terrapin's explanation that this was because moonstones were both more plentiful and less in demand than before was not accepted.

One warrior said, "Animals and plants can become more plentiful, but rocks cannot! And how can they be less in demand? What people use, they use."

A goblin woman said, "The value of a thing does not change from year to year."

Captain Terrapin replied that the true value of a thing does not change, but the market value does, from place to place and from time to time, and without this variance in market value, trade would not exist.

Or at least merchants would not exist, Rockdream thought to himself. He could understand both the human and goblin viewpoints, but did not know how to reconcile the two.

Meanwhile, Salmon was telling Coral that Sorrel's birthing had gone smoothly, and the infection in Graywool's leg was healed enough that he could hobble around on crutches. "Moonwort and I still have our disagreements, but I greatly respect her knowledge."

"How long did it take you to get here?" Bloodroot asked Rockdream.

"Ten or eleven days, I think. I lost count. What day is this?"

"The 18th," replied Bloodroot. "This is our fifth day from Newport. The captain still wants us to reach Upriver by the 35th, but I think it will take several more days, even with good wind. The current is strong."

"The river is actually higher than it was two weeks ago," said Rockdream. "Drakey timed our journey just right, between the end of the heavy rains and the melting of the mountain snows."

The trading was completed quickly, for Terrapin wanted to take full advantage of the afternoon westerly. Rockdream and Coral said goodbye to Salmon and Bloodroot, then joined the goblins in welcoming Beartooth back to camp.

Later that afternoon, the women had trouble using the new bronze grill, which tended to burn the flatbread, until Coral suggested they raise it higher above the fire. It was still less satisfactory than the tile grills, but Coral said, "Remember how much trouble I had at first with tile grills? This just takes getting used to."

"Why change a thing that is already good enough?" asked one of the older women.

"This might be better, once we learn how to use it," said Cicada.

At the main fire after dinner, Beartooth told the story of his stay in Newport. He described Bloodstone's Tower as "twice as high as our totem pole, three times as wide as our biggest tent, and the walls are this thick—" He spread his arms wide.

"They have many towers that big. They have a few that are much bigger.

"At first I thought the humans were foolishly afraid. I know the old stories we tell about dragons. If dragons now grow as big as the humans say, they are much bigger than they used to be. If dragons really play thought-listening games to outwit the humans, they are much smarter than they used to be. Or maybe a new kind of dragon has come to this land, following the humans. They say dragons have always been like this.

"But then I thought about how humans split life into small pieces. The warriors' work is to worry about dragons. They are experts at fighting dragons. They say no dragon is too big to fight. Maybe the dragons have learned how to fight back.

"But why do they worry about a thing that comes only once in thirty or forty years? They do this because they are rich in things they can lose. They have their city, their belongings, their animals, their orchards, their farms. Even if a dragon does not kill them all, it can take or destroy all these things. So when a dragon comes, the warriors must fight.

"But other people in the city do not think so much about dragons. They do whatever piece of life they do. Some do nothing but grind flour and bake bread. They make many different kinds of bread. Some are sweeter than the ripest berries.

"We call the riverboat humans mean-spirited because they argue about value, and seldom stay to eat or dance. But their piece of life is to sail up and down the river and trade. For them, getting a better deal means what better hunting means, to us. They have to do a whole year's worth of trading in less than eight moons. When we see them, they have no time for anything else.

"The chiefs of trading are the merchants, who we never see. They seem very greedy for wealth. But the merchant I talked to told me that he needs this wealth to build the big riverboats and ships. Maybe this is true."

Beartooth went on to list as many different occupations as he could remember, some of which seemed amazing and funny to the goblins, who afterwards made jokes about which pieces of life certain goblins might be best suited for.

But even though Beartooth considered the human way of life unbalanced and needlessly complex, he had developed a taste for human breads and stews, and since Coral knew little about baking, he asked her to show the women how to make a stew that was really delicious.

"The biggest difference between our stews and yours is onions and garlic, which have to be grown in gardens, or else traded for. But there are herbs growing wild here which might be used to season a stew. I will see what I can do."

So Coral went herb-gathering with Glowfly one more time, this time searching for wild spices. The stew she made was almost as distastefully bland as the stuff the goblins made when hunting was bad, but they were actually quite pleased with it, except for Beartooth and Drakey, who had tasted much better.

The day after this, a boat from Upriver, the *Wandering Elk*, sailed down the river with passengers and goods bound for Newport. Upriver boats did not often stop at goblin camps on the way downstream, but the goblin boys who were fishing on the shore saw the boat in time, and signaled for it to stop, as they had been told to do.

Rockdream and Coral were both in camp, and in moments, they were packing and saying hurried goodbyes to Drakey, Beartooth, Cicada, Screaming Spear, Glowfly, and all the others. Gray Lizard paddled them to the middle of the river, where they climbed aboard the anchored riverboat.

"Thank you for stopping," Rockdream told the captain.

"Diplomats from Newport, I suppose?" she said. "I will make the fare three treemarks for both of you."

"A treemark is the same weight as a Newport singlestar, is it not?" asked Rockdream.

"Near enough," the captain said, then shouted, "Pull the anchor and set the mainsails!" while Rockdream counted out twelve quarterstars.

37.

Rockdream and Coral were given an audience with Lord Herring, Baron Oakspear, and several important diplomats, in the common room of Eastgate's north tower, which was the first time Coral had ever been allowed inside either Eastgate tower, much less been in the presence of the lord.

He was then a man of fifty-seven summers, several years younger than Drakey, but he looked much less healthy and happy than the old goblin, for all the magnificence of his clothes and surroundings. But Coral knew better than to even hint that she could help him with medicines or treatments.

Lord Herring frequently interrupted their presentation to ask questions or tell them what was irrelevant. He was interested in mundane details, such as how goblins arranged their possessions inside their tents, and how they protected their grain supply from mice and rats, but he was not at all interested in their religion, magic, or philosophy, which was what the young humans thought they had gone there to study.

But at the end of the audience, he told them that, if they wanted, he would arrange a formal storytelling for them, later in the week, where they could talk about goblins their own way. And so, a few days later, they found themselves again in the Eastgate common room, facing a cramped audience of over a hundred humans, mostly squires from the castle, but with some warriors and tower lieutenants, and a few diplomats, storytellers, and minstrels.

Rockdream spoke first, narrating the canoe journey, with comments from Coral, who then recounted their receptions at the two different goblin camps, including a summary of Glowfly's story of Raven the Shamaness. They took turns describing the routines of life, the spiritual practices, and explaining the philosophy behind both, as well as they understood it.

After they finished, one of the storytellers invited them to speak at his own story circle, and Loon the Minstrel, who had traded Coral the lyre, complimented their presentation, and said she would like to meet Glowfly and learn some goblin chants.

The next day, Rockdream resumed his duties at Eastgate, which was busy with farmers going out to work the fields, and miners bringing back cartloads of ore, which had to be inspected and tallied. Coral did some healing work that spring, and she and Rockdream repeated their goblin lecture several times, to story circles in various parts of the city, and once to an audience of sailors and fishcatchers in the Tidewater Tavern. Salmon and Bloodroot returned home for a few days about this time, then left again on the *Golden Turtle*'s second trip to Upriver.

The month before the solstice, Coral's cramps and pains came back, and the baby was kicking more often, so she worked less, and spent more time at home, playing the lyre, or reading borrowed history books, or simply sitting on the log in front of the cottage, admiring the beauty of the forest.

Salmon and Bloodroot came home again just two days before the solstice, and danced with Rockdream and Coral in the Rose Garden on solstice night. Coral's belly was swollen large, and she was awkward on her feet, but dancing felt good even so, at least for a short while. She and Rockdream went home early.

When the *Golden Turtle* left for its third trip the next day, Bloodroot went, and Salmon stayed, to be with Coral for the last weeks of pregnancy and the birth.

6

YEAR OF THE COMET

38.

A week before Midsummer's Day, a merchant ship from Godsfavor, west of the sea, sailed into Newport Harbor. Their interpreter had died at sea, and most of them did not speak the local language well, if at all, but Newport had storytellers and clergy who could understand and speak the Godsfavor language well enough to conclude trade, including a small fee to cover this service.

However, translating and understanding the strange tale that Captain Catch-Plenty and the crew of the *Diving Pelican* told of their voyage was much more difficult.

About a week before arriving in Newport, the *Diving Pelican* encountered two dragons, much bigger than any dragons west of the sea—longer than their ship, and with wings that covered the sky. Dragons were seldom seen so far from land, and almost never more than one at a time.

It was a bright, clear morning with a brisk, favorable wind, the sort of weather when no one would expect to see a dragon, but they did, a rust-colored dragon flapping its wings in the distant west, moving closer as if it was chasing them.

Captain Catch-Plenty ordered his crew to the dragon guns, but the dragon stopped moving toward them and flew in a circle, then suddenly swooped, splashed the waves, and flapped furiously to rise again with what looked like a porpoise in its front claws, which it quickly bit in half and swallowed in two bites. At first, they thought it must have been a young porpoise, because no dragon could have a head that large, especially not this dragon, whose head seemed disproportionately small for its body.

It did not at first come closer to the ship, but rather flew what looked like miles in random directions, or at least far enough to shrink it to a speck. This might have been a hunting technique to fool the porpoises, though no one had ever heard of a dragon catching porpoises before.

It was again relatively near the *Diving Pelican* when it caught another porpoise. This time, it folded its wings and plunged into the water. Dragons do have a large flight bladder filled with firegas, which is lighter than air, so it was not impossible to believe that it bobbed back up from its dive, with the porpoise in its mouth, clear out of the sea and into the air, where it flapped its wings to gain altitude.

But though this might be possible, it seemed unlikely to the translating storyteller, and she noted that this might be marine exaggeration.

Captain Catch-Plenty held his course. There was certainly no way his ship could either hide from the dragon or outrace it. Then one of the mariners shouted, and pointed in the opposite direction. Their attention had been focused on the red dragon, and no one aboard had noticed the green dragon until it was quite close.

It was flying no higher than twice the height of the tallest mast, and it was huge, easily big enough to swallow a full-grown porpoise without even bothering to bite it in half. This was probably not marine exaggeration. No one had seen the dragon Riversong of Moonport for several years, but he was nearly that big, and also a dull coppery green. Yes, this dragon was male, Catch-Plenty could not doubt that, but if he was Riversong, he was far from his normal territory.

There was no time to re-aim the dragon guns, no time to do anything. But the green male breathed no fire, not even at the sails, usually the most tempting target, and did not even say anything, which was doubly odd. No dragon in its right mind would come so close to armed humans unless it meant to attack, but if it did not attack, surely it would speak some message of fear to be delivered wherever the ship was going.

But all the green dragon did was pass over the ship, then flap quickly to gain altitude, making a blast of wind that cracked the second mast, which was already damaged from a storm.

Now the red dragon bellowed, and flapped its wings to rise. The green one chased it, but when it came close, the red changed direction to circle it, and then the red was chasing the green.

Captain Catch-Plenty ordered his crew to watch both dragons, which they were already doing, and also to watch everywhere else, because where there were two dragons, there just might be three or more. This pattern of chase and circle could be a mating dance, but it could also be a contest between two males for a nearby female. The red was never close enough to the *Diving Pelican* for anyone to see its sex.

Both dragons now stayed well out of range of the ship's dragon guns, though they chased each other all around the ship. After a while, they stayed to the ship's stern, and after what seemed an eternity, they were out of sight. Some hours later, the sun reddened and set.

This incident was much discussed in the towers, taverns, and markets of Newport. Rockdream first heard about it at Eastgate, and Salmon visited the harbor and the Tidewater Tavern the next day, to learn all the details.

"It is a rare glimpse into dragon life and behavior," she said. "I think the male was trying to impress the female with his prowess, to show her that he was not afraid of the humans and their dragon guns. Notice how *she* always stayed out of range."

"That makes sense," said Rockdream, "and he would not waste his strength actually attacking the ship, for the other dragon, even if she was his prospective mate, was the greater danger to him."

"It could not have been a territorial struggle," said Salmon. "They were both much too far from home."

Coral said, "At least I had no nightmares about Riversong last night. When I was six, I dreamed again and again that he burned my parents' cottage, and when we ran outside, he was waiting for us. Sometimes he would just be walking down the road with his wings folded, ducking his head under the overhanging trees, and I would see him, and he would see me, and I woke up terrified. For five years I had the same dreams, every time people talked about Riversong attacking ships. But I prayed to the Second Son, Cloud the Wizard, before I went to sleep last night, that he send me a clear message if there was any immediate danger, and my dreams were peaceful."

Rockdream said, "If you ever do have prophetic dreams about a dragon attack, try to get a sense of its tactics, so that the city can prepare a good defense. Foretelling doom is illegal, and with good reason, but foreseeing enemy tactics is just good strategy."

"What if the tactics cannot be countered?"

"Any tactic can be countered," said Rockdream. "Mugwort destroyed Turtleport by twisting and diving in the sky to evade the dragon guns. Wentletrap's crossbows made such evasion impossible. Riversong destroyed Moonport despite crossbows by burning the buildings on foggy nights. Our own city, without wooden buildings or thatched roofs, is proof against this kind of attack. But some dragon may think of a way around our present defenses, but if some Newport citizen foresaw these tactics—"

"Yes," said Coral.

"Our biggest weakness is that if a dragon ever does conquer Newport, we have nowhere to go," said Salmon. "The cities of the Two Rivers Valley might let us live there as bonded servants; Upriver could not support us at all, and founding a new city anywhere else would start a new goblin war. I think it was and is a mistake to let Riversong keep Moonport. He is there, Redmoon holds Southport, and even one major city lost to a dragon is too many."

"I think it would be an excellent job for someone else to do," said Rockdream. "If I must fight a dragon, let me do it from this strong place, with a thousand other warriors to help."

"That is just the kind of thinking that is losing us—and I mean all humans east of the sea—our cities. Wentletrap killed Mugwort with about three hundred warriors. I am no great strategist, but if someone who was, wanted to get together an army of several hundred to go after Riversong, I would join it gladly."

"Unfortunately, it was the kind of goblin war that we all want to avoid that made Wentletrap such a brilliant strategist," said Rockdream.

Salmon sighed. "Yes, and Newport alone could not spare so many warriors. We would need the full support of the Lords of the Valley, which we are not likely to get. They remember

how the warriors of Wentletrap's private army almost per-
suaded him to try to conquer Moonport or Midcoast when they
learned that Turtleport could not be rebuilt.''

39.

Half a month after Midsummer's Day, Coral awoke with
sharp pains, sat up in bed, and looked down at her stomach.
"How are you ever going to come out of me?" she said,
forcing herself to take deep, regular breaths. "I know you will.
I have helped enough women through this, myself, but—" She
moaned and lay back down.

Salmon pulled aside the tapestry and Rockdream nodded his
head yes and got out of bed to make room for her to sit. All
three of them were naked. "You are ready," Salmon said,
when she felt the contraction in Coral's belly with her hand.
"Get Moonwort," she said to Rockdream.

Rockdream pulled on his pants, shirt and sandals, and stepped
outside. Already it was another sweltering day. He heard Coral
ask Salmon to wear her plainest dress as he walked away, and
as he approached the cottage of Coral's parents, he could hear
Moonwort chanting.

He knocked lightly on the wall, and pulled aside the tattered
blanket that served for a door. "Excuse me, but Coral is having
pains," he said.

Moonwort twisted her frown into a half-smile, and got up
from her stool. Cliffbrake was still in bed, but awake. "I am
becoming a grandfather," he mumbled. Moonwort stepped
outside.

"It is hotter than a curse today," she said.

They found Coral propped up with pillows, breathing steadily and heavily, while Salmon massaged her stomach. "Her
womb is clenching every few minutes, but still closed," she
said.

"It will open, in its own time. How do you feel?"

Coral nodded her head yes, and kept breathing.

"Good. Just keep breathing that way."

Every few minutes, Coral would groan, or scream, and
afterwards she would say, "I am fine," in a harsh whisper that
seemed to belie her words, or else she would try to smile. She
grabbed for Rockdream's hand. Hers felt cold, hot, trembling,
sweaty, and she squeezed so hard it hurt. "I am going to live

through this,'' she said firmly. ''I am—'' She interrupted herself to breathe.

''You do not have to talk, just breathe,'' said Moonwort.

This continued for what seemed like hours, until it actually was hours. The heat of the day, and the small fire in the hearth, heating the water, made the room so hot that sweat ran all over Coral's body. Rockdream took off his shirt.

Salmon said that Coral's womb was beginning to open.

The contractions were a burning torment. Coral was screaming, breathing, crying silently. ''Wipe me off,'' she tried to say, and when Rockdream wiped her face with his handrag, she smiled and coughed, trying to laugh. ''I meant all of me.'' He began wiping her shoulders and breasts, but she tensed, grunted, and tried to push.

''Patience,'' said Salmon. ''You need to open up more first.''

''Let me put some heat on your belly,'' said Moonwort. ''Give yourself up to the sweat and try to relax. Your muscles are fighting each other.''

Coral shuddered at the heat of the wet cloth, but after a moment realized that it did feel good, and the sweating also felt good. Her heavy breathing lapsed, and she was falling, falling into nothingness.

''Keep breathing,'' Rockdream said, while wiping her face with the damp cloth.

For a moment she relaxed, then screamed and thrashed at the pain of a red-hot sword between her legs. Salmon firmly held her feet and said, ''Two fingers.''

''Is that *all?*'' Coral asked. The contractions and pain were continuous. She panted, pushed, panted, pushed, and screamed from the pain that was ripping her in two. For several moments she lost awareness, then returned to pushing and pain. Would this ordeal never end?

A tiny, blood-smeared, and slightly bluish human face popped out, and Moonwort reached for the shoulders and pulled gently. He was a boy. Moonwort gave him a light smack to start his breathing while Salmon tied the cord. Coral was bleeding far too much, even before delivering the afterbirth. The pressure was gone, but the pain was a molten river.

''Let me hold my baby,'' she gasped. He was choking, coughing, and sneezing like someone with a bad cold. Salmon had wiped off the blood, and his skin was a flushing pink.

"Oh, you are not so big," she told the baby, who momentarily opened his eyes wide to look at her. "You remember Mommy's voice, yes? I love you, you know that." She was crying with frustration because she could hardly raise her arms to hold him. Salmon was holding a compress against her crotch. "How badly am I bleeding?" she asked.

"You are going to live," Rockdream said firmly, trying to hide his fear.

"Not as much as a few minutes ago," said Salmon. "It will stop. Do you want a cover?"

"I still feel hot."

"You do not want to risk being chilled," Moonwort said, helping Salmon spread a sheet and blanket. "You lost a lot of blood, and it may take you some time to regain your strength."

"I know that, Mother."

"Good. You still have a bit of spunk and sarcasm left. But do stay in bed as much as you can."

The baby pursed his mouth, making little gasps, and Coral moved him to her nipple, stroking the fuzz on his tiny head. "I will call you Wedge," she said, "for you nearly split me in two."

40.

With Salmon there to help care for Coral and the baby, Rockdream had no real reason to take time off from his duties at Eastgate, and both women encouraged him to return to work on schedule, the second morning after the birth. He was frustrated at how little he could do to ease his wife's pains, and needed to have other concerns.

Coral was making enough milk for little Wedge, but her skin was pale, and she got dizzy whenever she sat up in bed, much less tried to stand. Had she borne him in winter, she might have sickened and died of some minor complaint, weak as she was, but in the heat of summer, with Salmon's constant care, and Moonwort's potent herbal teas, she slowly regained her strength.

"I think I would get my strength back all at once, if only I could get a full night's sleep," she told Rockdream one morning.

"You both seem to sleep most of the time."

"So I wish! *He* may sleep most of the time, but he wakes up wanting to nurse just when *I* manage to fall asleep." She kissed the drowsing baby's forehead and said, "I love you, even if I grump a lot."

"You complain very little," said Rockdream.

"Just wait till I get my strength back. Then I will complain much more."

By the time Wedge was three weeks old, Coral was on her feet again and doing an increasing share of the household chores, but her crotch still stung when she passed water, and ached when she walked very far.

She resumed giving Salmon witchcraft lessons, beginning with techniques for opening and strengthening a patient's etheric roots, and for easing chronic pain without herbs. Salmon's efforts helped her, even when interrupted by demands from a suddenly awakened Wedge, but it was the act of teaching witchcraft, more than anything else, that made Coral feel like her usual self again.

Wedge got bigger, cuter, and more interesting each day. He liked being held, carried, rocked, sung to, and sometimes he liked being tickled. He preferred Coral to Salmon, and Salmon to Rockdream, which sometimes made the young father feel like a stranger in his own home.

"You are a lucky little boy," he said, tickling Wedge's tiny palms. "You have a momma and Salmon too. Yes. You do. And even a poppa. Yes. And you know what? I used to think it was so silly when Birdwade talked like this to her baby. But now I am doing it too. Yes, I am."

Salmon laughed at this.

"He brings out the child in each of us," said Coral, and at the sound of her voice, Wedge flopped his head toward her, and began starfishing his arms and legs and crying. Rockdream gave him to Coral, who freed a breast from her unlaced bodice and began to nurse him, while singing the wordless chant to the Nameless Mother as a lullaby.

When the harvest season began, Salmon hired out at Eastgate as an extra guard, and arranged her schedule so that she and Rockdream worked separate shifts, and one of them was always home with Coral and Wedge. This way, Rockdream spent more time with his family, and Salmon did some warrior's work, and both were more satisfied. Lieutenant Coaljay objected no more to Salmon's witchcraft studies than she did to Rockdream's marriage. In a gate guard, these things did not matter.

About this time, Rockdream's parents came to the cottage

for a visit. They were delighted with their grandson, who
smiled, waved his arms, and gurgled at them, and they were
reasonably polite to Coral, and seemed concerned about her
health. Rockdream avoided being drawn outside to a private
talk with them, where they probably would have said something offensive, and soon enough, they were gone.

41.

A few nights after the fall equinox, some of the warriors
standing dragonwatch noticed a strange star in the east, rising
about two hours before the sun. It rose somewhat later each
night, and seemed to be brightening. The next few nights were
foggy toward dawn, after which the star was too close to the
sun to be seen. A week later, it reappeared in the west as a
brilliant comet, between the setting sun and the double twilight star. As it moved farther from the sun, it became even
bigger, and its tail changed shape each night.

The farmers bringing in their harvest talked about little else.
At first they called it an omen of ordinary hard times: a cold
stormy winter, a lean harvest, and maybe an outbreak of serious illness. But then rumors spread through the city of several
dire prophecies made by a priest in deep meditative trance: a
dragon attack, an earthquake strong enough to topple stone
buildings, a war with goblins, an attack by foreign pirates
armed with a deadly new weapon, and rocks falling from the
sky, pieces of the comet itself.

When Rockdream's duty ended each day, he would climb to
the tower ramparts for a good look at the comet before going
home. Coral saw it much less often, for it could not be seen
from the forest, and the walk on Apple Road to the nearest
open field tired her.

But Moonwort came one evening just before sunset, and said
that she knew a much closer place to view the comet, which
had become truly spectacular the past several nights, and so,
while Salmon watched Wedge, Coral walked with Moonwort
through the woods, on a trail she had not much used since
childhood.

"Why do I keep thinking you are hiding thoughts from
me?" Coral asked. "This reminds me of the times you used to
walk me out to some unfamiliar part of the woods to teach me a
new spell."

"If anything, I do not want to teach, but to learn," said Moonwort.

"Mother, I just came out here with you to look at the comet for a few minutes. I have neither the strength nor the concentration to attempt anything unusual."

"Then come, have a look."

From where they stood, at the edge of Brownbark's wheatfield, the comet was directly above the walls and towers of Newport.

"Why, it is at least half the size of the moon!" said Coral. "And look at the tail!"

"Lord Stock's comet was dim and small in comparison," said Moonwort.

"I do not remember."

"You were just a toddler then. What do you think about the prophecy?"

"I think it is almost funny."

"Might there not be some truth in it?" asked Moonwort. "After the other comet, Lord Stock died, and Riversong conquered Moonport, and there was a goblin war in the Dragonstone Mountain country—"

"—and probably a few bad harvests and shipwrecks, if you count all the other troubles of several years," Coral said. "Mother, you are the one who always warned me against foreseeing death and destruction. And you were right; unless the warning is as clear as Raven's dream, it is not of much use."

"Who is Raven?"

"I told you about her last spring. She was a goblin shamaness who foresaw a dragon attack in a dream—"

"Yes, yes, I remember now," said Moonwort. "But that was just an old story. Prophecies are always more clear in the old stories than in real life."

"That might be true," Coral admitted.

"Dreams are debatable at best, even when they do seem clear. But that comet is an undeniable manifestation, a message for those who know how to read it."

"That comet is a mountain-sized lump of rock and ice circling the sun, even as our world and the planets do, and when it comes close to the sun, the ice melts and boils away as steam. That is what Pip the Elf told Hornbeam, anyway, and it seems as likely a tale as any."

"Try looking at the comet with your trance-eye," Moonwort said.

This seemed like a simple enough suggestion, but for some reason Coral felt hesitant. "Mother, are you sure this is wise?"

"I think you are one who can see the truth about this omen," said Moonwort. "From here, the comet is aligned with the city. How are they connected? Look with your trance-eye."

"Have you tried this yourself?"

"I saw nothing. My mind wandered. But I think the concept is valid."

"Possibly there is nothing to see," said Coral. "All right, I will try it."

Coral closed her eyes, and began to relax and root herself in the Nameless Mother, then created a protective egg of golden sunlight. She did perceive a strong rope between the comet and the city, but was not sure which way the energy was flowing. Folded inside this rope were futures, likely and unlikely.

Something warned her to pull back and check the condition of her etheric roots and egg. The roots were shriveling, and the egg was thickening and turning blue, darkening toward the color of the night sky. She had to hide. She had to run. She could not think.

She was running, really running, stumbling through the shadowy forest to the starlit dirt road. Panting and wheezing, she tripped and fell on the path to her own front door.

Salmon helped her to her feet and half carried her inside, where she collapsed on the bed, awakening Wedge, who responded to her panic by crying and thrashing. She ripped her bodice, fumbling to unlace it, and held the baby to her breast with trembling hands.

"Easy, easy," said Salmon.

Coral cried freely and silently while she tried to nurse Wedge, who took a few sucks, then startled and began crying again. She sat up and tried rocking him in her arms, and after a minute of this began improvising a lullaby:

> Hush, little babe,
> go back to sleep.
> I will rock you, rock you,
> back to sleep.
>
> The door is closed,
> the cottage is warm,
> and Momma is holding you
> in her arms.

Sleep, little babe,
sleep comes soon,
dream sweet dreams and
sleep till noon.

She repeated this with variations until Wedge became drowsy.

Salmon put her hand on Coral's knee, and asked, "What frightened you so much?"

"I do not know. I panicked. One of us should go tell Mother I am all right."

"She knows her way better than either of us. If she is really worried, she will come here to get my help."

Coral studied Salmon for a moment as if for the first time. She was several inches taller than either Coral or her mother, and heavy for her height, and much of this weight was muscle.

"So tell me what happened."

At that moment, Moonwort knocked, and came inside, her face wrinkled with concern. Wedge startled awake, but Coral gave him to Salmon, and hugged her mother. "I am fine, I am fine," she repeated. "Have a seat."

Moonwort's eyes were tear-filled. "You disappeared! I mean, in the blink of an eye, you were gone."

"I panicked and ran home. It was dark."

"But I did not hear you running. You cast a perfect glimmer—one that made you appear to be nothing."

Coral stared at her mother with disbelief. "Oh, nonsense! Salmon had no trouble seeing or hearing me when I stumbled on the walk."

Wedge was drifting back to sleep while Salmon rocked him.

"Well, why did you panic?" Moonwort asked.

"When I saw the rope between the comet and Newport, I felt something urge me to check the condition of my egg and roots. The roots were gone and the egg was thickening and becoming a dark blue like the sky. I felt the way I did in those dreams I had when I was little, when I had to run and hide before the dragon heard my thoughts about running and hiding."

"You ran and hid very well," said Moonwort. "So the connection reminded you of a dragon, did it? I remember you talking a few years ago about some of your dreams, and you said that they might mean Newport will be destroyed by a dragon."

"That was not prophecy, but fear," said Coral, "and so is the rope between Newport and the comet."

"Are you certain that you can tell the difference?" asked Moonwort.

"Fear spreads like a winter fever, from person to person. I caught that fear when I looked at the rope."

Salmon lay Wedge down on her own bed and closed the tapestries. "I will tell you what I think," she said. "If enough of us think we are doomed because of that pretty light in the sky, maybe some dragon will hear these thoughts and think we are vulnerable to attack. And if the humans who believe that witches and wizards think the loudest are correct, all three of us have a duty not to be afraid."

Moonwort and Coral both agreed with this, but later after Moonwort went home, Coral wondered whether there might be another explanation for her fear. If the rope was a valid prophecy of a dragon attack, and if she had looked at the rope deeply with her trance-eye, the dragon might well have noticed her, and might think she was a witch powerful enough to be a serious enemy, and would seek her out to kill her when it did attack the city, or worse, maybe it would try to dragonbind her. The unexplained thickening and darkening of her egg of light, and her sudden urge to flee, may have protected her from this.

Salmon moved Wedge back to Coral's bed, and was getting ready to go to sleep in her own, when Coral voiced these speculations to her.

"One of your first lessons to me was not to do anything that feels wrong, when I am healing," Salmon said. "That would certainly apply to every other kind of magic."

"Yes," said Coral. "What I was trying to do did not feel quite right."

"Learn from your mistakes, but do not be obsessed with them. That is what the warriors tell the squires. I have to be at Eastgate at dawn tomorrow, and I need to go to sleep. You need to get your mind on something else. Sing me that lullaby you just made up. It was really pretty. Better yet, take down the lyre and work out an arrangement for it."

"All right," said Coral, and she unwrapped the lyre and searched for the melody strings. She was still working on the arrangement when Rockdream came home.

7

DRAGON ABOVE

42.

The winter after the comet was a severe one for Newport, with heavy rains, high winds, and three snowstorms before the solstice. Coral's father, Cliffbrake, called this "a real Swordwall winter," after the northernmost human city east of the sea. He himself had never been farther north than Moonport, and this many years ago, before Riversong came, but he knew that this winter was too severe even for Rockport, so it had to be a Swordwall winter. More than a hundred Newport humans, including eleven warriors, had already died of winter illnesses, and more would surely follow.

Coral had not intended to practice healing at all that winter, but she had friends she could not refuse, and Salmon was no longer working at Eastgate and was eager to learn and assist. By the month of the solstice, she was bundling Wedge onto her back, and her medicines onto Salmon's back, and riding to the city at least twice a week, sometimes more often.

When Rockdream expressed concern about Coral or Wedge catching an illness themselves, she said, "I am more than strong enough to work. The same energy I use to heal my patients flows first through my own body, healing and strengthening me, and I also cycle some of this through Wedge."

About two weeks after Midwinter's Day, during the winter's fourth snowstorm, a tragic accident showed a dire weakness in Newport's current defense strategy. Two warriors standing night

dragonwatch at a tower on the North Wall burned to death in
the snow. Probably they had huddled too close to their fire, and
their leather clothes, oiled to keep them dry in the sleet, caught
fire, but it was possible to believe that they had been burned by
a dragon swooping out of the snow.

Their screams brought other warriors from the tower, but not
soon enough to save their lives. Warriors elsewhere on the wall
saw the sudden blaze, assumed the worst, and sounded the
triple alert. In moments the church bells rang triple alert all
over the city, and at least six warriors from every tower dressed
hurriedly and ran to the roof. A few fired steel arrows at
shadows in the storm.

At the hearing held the next morning in a castle audience
room, Baron Oakspear argued, "If a dragon had been attacking
the city, it could easily have burned a large number of warriors,
for most of those who answered the alarm also wore water-
proofed leathers. This clothing must be outlawed immediately,
and we should petition the Church to offer prayers of thanks to
Fire, the war goddess, for revealing this weakness to us, and
prayers to Mountain the Priest, that the spirits of the two who
died may find happiness and peace."

"That sounds well to me," said Lord Herring. "Lieutenant
Conch, you have a question."

"This replaces one problem with another," Conch said.
"Even as things have been, often as not two or three of my
warriors have colds or worse illness. If we must stand
dragonwatch these long cold nights with less protection from
the weather, we may lose warriors' lives."

"Lieutenant Canticle," said Lord Herring.

"I had a warrior who caught a fever and almost died from
standing dragonwatch on a night like last night, and he said, 'It
is backstabbing folly to stand dragonwatch in weather so bad no
dragon could fly,' and I think he has a point. I would suggest
that we limit the dragonwatch on stormy nights when it is
below freezing or even near it."

Baron Drill said, "That would be a dire mistake."

"How so? Come, speak up," said Lord Herring.

"I know you do not take the prophecy seriously, but—"

"You are out of order. We are not discussing prophecies,
but trying to mend an evident and serious flaw in our defenses,
which may well mean reducing the watch at certain times."

Lieutenant Coaljay waved her raised hand. "My lord, there

is some possibility that a dragon is already plundering Newport's herds—and one big enough to carry a cow in flight. A number of cattle, sheep, and goats have disappeared from the herds without trace—no carcasses, no predator footprints. Even the herders who hunted and killed Old One Ear last winter could find no clues.''

"I have heard about this matter before, and will select a party of warriors to investigate when the storm ends," said Lord Herring.

"Likely as not, it is flying them over the river," said Coaljay.

"Likely as not, it is hungry wolves or something of the sort, but we will find out," replied Lord Herring. "I propose a new law: Warriors may not wear oiled leather, on or off duty. All oiled clothing and boots must be soaked and scrubbed. The whole purpose of wearing leather is that it burns less readily than cloth. In heavy rains, herders wear wool, and they are exposed to more hours of bad weather than anyone standing dragonwatch. Since sopping wet wool will not burn, I suggest we wear the same in heavy rains. Once we learn what is killing the animals, I will consider the merits of reducing the watch.''

The warriors who went to search found scattered cattle bones with signs of wolves, organized a hunt on horseback, and managed to kill the leader and most of the pack. Some herders said that the dragon might have dropped the leftovers of its meal where the wolves would find them, and where the warriors would find the wolves, just to mislead everyone, but this was more herders' humor than serious speculation. After the wolves were killed, there were fewer animals lost.

But Lord Herring decided against reducing the watch, for now the fishcatchers believed that a dragon was nearby. The weather was at last getting milder, and some of the larger fishing boats were making short trips out to sea to try their luck, and some did not return.

By the week before the spring tournament, the merchants were also discussing the unseen dragon, for not a single ship had yet sailed into Newport harbor despite mild weather. When a small plume of smoke that could only be a distant burning ship was seen from the ramparts of the great tower, it was time to do something about the dragon's blockade.

The merchant Fairwind wanted to convoy three ships, each lent to the cause by a different merchant, and each with a crew including forty warriors armed with crossbows, but Lord Herring would not allow this.

"This dragon is unusually clever and efficient, or someone would have seen it before this. It is trying to lure our forces away from the walls to places where it would have the advantage."

Baron Oakspear said, "If that is its strategy, then before it attacks the city, it will also burn our farms and orchards, devour our herds, and possibly swoop into our harbor some foggy night to set the ships ablaze."

"We cannot risk a hundred twenty warriors at sea," said Lord Herring.

"How many warriors do you and the other merchants have working as ship and boat guards?" Baron Oakspear asked Fairwind.

The merchant's bookkeeper and secretary, a young man named Ironweed, replied, "We employed twenty-nine warriors last year. Ten of these are overseas now, which leaves nineteen. All the other merchants together probably employ no more than twenty warriors who are in Newport now."

"That makes almost forty," said Baron Oakspear. "But how skilled are they?"

Fairwind said, "I would not invest my money in unskilled warriors. All have passed their warrior's tests, and some actually have battle experience."

"With a dragon?" asked Oakspear.

"No, with pirates off Cape Horn. Their ship was heading for Prosperity Bay and got blown off course by a storm."

"Do you think forty warriors armed with crossbows could kill a big dragon?" Lord Herring asked his son.

"If I had fifty warriors on one ship, I could kill this dragon, or both dragons, if the two that those foreigners saw last year are doing this together. If no dragon attacks us, I will sail to Midcoast, and ask the Lords of the Valley for assistance, which I think they will give us."

"And if the ship is destroyed?"

"Think about it, Father. What ship has ever been so heavily armed against dragon attack?"

"You make it sound feasible," said Lord Herring. "If you choose your company primarily from ship and boat guards, I would say your plan is approved."

Salmon was one of the warriors Baron Oakspear chose.

43.

"Of course I am going," Salmon said. "I was even going to ask Rockdream if he wanted to volunteer to join the company."

"Do not even think about it!" said Coral.

Bloodroot was slumped in his stool, staring at the rugs on the cottage floor. He looked at Salmon with tear-filled eyes. "If you die—"

"I am not joining Baron Oakspear's company to die, but to kill a dragon—or at least get help from Lord Crossing of Midcoast, and maybe some of the other Lords of the Valley. Am I the only one here who understands that?"

Wedge, who had been crawling around on the floor with a cloth toy cat in one hand, pulled himself up onto his wobbly legs by grabbing a leg of Coral's stool, and babbled something like "Baa-woo weh-weh," over and over.

"Bloodroot weh-weh!" said Salmon. "He says you are crying."

"Did you say that? Did you say Bloodroot weh-weh?" Coral asked Wedge, who smiled, shrieked, and repeated his babble.

"Would you prefer me to swallow my fear, or pretend to love you less?" Bloodroot asked.

"That is the kind of love Wedge feels for his mother," Salmon said, "not the kind a warrior would expect from her husband."

"Love is love," said Coral. "When I first met you, you were terrified that your husband would die of that sickness. His fear is no different."

"I am sorry," Salmon told Bloodroot, making him look into her eyes. "This is very important to me. I am a warrior, and it is my time to fight. Our company has the best mariners, the best ship, the best ship's warriors, and the best leader that Newport has seen since Wentletrap."

"How much are you getting paid for this?"

"Just twice the usual amount for a round trip to Midcoast, but remember there are a lot of us to be paid. But if we kill the dragon, I will get eight pounds of gold, and if we kill two dragons, sixteen pounds."

"Two dragons?" asked Bloodroot. "Well, yes, I guess there could be two dragons."

"In addition to all the crossbows, the ship has four gear-

locking dragon guns with sights. A hundred forty years ago, all
of Turtleport only had three dragon guns, and those of course
did not have gear-locks.''

"Rockdream thinks dragon guns are not very good weapons," said Coral.

"These are new ones, from Godsfavor, the same kind they
used to kill Swordrot, the dragon of Cherry Blossom City."

"Well—" said Bloodroot.

"Eight pounds of gold is enough to buy a good riverboat,
and several loads of goods. By the time the rivers drop, you
could be a captain, maybe even a minor merchant."

"All I pray for is your safe return," said Bloodroot.

"I will do the same," said Coral.

44.

Salmon was one of the last of the crew to board the *Great
Circle,* early the next morning. It was a sixty-foot, three-
masted trading ship with seven ribbed sails, and armed with
four Godsfavor-style dragon guns, one forward, one aft, and
two midship. The crew was twenty mariners and fifty warriors.
Salmon knew few of the mariners, but recognized most of the
warriors, and some of these were her friends.

Baron Oakspear was saying, "The best strategy against an
enemy who can hear your thoughts is to make no plan, but to
react quickly and correctly to whatever the dragon does. And
even in battle, especially you mariners, keep a watch on all
quarters of the sky, for we may find ourselves facing two
dragons. But if any dragon swoops low enough to attack this
ship, we will shoot it down!"

And Salmon cheered with the rest of the crew, feeling the
thrill and power of a historic moment.

Now Captain Reed spoke, explaining the order of command.
Then he beat the drums, for the mariners to row the *Great
Circle* out of the harbor, where the swollen Turtle River distrib-
utary carried it swiftly out to sea, where the mariners set sail to
the morning offshore winds that were scattering the fog.

Since Salmon had not gotten enough sleep the night before,
with Bloodroot's worries and long lovemaking, she volunteered
for the evening watch and went below to sleep. There were
three dozen regular bunks, and thirty additional bunks built
into the cargo area, which had more headroom but no storage

lockers. Salmon chose one of the regular bunks, stowed her gear, and went to sleep in her clothes, in case she was suddenly summoned to battle.

With the coastal current flowing south, and strongest about thirty miles offshore, most ships leaving Newport for northern destinations first moved southwest, until well out to sea, but the *Great Circle* sailed the morning wind against this current, and moved due west. When the wind changed, the mariners tacked as necessary to hold this course.

Salmon woke late that afternoon, when the ship was beyond sight of land and sailing northwest by north on a southerly breeze, and the fogbank was closing in.

A dragon flying over a fog at sea might overhear the thoughts of a crew, and learn that a ship was somewhere, but this would not betray its exact position. Even voices could be misleading, but voices were a better clue, so the crew talked as little as possible while sailing through the fog, even when eating meals. The most dangerous time would be when the fog began to thin, when a dragon might glimpse the ship but still use the fog to hide the twists and turns of its attack.

Salmon stood the night dragonwatch with nineteen other warriors. At midnight, ten of these were replaced quietly by ten others, and Salmon was among those replaced a few hours before dawn.

She woke at midmorning the next day to cries of "Dragon above!" and the alarm gong ringing. She pulled on her boots and grabbed her crossbow, while other warriors around her did the same, and they all hurried up the ladder to the deck.

"Change course!" bellowed Captin Reed.

"Warriors: guard all directions and be ready to shoot!" shouted Baron Oakspear.

Salmon loaded and cranked up her crossbow. The dragon was hidden above the fog. A tense minute passed, but still it did not swoop low to try to burn the sails. The *Great Circle* changed course twice, and the fog continued to dissolve.

"Maintain full alert!" ordered Oakspear.

And there was the dragon, silhouetted against the blue sky overhead out of range, flapping its wings to match the motion of the ship. It dropped something round. Captain Reed ordered another course change, but not soon enough. A gray boulder at least three feet in diameter struck the stern, punching a hole through deck and hull, and the *Great Circle* tipped to one side and began going down.

More than half the people were knocked down by the impact, and some of the cranked-up crossbows misfired. One warrior woman was struck in the side by a steel arrow and fell into the water dead, and one man was struck in the leg, and stumbled on the deck, slipping into several other people. The other arrows flew over the side, and one ripped through a sail.

Captain Reed shouted, "Sailors: free the aft skiffs and get them afloat! Stay near the ship!" About ten mariners jumped overboard to do this, for swimming was quicker than wading and stumbling on the submerged rear deck.

Baron Oakspear shouted, "Warriors: stand firm, if you can, and be ready to shoot!"

Salmon had thought enough to set the safety catch of her crossbow when she saw that the rock would strike the ship, so hers was still loaded and ready to crank up again, even though she had stumbled. So were the crossbows of about half the others.

The dragon, a vast male the green of tarnished bronze, pulled out of his dive and flapped his wings to circle high above the foundering ship. He bellowed, a fearsome sound, but far more fearsome were the words of his thought, which ached inside the mind of each warrior and mariner: *Your ship is sinking. The small boats will not hold all the crew.*

When several humans jumped overboard to swim to the skiffs, Baron Oakspear shouted, "Who do you trust, the dragon or me? He wants you to panic and abandon ship. Do not fall under his fear-spell!"

Captain Reed added, "If you swim while you still have a place to stand and fight, you are backstabbing fools!"

The *Great Circle* had stabilized with three quarters of the deck below water, and was less tilted than before. Two of the dragon guns were still usable, but the dragon continued to circle cautiously out of range.

"Riversong, you are a coward," Baron Oakspear said in a normal voice, knowing the dragon would hear him.

Human honor interests me less than the taste of human flesh.

At a moment when Riversong sensed that most of the warriors, and especially their leaders, were less attentive, he swooped down to attack, but they were ready, and fired their crossbows, and one of the dragon guns. To evade this volley, he flapped his wings in reverse while curling his body into a ball, then straightened his body, folded his wings, and fell head first into the sea. The sails of the *Great Circle* caught the wind of his wings, tilting the ship suddenly, then his splash jolted the ship again, knocking most of the humans off their feet, and some into the water. The dragon was only submerged for a few seconds before he bobbed back into flight, and as he had hoped, the warriors were not ready. He belched flame at the sails and bow. No one shot another arrow at him. All was flame, black smoke, and panic.

In the confusion, Salmon jumped into the flooded hold, and swam beneath the forward deck, where there was air. She felt immediate relief to be out of sight, in the dark, and alone. She felt to make sure she had her knife, then unbuckled her sword and let it sink. She had no hope of surviving, let alone winning, this battle as a warrior, so she let her witch's instincts take over, and surrounded herself with a thick egg of blue light, the better to blend with the bright ocean.

She heard people shouting and swimming, footsteps on the deck overhead, and a dragon gun's characteristic thunk and whoosh, then a scream of pain suddenly cut off when Riversong caught and killed someone. She opened her heart to all the fear and grief of the others' painful deaths as she heard them happen, so that her thoughts would be no different from theirs, and Riversong did not sense her presence inside the ship.

Salmon lost sense of time, until the underside of the deck began to smolder, then took a quick breath and swam underwater through the hole in the hull, then bobbed to the surface and treaded water. Several hundred feet away, the dragon flamed and swallowed a human in his mouth. Salmon forced herself not to look at him again, and forced herself to be calm. When she looked at the burning ship, she realized how cold and numb her body was getting.

After an apparent eternity, the fire burned out at the water-line, and by this time, the dragon was gone. Salmon swam back to the wreck, and somehow made a workable raft from the remains of the bunks in the captain's cabin. As far as she could see, there were no other survivors. She salvaged a paddle and a big waterbag, and a heavy wool blanket she thought might serve for a sail. Then she found a canvas tarp, but she kept the blanket. She even found some fishing gear.

Salmon climbed aboard her raft, secured everything with

twine and rope, and stretched her canvas to the afternoon westerly. When the wind died after dusk, she offered a prayer of gratitude for her survival, then slept for a few hours, warmed somewhat by her wrung-out blanket.

45.

The fog was thick when Salmon woke, but she found herself able to see the direction of the current with her trance-eye, and used this to guide her paddling.

She slept again, woke to a sunny day, and paddled most of the morning, trolling her fishline, but she had no luck with this till she thought of cutting a sliver of leather from her tunic to use as bait. Then she caught a silver scuppie, cleaned it, and ate the raw flesh slowly. She rationed her water. Just before sunset, when she was sailing by the afternoon wind, she thought she saw mountains ahead on the horizon.

Another night and part of another day passed. She caught another fish, a herring, but the afternoon wind was stronger and whipped up swells, which made her seasick. By the time she saw the low cliffs of the shore, she was only half conscious. She did not remember landing on the beach, but woke up groggy to the sound of children's voices.

"She lives."

"She saw him, but she is still free."

"That is a nice thought. The rest is much too sad."

"Much too sad."

"The wizard might help her."

Salmon shook her head to bring herself back, staggered to her hands and knees, and found herself face to face with a little furry pook man.

"Could you mean—Treeworm?" she asked.

He laughed, as did several of the others.

"I am apprenticed to a friend of his," Salmon explained, twisting herself around to sit up.

"Coral! You know Coral!" exclaimed a half-grown pook girl. "Go get the wizard, right away!"

The other pooks looked at each other, then one of the men ran up the beach. Salmon tried to stand up, but her legs felt like they were made of butter.

"You are too cold and too hungry," said the other man.

"Just crawl up to the dry sand and lie down. The wizard will help you."

Even though the sun was getting low, the sand felt comfortably hot and out of the wind. Salmon drifted in and out of sleep, until she was roused by an old man dressed in robes like a priest, but his were blue instead of red, and his white hair and beard were long.

"I am the wizard Treeworm," he said, and poured some hot peppermint tea from his water-pouch into a cup, which he offered to her. "I know your mouth feels like old feather-stuffing, but drink this slowly."

After sitting up and taking a few sips, she said, "I am the witch and warrior Salmon, apprentice to Coral, and I am honored to meet you. My ship was destroyed by the dragon Riversong. I may be the only survivor."

"She is sad and unable to dance," said one of the pook women.

"I am not even sure I can walk, let alone dance," said Salmon.

"The tea will stop your dizziness," said Treeworm.

Salmon finished the cup, stood up carefully, and took a few steps. "I think I can manage. The tea did help."

They walked south along the beach, around several rocky prominences, which the pooks playfully climbed over, until they came to a sizeable stream, which they waded, then followed its valley above the cliffs, where a broad rolling meadow spread between forest and sea, and where Treeworm's cottage was cleverly concealed. Inside was a warm fire, and heated water for a sponge bath which the wizard moved behind a screen, and a spare robe for Salmon to wear while her own clothes dried, and a delicious meal of abalone chowder, raisin cake, and more peppermint tea.

"Well, I am alive, I feel better than I have since the battle began, and I am deeply in your debt. You want to hear my story. When I reach the city, I am going to have to tell this story again and again, and try to be objective and professional, but when I think of all the others burned and bitten to death, I just want to cry and cry—"

"Then do so, whenever you need to," Treeworm said gently, and squeezed her hand.

"I know what my husband will say, but we were right to attempt the voyage. Someone had to do it, if only to identify

Riversong and learn his tactics." And Salmon described the *Great Circle*'s armament and crew, what she saw and did in the battle, and how she escaped.

"This is bad, very bad," said Treeworm. "Already, Riversong has isolated Newport. Next he will burn the farmland, and when everyone is huddled inside the city, he will start dropping rocks. It fits the prophecy perfectly. Even the goblin war seems likely, once the survivors try to rebuild somewhere else. I see the whole pattern, but I do not see how to break it."

"The city will be harder for him to destroy. He cannot knock the ground from under our feet, or even the walls, the way he did with the ship."

Only one pook, the girl, had stayed inside the cottage to hear Salmon's story, and now she spoke out. "What are you saying? Have you learned nothing? You cannot face him again. You must leave the city right away!"

Salmon sighed, and began crying again. "I cannot face him again, yet I must, or I am dishonored. My duty as a warrior is to defend the city."

"You must leave also," the pook girl told Treeworm. "Up in the forest, you can eat roots and grubs, and catch minnows, till the nuts and berries ripen."

"Oh, stop it!" said Salmon. "Humans are too big to run and hide like pooks. And how can you be so certain that Newport will be destroyed? What we need is a weapon to strike that backstabber high in the sky."

The girl glared at the woman warrior. "The big ones who used to live here, the goblins, ran and hid whenever a fierce one came, and very few of them were ever killed. But your people, who fortify and fight—"

"I just thought of a way to do it!" Salmon interrupted. "Turn the sky itself against him. Make a storm. Can you do it? Someone among all the city's witches and wizards must have the knowledge and the power."

"To raise a sudden storm or make lightning strike requires rage," said Treeworm. "When I was young, the study of such magic was firmly discouraged, and for many years, it has been forbidden."

"But you know how to do it," said Salmon.

The pook girl said, "If you become fierce to kill the fierce one, he has defeated you; but if you are happy and able to dance, he cannot defeat you, not even if he kills you or drives you from your home."

Treeworm sighed. "I appreciate your wisdom, little friend. The dangers are severe. Channeling angry or destructive energies through my body could sicken or kill me if I am not very careful, and of course it is much easier to start a storm than to control it. Worst of all, trying to fight a dragon with magic would make me receptive to dragonbinding."

"You are too honorable a man for that," said Salmon.

"But to make a storm, I must become a storm, and a storm has no honor. In the rage, wind, and fire, when my naked soul is shredded by pain, the dragon will try to help me, to become my source of strength, healing, and love, to twist my storm to his own purposes."

"Then it cannot be done."

"Not by me," said Treeworm. "I am not a warrior, and I am old."

They sat in silence for several moments, then the pook girl said, "You humans make everything too sad. I have to dance," and she hopped off the workbench, skipped across the carpets, and disappeared into a hole in the corner.

"You cannot run away from sadness," Salmon said, but the pook was already gone.

"She just did," said Treeworm.

"But she will have her own sorrow, which she cannot run away from, when someone dies who she loves, will she not?"

"When a pook dies, they dance, to remember the dead one. Their dances connect their spirits with each other and with the rest of the world in ways I can hardly imagine, and I have danced with them. They remember, not just their own, but each other's previous lifetimes, and between-life times. Our separateness, and forgetfulness, make death a much greater sorrow for us, and when we live in cities, we can die by the thousands."

"When we live in cities, we can defend ourselves," said Salmon.

"The pookish way of life is not for you," said Treeworm. "I will miss them very much when I leave this place."

"I am sorry. I have been a wretched guest. The pooks helped me, you helped me, and after bringing you terrible news, I criticize you because you are not like me."

"I accept your apology," said the wizard. "Let me make up

a bed for you," and he piled a mattress of carpets and gave her a fur for a cover.

When she woke, late the next morning, he was gone, and more belongings than an old man could carry were also gone. All those books—could he have burned or buried them? Her leather clothes were folded neatly on the workbench, and beside them was a loaf of waybread wrapped in cloth, evidently meant for her. She ate some of this, tied the rest to her belt, stepped outside, closed the door behind her, and walked south toward the city.

46.

After passing through Northgate and Old Northgate just before dusk, and talking to the guards at the castle's outer and inner gates, Salmon was sitting alone in an audience room, waiting. When the door finally opened, she stood up, and to her surprise, two midpriests walked in.

"I am Father Stonelight, and this is Father Starmoss," said the older one. "I hope you will not find this offensive, but we must examine your spirit, to make certain you are not dragonbound."

"What do you mean?" asked Salmon. "Of course I am not dragonbound."

"Then you have nothing to fear. Please stand here, in the center of the room, keep your eyes open, and be your normal self. This should only take a few minutes."

"I do find this offensive, but if Lord Herring believes it necessary, I suppose I have little choice."

Father Stonelight sat in a chair facing Salmon, while Father Starmoss, who almost looked too young to be a midpriest, knelt beside her, and began moving his hands on a contour about a palm's width from her legs. He paused for a moment near her crotch.

"Who I make love with is not your concern," she said irritably.

"The other end of the rope is human. Proceed," said the older priest.

Each time Father Starmoss found a rope, Salmon found herself thinking of someone important to her, most often either Bloodroot or Coral, but there were also brief thoughts of her mother, her father, and Fairwind. Then the midpriest's hand stopped near the center of her stomach, she had a brief image of Riversong above the ship, and her heart skipped a beat.

"I want to kill him!" Salmon said. "He killed my friends. He killed my commander. I am not dragonbound. You must know that. You must." And she began sobbing.

"Please calm yourself," Father Starmoss said, and tapped her spine in certain places.

"Tell me I am not dragonbound. Tell me."

Father Stonelight said, "This rope feels like an influence. You were frightened, and you try to smother your fright with anger. Would you like us to help you heal this wound?"

Salmon did not know how to answer, but Father Starmoss opened his left hand to the window, and with her trance-eye she could see a stream of gold and blue sparkles passing into his hand. His other hand was on her stomach, and she felt the pulsing heat penetrating her tunic and skin.

Father Starmoss said, "Imagine that there might be a place where the humans Riversong killed can find peace and healing. You can even imagine that in this place, they can do everything they would have done, had they not been killed."

"I hope such a place exists," said Salmon.

"I can look at the beauty of a single rose, and know the reality of heaven (to give the place its customary name), for the beauty of the rose is but a reflection of the beauty of heaven."

"Heaven seems very remote to me. I wish this ritual was over, and my audience with Lord Herring was over, so I could go home and snuggle into my husband's arms."

"Proceed," said Father Stonelight, and Father Starmoss continued to feel the air around Salmon's body, searching for every important connection.

"You have made some study of witchcraft, but you are not dragonbound," said Father Stonelight, and he opened the door and spoke to the warrior standing guard, and the squire who left as messenger.

Less than a minute later, Lord Herring entered the room, with Lady Whitewing, Baron Pelican, and Baron Oakspear's wife, Madam Curlew. Salmon's story was interrupted by one hard question after another: Exactly how big was the rock? What kind of rock was it? How quickly and sharply did Riversong change the direction of his flight? Was he wounded by any of the arrows? What was the exact wording of the captain's command? When and where did Salmon last see the baron?

Why did she jump into the hold? How big was the hole in the hull? Why did she not look at the dragon?

"Because if I looked at him, I would think about him, and attract his notice. I let the cold water numb my mind, and looked at the burning ship when I needed to look at something. Eventually the ship burned to the waterline, and the dragon was gone. I made a raft—"

"Did you see the dragon again?" asked Lord Herring.

"No, my lord."

"Then I believe I have the facts. I order the dragonwatch doubled immediately, and I summon a council of tower lieutenants, to meet as soon as they arrive. Select twenty of the forty-five at random, but be certain to include Canticle and Coaljay. Baron Pelican, see to it."

"Yes, my lord," he said, and left the room calling for messengers.

"I summon the master Architect—"

"I will find her for you, my lord," said Madam Curlew.

"Are you calm enough to run messages?"

Her eyes were full of tears and her lips trembled. "I need to do some useful work," she replied.

"As you wish. Bring me the master weaponsmith as well."

Just then, Baron Swordfern and Fairwind the Merchant entered the room, both trying not to stagger. "Your pardon, my lord," said Baron Swordfern, "we—"

"—were carousing in the Tidewater Tavern no doubt. Well, I have hard news for you."

Madam Curlew left the room, and Lord Herring described Riversong's destruction of the *Great Circle*.

Fairwind looked at Salmon, hugged her fiercely, and muttered, "Bloody death," over and over. "My lord," he said at last, "I have not had nearly enough to drink."

"You have lost ships and people before," Lord Herring said. "This is no time for you to fall apart. I lost my son."

"You should have sailed a convoy, as I originally proposed. Riversong dropping boulders! Bloody death. I had eight ships. Five are overseas, and due back this spring or summer, each with a crew of three dozen, and I have no way to warn them. The *Great Circle* was the sixth. I have lost, or almost certainly will lose, over two hundred humans. I really thought Baron Oakspear's plan would work."

"We must save the people we can save," Lord Herring said.

"Cheer up, master merchant," said Baron Swordfern. "By the time those ships reach the vicinity, Riversong may well be dead."

"I have a question, my lord," said Salmon. "Are you going to save the witches and wizards, or abandon us to exile or death?"

Lord Herring looked directly at Salmon's eyes. "You, unquestionably, may live in the city. As for the others—let them in."

Father Stonelight looked surprised. "My lord, are you certain this is wise?"

"Yes. Newport needs them. Last winter they saved I do not know how many lives, and Salmon's survival proves that a dragon hears a witch's thoughts no better than anyone else's. Let the wizards and witches live inside the walls. I will make this part of my official proclamation."

"May I be assigned to Eastgate, my lord?" asked Salmon. "I worked there last fall as an extra guard."

"I will see what I can do, but I cannot promise anything. Some of the other towers may be understaffed. Report to Lieutenant Coaljay tomorrow and she will have your assignment. You may go. Merchant Fairwind, you may go also."

While they walked down the hall, Fairwind kept wiping his eyes.

"Go ahead and let yourself cry," Salmon said. "Believe me, I did. It was horrible."

Even before they passed through the castle's inner gate, they heard the church bells ring the double alert.

"I have to hurry home," said Salmon. "Bloodroot may hear the rumors wrong, and believe that I am dead."

"I will be fine," said Fairwind.

Salmon was tired and sore, but she ran, at least part of the way through the old city. The alert bells, and the messengers and tower lieutenants riding here and there on horseback had given most people the idea there was some danger, so Castle Street was almost deserted. She passed through Churchgate, and the newer part of the city, walking most of the way now. At Eastgate, she saw Rockdream standing guard at the lesser gate.

They hugged, and kissed each other on the cheek.

"I am so glad to see you alive," Rockdream said.

"Riversong sank and burned the *Great Circle*," she said. "I may be the only survivor."

"I knew something was up."

"We can live in the city now," Salmon said. "I talked Lord Herring into changing the sorcery law."

"That is good. We live on the second floor of a house on Salmon Street, the third one on the left after Bakery Street."

"We do?"

"Coral had a dream about the cottage burning down, two nights ago, and that was enough for all of us," said Rockdream. "Bloodroot is at the apartment, with Coral and Wedge, and Coral's parents. It is crowded to say the least, but we are all relatively safe."

"I should go there at once. The third house on the left, upstairs, is that right?"

8

BATTLE ON THE DELTA

47.

Lord Herring's proclamation of war against the dragon Riversong included directives to the citizens of Newport, to remain inside the walls as much as possible.

There would be no spring planting, no mining, and no fishing except in the river immediately upstream from the harbor. All cattle, sheep, and goats would be grazed within three miles of the city, and remain within shooting distance of the ramparts at night or in times of fog. Breeding animals would be penned in the main courtyard of the castle, and fed hay. All wizards, witches, and other people who lived outside the city would either move inside, or take exile for the duration of the siege.

Anyone who refused to obey the spirit of these directives could either take exile or stand trial for lesser treason.

The directive concerning the Church was prefaced by an architect's analysis of the building's vulnerability to falling rocks. In particular, if the buttresses were broken, the entire building might collapse, and if this happened during a well-attended chant and prayer service, thousands of humans might be killed at once.

Therefore, the Church Council, in cooperation with Lord Herring, whose wartime authority did not include such matters, agreed to limit attendance at each service to eight hundred, and the number of services per day would be increased. Private services for the warriors, who were advised against attending Church, would be held three times a week in the common rooms of certain towers.

Gathering together the cattle, sheep, and goats took most of that day and the next, even though many herders were already grazing their animals closer to the city than usual. By this time, the wizards and witches had all either moved into the city, or disappeared completely, as Treeworm had done.

Shortly after the midnight bells on the third night after the proclamation of war, Rockdream was standing guard at the lesser gate, and heard the small gong, signaling an increase of the dragonwatch. He stepped outside the wall to have a look at the sky, which was moonless and partly cloudy. One of the herders whose cattle were bedded down north of the road was pointing up at something, and Rockdream moved farther from the wall for a better view.

"Do you see him, guard?" asked the herdswoman. "He is studying the lay of the city from a safe distance."

The dragon was small, and hard to see against the cloud except when he flapped his wings.

"When the fog comes in, he will try to pick up a straggler," said the herdsman. "Then you have a chance of getting him."

"He loves to eat cows, but he is cautious," said the woman.

"He will get bolder now that we are on our guard. He may be clever, but he is ruled by his predator instincts."

"The warrior does not need you to be telling him about dragons," said the woman.

"Nobody knows very much about dragons," said Rockdream. "Any reasonable guess about their motivations is worth mentioning."

The dragon circled away from the cloud and moved lower, though still far beyond crossbow range. Rockdream ran back to his post, put on his quiver, exchanged pike for crossbow, and ran back outside, but the now plainly visible dragon came no closer, and after completing a third slow circle over the city walls, he flew south over the delta and out of sight.

Rockdream returned to his post, and stood there through the long hours of late night, expecting fog, expecting the dragon to return, but neither happened. Pinchgrip relieved him at dawn.

"It seems odd to be the only guard at the gate, on a morning like this, clear and soon to be sunny," Pinchgrip said. "I know about the dragon. Was there any traffic through the gate?"

"No one came in, and no one went out," said Rockdream. "No one is even allowed in or out at night except herders, and when they are on duty, they stay out. The gate may as well be closed at night."

"Coaljay thinks the same. You may be on the ramparts tonight."

"What hour?" asked Rockdream.

"Midnight."

"Good. I was afraid you would say dusk."

Carrying his crossbow and wearing his quiver, Rockdream walked up Castle Street toward the Old Wall, where the streets were busy with people leaving the dawn chant and prayer, or going to the morning chant and prayer.

"The way I heard it, the dragon swooped low over the towertops, so swiftly that none could take aim at him," one woman was saying.

"I saw him," said Rockdream. "He was at least as high above the ground as the distance between Churchgate and Eastgate, and he was looking everything over, flying slowly."

"I told you so," said one of the woman's friends.

"Even so, they should have rung an alarm. We have a right to know when a dragon is above."

"I can tell you what I saw last night, but I cannot discuss our defense tactics. I am sorry," Rockdream said, and continued walking, through Churchgate and past the Church itself.

"Rockdream!" said a woman with a foreign accent, Loon the Minstrel, who was with her husband Feathergrass. "I see you and Coral so seldom, but now you must live in the city, yes?"

"We live upstairs in a house around the corner from the bakery."

"Then let us go to the bakery, and have muffins and tea together. We are just leaving chant and prayer. The priestesses were wonderfully blunt about the truth today. Yes, we may all die; we will all die sometime, if not soon; but what matters is how we live. This inspires me to write the tragic song about Baron Oakspear."

"Is this not too recent and painful a story for song?" asked Rockdream.

"No, no, that is the problem with the old ballads. They were all written when the intensity was over. They lack the passion of the truth. Did not Spiral the Sculptor carve her greatest work, the goddess of war in the Rose Garden, when she knew she was dying?"

"You are either crazy, or you understand something that I cannot," said Feathergrass.

"His mind does not understand, but his body and heart understand," Loon told Rockdream. "Maybe you are the same."

They opened the door to the bakery, and walked into the rich smell of baking bread and cake.

"The service this morning upset Ripple very much, and I did not like it either," Birdwade was telling her mother. "I think the priestesses who led the chant and prayer have seldom done this before, and their attitude was wrong. I wanted to hear some rousing prayers for the strength of the city, and instead, they seemed to be trying to prepare us for our deaths. That old midpriestess who introduced the Canticle of Fortune just terrified Ripple. She was still crying and trembling when I left her with Brownbark."

"Go help the customers," said Orchid. "I will knead the dough."

Birdwade stepped to the counter.

"Could we have muffins and tea?" asked Rockdream.

"You can have raisin muffins right now, and in about ten minutes you can also have honey walnut muffins."

"A raisin muffin will do for me," he said, and Loon and Feathergrass agreed.

"Were you at the gate last night? Did you see the dragon?" Birdwade asked, while putting the muffins on a tray and pouring the cups of tea.

"I only saw him by starlight, and not very close, but I was impressed. He—"

At that moment, Coral walked into the bakery, said hello, and stood on tiptoes to give Rockdream a kiss. "Wedge is with Moonwort. How was your night?"

"Uneventful, except for the twenty minutes or so when Riversong was circling over the city."

"Really? But there was no alarm," said Coral.

Feathergrass said, "They are ringing no more alarms on the church bell, because that would give him good reason to destroy the Church."

"I cannot discuss our strategy," Rockdream said, "but I can tell you what I saw. The dragon was maybe a mile high at first, and almost impossible to see against a cloud by starlight, but then he came closer, maybe half a mile high, and circled the city three times before flying off over the delta.''

"How did it make you feel, to see him at last?" asked Loon.

Rockdream considered for a moment. "I was alert and ready for combat, yet somehow it felt like a dream."

Coral said, "He may have been working some sort of magic, to strengthen that part of himself who lives inside the spirits of all of us."

Birdwade looked at her. "That was what was wrong with the priestesses this morning! The dragon has corrupted them from inside, and they made a chant and prayer about being ready to die."

"No, no," said Loon, "it was about living our lives in the best possible way, because we will die, sooner or later, dragon or no. We all go through conception, birth, life, death, after-life, yes? This is the truth, not a corruption. You are upset because your daughter is frightened. Give her a chance to learn."

"I am not taking her back to Church if she does not want to go, and that is that," said Birdwade. "Coral, would you like a muffin and a cup of tea?"

"Yes, please, and four other muffins wrapped up."

They paid Birdwade, who took their tray to a table. Several other people came into the bakery, wanting muffins or rolls or loaves of bread.

"We sold out of yesterday's goods," said Birdwade, "but the bread will be ready soon. Cinnamon rolls we do not have, because there is no more cinnamon at any reasonable price."

48.

Only two sizeable forests stood within three miles of the city, one north of the main east road, the other surrounding two recently abandoned witches' cottages on Apple Road. No one suspected that Riversong, after flying over the delta the night before, had crossed the river again farther upstream, and walked around behind the forest to Apple Road, and followed this to the nearer edge.

Here he waited through dawn and morning, a huge but dull green dragon shaded and screened by foliage, through which he watched the cattle at last graze closer and closer, guarded by herders armed with longbows, and one warrior with a crossbow.

The herders' quivers were filled with steel longbow arrows, a new and secret weapon known to few but the smith who made them, and the herders who used them. They were longer and more slender than crossbow arrows, and like them had fins instead of feathers. Their range was limited, but a skilled longbow archer could fire several while the crossbow archer was still cranking up.

The warrior did not know about these special arrows, but he was clearly in command, and if Riversong was listening to the humans' thoughts, he weighed the warrior's inaccurate opinions about their weaponry more heavily than the confidence of the herders.

The dragon rushed out of the forest, breathing a long jet of blue flame at the warrior, who became a screaming red fireball, then he flapped his wings and jumped into flight toward the startled cattle, and seized one with his front claws. The herders ran toward him, and shot their arrows, which to his surprise did not turn to ash in his spray of flame, but pierced the muscles of his wings.

He screamed, and burned his pain and rage into the herders' minds, but still they shot at him. Each flap of his wings was another roar of pain. He dropped the cow, and now he belched firegas, and breathed a thin jet of flame which made the gas explode in a sudden fireball. The grass was too short and green to burn well, but the distraction was enough.

Twisting his flight to avoid a volley of arrows, though one went through his right wing membrane, he flew higher and higher toward the river, roaring and screaming with pain. Once across, he seemed able to bear the pain of flapping his wings no longer, and landed awkwardly in the middle of the forest, on the delta's closest island, just three miles south of the city walls.

By the time the herders' messengers arrived at Eastgate with news of the battle, an army of two hundred warriors, under the command of Baron Swordfern, was already boarding riverboats in the harbor. Lord Herring, who had reached the ramparts of the great tower in time to see Riversong's flight across the river and awkward landing, was convinced that his enemy was critically wounded, and the warriors standing dragonwatch on the east and south walls, who had seen more than that, were eager to finish him off.

Salmon, who was standing dragonwatch on the south wall,

could not think of a good way to voice her vague doubts without seeming cowardly, but she did not volunteer to join the force.

They anchored their boats in the shallows, left a guard, waded ashore, crossed the mudflats, and entered a forest of alders and willows, spreading out to give each warrior a clean shot at the dragon. Ahead they heard his raspy breathing, his rumbling groans, his sudden bellow that turned into a cough.

I am not so badly wounded as you think, the dragon said, as if trying to bluff them away. Closer and closer they came, but the trees offered no clear shot.

Then the dragon spread his wings and jumped into flight, proving the truth of his words. His first blast of fire struck Baron Swordfern, and the dead, dry lower branches of a big alder. His second blast burned three other warriors, and kindled some dry brush. His third blast burned a pitch-pine split by lightning. Even a dragon Riversong's size had but a limited amount of fire, and the forest was too green to burn easily, but he chose the targets that would blaze the hottest, until he had a smoky brush and crown fire between the warriors and their boats.

They shot at him, but few arrows found their mark, and none hurt him seriously, and before they could crank up again, he swooped low to hit them with blasts of flame, and his dragon laughter echoed in their minds. He landed, and quickly gulped down the fallen and dead. Digesting this fresh meat would soon replenish his supply of firegas. When some of the warriors charged, he jumped into flight and burned the leaders. Then he circled widely, to attack the warriors who panicked and ran.

Before long, the spreading fires made so much smoke that the dragon could no longer come near the trees, so he contented himself with attacking the warriors who had reached the coastal mudflats. He stayed well away from the anchored riverboats armed with dragon guns, and so, the warriors who made it through the fire to that shore did escape, about fifty, or a quarter of the original force. Some of these died later from their burns, or from smoke in their lungs.

"I understand now the grim despair in merchant Fairwind's heart," Lord Herring muttered, while he watched the tiny dragon circle the burning island, "but I will not succumb to it," he added firmly. "Madam Curlew, send messengers to see that people do not crowd the harbor or the area around the

market, or better, urge them to stay in or near their homes. I do
not want anyone getting trampled in a panic, if the dragon
makes some sort of attack when the boats return. I will make
an official proclamation about the battle as soon as I have a list
of survivors, wounded, missing or dead. The gates are pres-
ently closed, are they not?''

"I am not sure,'' said Madam Curlew.

"I want every gate in the city closed, including the castle
gates and the gates in the Old Wall—''

"My lord, that might cause the panic you wish to avoid,''
suggested Bronzeberry, a warrior who had escaped Riversong's
devastation of Moonport.

"If people panic, they panic, but this will minimize the
danger of them getting hurt. Madam Curlew, see to it.''

"Yes, my lord,'' she said, and hurried to the tower stairs.

"We have not lost the battle yet,'' protested Springweed,
who was Baron Pelican's oldest son and a squire serving the lord.

"Yes, we did. You can see survivors moving toward the
boats. Baron Swordfern and Madam Skewer were probably
killed by the first flashes of fire.'' Lord Herring's hands on the
parapet were trembling. "Folly is easy to recognize after the
fact. Could a few herders' steel arrows seriously injure the
mightiest dragon east of the sea? Could any forest be too green
for him to burn? We believed what we wanted to believe, yes,
what he wanted us to believe. We will not make that mistake
again.''

You will make other mistakes, whispered a doubt in the
lord's mind, or was that the dragon's mental voice?

The first boat began moving across the river, and Lord
Herring rubbed his eyes. "I must talk to Mother Mallow,'' he
told Bronzeberry. "I will return soon.''

49.

Rockdream woke groggily in the dark to a caress and Coral's
whisper, "Can we make love before you go? We have time.''

His jumble of thoughts and questions, about Riversong and
the battle on the island, melted in the warmth of her wet kiss.
Quietly, quietly, not to wake up Wedge, she sat on top of him
and slipped it inside. Her ring of muscle squeezed lightly. His
hands moved up and down her spine while she kissed his
mouth and face.

After a timeless time of slow joy, they heard the baby grunt, and stopped moving, hoping he would not wake up, but the next moment he started crying.

"If you are near your streaming, go ahead," Coral whispered, and kissed him, but Wedge was too insistent even for this.

"Maybe give him the chewing leather," Rockdream suggested.

"I need the light to find it." She stood up and scooped Wedge from his cradle to nurse him, while Rockdream snapped the sparker to light the lamp. "Ow!" she said, and pinched the baby's nose. "You must not bite me."

Rockdream handed her the chewing leather, but the baby knocked it out of his mouth.

"He is furious now," Coral said, rubbing his stomach. "I am sorry, Rockdream. Now that making love feels good again, we keep having interruptions. Yes, we do," she told the baby. She was changing his diaper when the Church began ringing the midnight bells.

"I must go," said Rockdream.

He dressed hurriedly, kissed them both goodbye, picked up his crossbow, and walked downstairs to the dark, empty street. Even the lights on Castle Street were unlit, no doubt a new precaution. Churchgate was black as a cave, but at least it was open. Eastgate was closed, and the door to the north tower was bolted.

"Hello! Warrior Rockdream of Eastgate, reporting for duty."

"Coming down," said a woman's voice from the ramparts, and about a minute later, Lieutenant Coaljay opened the door, holding a lamp. "Come in," she said, and when they reached the common room, she hugged him. "I was so sorry to hear about your parents."

Rockdream stiffened.

"Have you not seen the list? I am sorry. Sit down."

"I did not even know they went to the island."

"They are said to have led one of the last attacks against the dragon, so they are almost certainly dead," said Coaljay. "They died bravely."

"Blood," said Rockdream, feeling tears swell up in his eyes. "I do not know what to feel. I was not close to them, not since I married Coral, who they would not accept. Even before that, I blamed them for my sister's death. They wanted Glint to become a strong warrior, and did not send for a healing priest nearly soon enough.''

"That is an archaic attitude," said Coaljay.

"I wanted to become a priest myself, and Glint was the only one who understood my aspiration. After she died, I went to the church, and actually got an interview with one of the high priests. He told me that I was meant to be a warrior, and that my spirit chose my parents for this reason. He said that when I was older, I would show them a better way to be a warrior than the way they knew." Rockdream sighed. "Are any people from Eastgate dead or missing?"

"Maplewing and Pinchgrip."

Now Rockdream clutched the tower lieutenant's hand and cried heavy sobs. He looked up and saw that her eyes were also tear-filled. "I should compose myself and stand my watch," he said. "What do I need to know?"

Coaljay rubbed away her own tears and made a tight-lipped smile. "For tonight, give no alert increase for fog, double alert for sighting, and total alert for attack. Dusk will be your partner, and you will both be relieved at daybreak."

Rockdream stood up, bowed to his lieutenant, and climbed the spiral stairs to the roof, where he reported to Dusk.

"You have done this before, have you not?" Dusk asked.

"Yes, and I watched Riversong last night, so I know what to look for."

"Did you get enough sleep this afternoon?"

"Yes."

"Good. I did not," said Dusk.

Rockdream studied the sky, clear but moonless, split in half by the dim Sky River, then leaned over the parapet to look at the animals. "Are the herders outside, with the gate locked?" he asked.

"They put the dragon to flight, and our people were killed, so they say. About as many stand guard as last night. It is their risk. I doubt that the dragon will return tonight. His belly is full enough for several days at least."

Rockdream's grief and anger boiled over. "Stab it, Dusk! My parents, and our close friends, are in his belly."

"This is duty. None of that," Dusk said firmly. "I will watch my tongue if you watch yours."

"I am sorry."

"So am I. We will both miss Maplewing and Pinchgrip. I

did not know about your parents. You never told me their names."

"Bane and Scallop."

"Blood! Bane was my younger roommate the last year I was a squire. I was sorry to see his name on the list. He was truly skilled with the crossbow, and won one of the first tournaments."

"And he never let me forget it," said Rockdream.

"He pushed you too hard," said Dusk. "Parents should not do that. Now, my oldest two are both overseas on one of merchant Forecastle's ships, with blessings from both me and Cypress, and my youngest is a squire in the castle, and learning well."

They watched the sky, even while they talked. The stars began to fade, and the Sky River disappeared. A dense fog moved ashore, foaming up over the cliffs and smothering the city, until even their own towers became vague.

"Well, this one is so thick, the dragon could not even see his own tail," said Dusk.

"On such a night, he burned most of Moonport."

"It may have been foggy, but not like this. Have you ever seen this stuff from above, say from a few miles up the miners' road? It looks like a sea of unspun cotton."

"He might approach on foot," said Rockdream.

"He must have done something like that last night," agreed Dusk. "We should keep silence."

They stared at the indefinite darkness for what seemed like hours, listening for any unusual sound. A herder's dog growled and barked, then another, then—

The sudden roar was loud, close, and terrifying, as much a sound of their own minds as something heard with their ears. Rockdream loaded and cranked up his crossbow, and clicked the safety catch to prevent a misfire, for he saw no target. The roar repeated, and he found himself shuddering the way Coral used to do when she woke from a nightmare. He knew that this enemy was beyond the power of Newport's warriors, knew that he would die if he did not flee at once, and knew that these were the dragon's thoughts, not his own.

"Beware the fear-spell," he told Dusk, with a low voice.

"It is not for us, but for the herds," Dusk replied.

Only now did Rockdream hear the thunder of hooves between the all-powerful roars. Other warriors hurried to the roof.

"What the bloody death?" asked Coaljay. "Never mind. It is another ploy to lure us—"

A blast of flame struck Coaljay's head and upper torso, cutting short her scream. The warriors shot at the source, a vague shape that was already gone, and before they could reload, they were scattered by a blind spray of flame. Rockdream and three others ran around the ramparts of the closer tower to load and crank up. The dragon laughter in their minds became a scream, magically distorted as the roar had been, and Rockdream heard the flapping of vast wings. Was Riversong wounded and flying away? The fog was maddening. Each second seemed a minute, each minute seemed an hour.

"Get a litter, someone. She is alive!"

Rockdream was near the door, and went inside with Bloodstorm, a stern, older man who sometimes reminded him of his father.

"Only one lamp," Bloodstorm said in a low voice while striking his sparker to light it. He turned down the wick to make it as dim as possible.

They went to the armory room, selected two stout pikes, laced on the leather litter, folded it, and carried it back to the roof. After moving Coaljay onto the litter, they picked it up, and Dusk hung the dim lamp from the head of one of the pikes. Rockdream and Bloodstorm carried Coaljay inside quickly, hoping the dragon would not notice the dim light, if he was still nearby. They bore the litter downstairs to Coaljay's room, placed her on the bed, closed the shutters, and turned up the lamp.

Her face was burned and scarred beyond recognition. It looked melted. The skin beneath her charred tunic was badly blistered, as were her hands.

"Let me get Coral," said Rockdream, trying to calm his queasy stomach.

"Nobody survives burns like these," said Bloodstorm. "If she regains awareness, she will be blind, and in endless agony until she dies."

"If she must die, Coral can help her with that."

"You do not want Coral involved."

"You are right," Rockdream admitted.

"A warrior may kill the fatally wounded to ease pain. You or I?"

"We should discuss this with the others first," said Rockdream.

"Their duty is to be ready for battle, as is ours. The dragon may return at any moment. No one would question this judgment after seeing the burns." Bloodstorm drew his sword and prayed, "Lord of Light and Darkness, who is embodied in the Holy Family, guide my sword and take swiftly the spirit of my dying leader and friend, Lieutenant Coaljay." He plunged his sword straight down through her scarred breast and heart, waited until the fountain of blood subsided, then withdrew his sword and wiped it on the sheet. He was sobbing when he sheathed it, as was Rockdream, who hugged him.

They heard the dragon roar again, not so loud as before, and pulled a sheet over Coaljay's body, hurried back to the armory where they had left their crossbows, and returned to the roof.

"He is driving the herds farther away," said Dusk. "How is Coaljay? Is one of the servants watching her?"

"She is dead, by my sword," said Bloodstorm.

"I had hoped her burns were not so bad," said Dusk.

The dragon roared again, but it was only a sound, and no longer the terrifying penetration of mind into mind.

"We must discuss this quickly, before he returns," said Bladeweaver. "I nominate Dusk as acting lieutenant. Any others?"

"Rockdream," said Mantleharp.

"I refuse," he said, then wondered whether he had made the right decision.

"Any others?" asked Dusk. "Then I am acting lieutenant. Each of you take a partner. You and your partner do not both shoot together, no matter how good a target you think you have. You alternate. This way we can spread out, yet maintain a fairly steady stream of arrows without being able to see each other. So spread out, stay near your partner, and do not go far beyond either tower."

"Good tactics," said Rockdream. "I was still trying to think of something."

50.

When the fog finally brightened to gray, a servant came to the roof to tell the warriors that breakfast was ready. Four at a time, they went down to the common room, ate quickly, and returned to the roof. The dragon's roars sounded far away.

But several minutes after the last distant roar, he spoke, and his mental voice was heard all over the city: *You know I am out*

*here. You know I am also inside your spirits. With each battle,
your numbers shrink. I will strike, and you cannot stop me.
You will try to strike back, but you cannot reach me.*

A boulder struck one of the Church's flying buttresses. The
people inside were unaware of the dragon, for they were chanting the Canticle of Mercy, which filled their minds and left no
room for the dragon's words. The boom was a horrifying
shock.

"Move smoothly to the doors and do not run!" shouted the
midpriestess who had been leading the chant. "Keep chanting
while you walk. We may yet know the divine mercy."

The congregation of five hundred had little trouble moving
through aisles and entrances designed for several thousand, and
most were outside, some still chanting, by the time a second
stone struck another buttress, and the vaulted ceiling began to
crack. Priests were running through the labyrinth below, some
half dressed and barefoot, and climbing upstairs to the exits.

The morning offshore breeze and sun removed the last traces
of fog when Riversong returned with a third rock, which
plummeted for five seconds of its ten-second fall before anyone
realized that this rock was aimed not at the church, but at the
center of the crowd retreating up Church Street. The rock, a
lump of granite as big as a horse's torso, struck the stone
pavement with the speed of a crossbow arrow. Fragments flew
in all directions, and two large pieces bounced and rolled
toward the front steps of the Church. Probably no one was
killed directly by flying rocks, though several were injured, but
four people stumbled and got trampled to death. One of these
was Loon the Minstrel.

A warrior on horseback bellowed, "Spread out! Keep at
least ten feet between yourself and everyone else. Keep moving! He will be back with another rock any minute."

"Loon, Loon, wake up!" cried Feathergrass. "Do not be
dead! Please, do not be dead."

"Is she breathing?" asked the warrior. "Spread out, I say!"
he told two priests and several other people who began to
gather around the body. "You could be next if you do not
spread out!"

"My wife is dead," said Feathergrass.

"Oh, I know her," said the warrior. "I have heard her sing
at feasts in the castle. I am very sorry. Spread out!" he

bellowed to everyone else. "Next time I pass this way, I should be able to gallop the length of the street!"

Riversong flew high over the east wall, then half folded his wings to swoop to a landing somewhere several miles away. Though much of Newport was built of rocks quarried from the seacliffs north of the city and floated to the site on great log rafts, the builders also made use of every rock upturned by a farmer's plow, for rubble if nothing else, so no large boulders remained within four miles of the city, which greatly slowed the dragon's bombardment.

A quarter hour later, he returned with a fourth rock, which struck the Church's vaulted roof, and with a vast rumble, much of the building collapsed to rubble and broken glass. The transepts at either end, though still standing, were both cracked, and likely to topple.

Again the dragon flew northeast and returned with a stone, which he dropped on a brick house on Herders Street, which was the second block west of Eastgate. It punched a big hole through the roof, the second floor, and a clatter of roofing tiles fell into the hole and onto the street, exposing rafters.

Your buildings are not completely brick and stone, said Riversong. *From close enough, I can set fires.*

The dragon flew away and returned, after a longer delay. Possibly he had to fly farther to find another boulder, and possibly he was getting tired. This one struck another brick house, on Elk Street near the Lilac Garden, breaking the top of a gable wall, as well as damaging the roof and inside.

Warriors on horseback were riding through the city, ordering people to come outside but stay near their homes. Dusk sent a messenger to tell one of these warriors about last night's battle, and Coaljay's death. An hour passed, and Riversong did not return. A messenger came from the castle with a signed note from Lord Herring confirming Dusk as lieutenant of Eastgate, and detailing strategy.

"The dragon seems to be taking his rest, so we will take ours, but I need two warriors to remain on duty, one to open the lesser gate and stand gate guard, so people can go out and gather spent arrows, and another to stand dragonwatch." Dusk chose these two, then asked for two more warriors to stand dragonwatch at nightfall, when the gate would be closed. He told Rockdream, "You return at dawn. All warriors living outside their towers are on day shift now."

On his way home, Rockdream avoided reading the posted proclamations, because he did not want to know about any more deaths, but he could not avoid the sight of the ruined church, and the small group of priestesses coming in and out of the still standing east transept, carrying books and statuettes.

"Everyone got out in time," a midpriestess told him. "We chanted the Canticle of Mercy even while we crowded through the west doors. Four humans were killed when the dragon dropped a rock on the crowd, and we pray for their spirits and grieve with their families, but it could have been so much worse."

Rockdream numbly nodded his head and walked away. At home, he found Coral in the common room with Moonwort and Wedge, where they were boiling down a pungent medicine in the big cauldron. "I knew you were all right," Coral said. "We are making an ointment for burns and abrasions— What is wrong?"

"Everything is wrong, and he needs to talk with you about it alone," said Moonwort. "I can watch the salve boil down, and Wedge as well."

"Thank you," said Coral.

In their room, Rockdream told Coral about the battle with Riversong in the fog, and carrying Coaljay downstairs on the litter. "She was unconscious, blinded, and horribly scarred. I wanted to send for you, but Bloodstorm insisted there was no hope, and—"

"I can see the scene in your thoughts," Coral said with a shudder. "I probably would have entered deep trance and spoken with her spirit before deciding what to do. I sense that she would have died without awakening to the pain. Hmm—" Coral closed her eyes, relaxed into trance, and spoke very slowly. "Coaljay wants to forgive whoever released her. She says, 'I am in the gray place, leaving the black cloud. I am bathed in love when I drift. Remember me as your friend.' I am telling her to follow the light to the center of the world of her heart. Her husband is calling her. She is gone." Coral opened her eyes.

"Could you do that with my parents?" asked Rockdream.

She hesitated, then said, "I will try," and settled back into trance. "I see dark gray and black, vague, twisting turmoil, distorted and changing. I am trying to make contact, but the closer I come, the more anger I feel. I try to speak from a distance. Bane and Scallop! You can find peace. Let yourselves drift away from this battle. It is ended, for you. Now I see a forest burning, all around me.'' Coral gasped, opened her eyes, and jumped off the bed. ''Rockdream, I am sorry, but I cannot do anything that might put me in spiritual contact with him.''

''You mean Riversong?''

''Please do not say his name. Yes. That vision was so strange. Whenever I approached your parents, I found myself getting angry about how unfair they were to both of us, but when I spoke to them from far away, this stopped. Then I was in the battle, saw him, and knew he was looking for me. Maybe this was only Bane's or Scallop's memory, but any vivid vision I have of him in trance can become a real contact, or at least there are stories which suggest this can happen.''

''It is better not to take the chance,'' agreed Rockdream.

9

CITIZENS' ARMY

51.

Each day, Riversong's aim became better, even when it was raining lightly or windy, but he dropped more rocks when the weather was fair. By the ninth day of his bombardment, he was doing as much damage to a stone house as he did at first to a brick house, and the brick ones just collapsed. Plainly he exhausted himself each day carrying rocks, then flew up to Herders Ridge, or Turtle Hill, or wherever he had driven the herd animals, to feast and rest. Many of the city's warriors wanted to seek him out and attack him then, but Lord Herring was absolutely against this.

"Trying to surprise a dragon asleep is a sure way to lose a battle we cannot afford to lose. Why would he keep a regular schedule, if not to lure us up there? We can afford to wait. He has been at us for nine days, and the city is still ours. Moonport fell the second day. Mark my word—he will lose patience before I do. For all the damage we have suffered, very few humans have died, not since the sortie to the island, and for that matter, the voyage of the *Great Circle*. The farmland is undamaged. He does not want to burn it, for that would spoil his hunting, but he will if we go out there. The city is just a pile of stones he is knocking down. Once we kill him, we can rebuild easily enough. But if he burns the orchards and woodlands, it will be decades before they grow back right."

"Once we kill him! My lord, how can we do that if we never go near him?"

"If we are patient, he will sooner or later come near us."

"He will not do that until he is certain he has the advantage."

"Yes, but he can be wrong about that," Lord Herring said, "but the fewer who know about our plans, the better."

"I understand, my lord," Bronzeberry said, with a stern look at the other warrior. But then she wondered whether Lord Herring really had any plans, and then she understood that it was part of his strategy for most of his warriors to doubt that he did. All she knew for certain was that she did not know very much.

The gongs rang. Riversong was returning with another rock.

The dragon passed high over the east wall and flew a twisted course over the city, so that no one could guess just where he would drop the rock. It was already falling, and Rockdream, who was standing dragonwatch on the ramparts above Eastgate, felt his heart skip a beat, for it hit somewhere very near his own apartment, and black smoke rose from the site.

The original strategy of having everyone stand outside their homes whenever the dragon was overhead with a rock proved impossibly disruptive, so now people took turns standing guard on each block, and would shout "Dragon rock!" whenever one fell toward the vicinity. Usually everyone got outside in time, but even if they did not, they were seldom killed or hurt.

The seven customers in Orchid's bakery got out with no trouble, as did Orchid, Brownbark, Birdwade, and Ripple, who had all been downstairs, but one of the three priestesses who had moved into the extra room on the second floor, tripped on her robe running down the steps. The rock hit the roof next to the main chimney, punched through the second floor, and broke the big oven. A shower of wood fell on the scattered fire, as did a big pot of butter, making quick flames and black smoke. The priestesses hurried out the back door, just when Brownbark and Orchid went back inside to look for them. In half a minute, the priestesses appeared on the street.

"Come out! They are all right!" shouted Birdwade.

"Stand back! Move away!" a woman bellowed, a mounted warrior on patrol.

"My husband and mother are inside, trying to rescue them!" Birdwade pointed to the priestesses.

"Bloody death!" swore the warrior. "This is beyond buckets. Everyone else, stay outside.'' She dismounted, handed the reins to Birdwade, tied a cloth over her nose and mouth, and went in. A moment later, she came out, coughing. ''The smoke is too thick. I fear they are lost.''

''Daddy!'' cried Ripple.

Birdwade caught her before she could run inside. ''Could they have gone out the back?''

''Not past that blaze in the kitchen,'' said one of the priestesses.

''We have to get Daddy and Grandma! Let me go!'' said Ripple.

Something crashed inside, and new flames and smoke shot out the hole in the roof. The warrior mounted her horse. ''Back away from this building, all of you! It could collapse.''

''Birdwade, are you all right?'' asked Coral, holding baby Wedge with one arm.

''Daddy is burning in the fire! And Grandma!'' Ripple said, crying.

''They are dead, and we are alive,'' Birdwade said with a hoarse whisper.

''Oh no,'' said Coral, looking at the billowing smoke.

Three other mounted warriors turned the corner from Castle Street, one of them Commander Conch, who had been promoted from tower lieutenant to commander of the castle on Baron Swordfern's death. ''Birdwade! How did this fire begin?'' he asked.

She tried to collect her wits. ''The rock must have broken the bread oven.''

''Be easy with her, sir,'' said one of the priestesses. ''She just lost her husband and mother. I was inside last. I saw the most. The rock broke the oven, scattered the burning logs, and the butter pot and some upstairs flooring fell on the fire, and it was spreading to the counters and cabinets when I dashed out the back door. I feel terrible about this. Had I not stumbled on the steps—''

''I do not mean to be harsh, and I am sorry about your family, but this is more urgent than you know,'' said Conch. ''Was the oven brick or stone?''

Birdwade cleared her throat and wiped her tears and said, ''Mostly stone. The hearth was lined with fireclay tiles, and the oven door and shelves were bronze. It was the best oven in the city.''

To the other three warriors, Conch said, "I want every forge, kiln, and oven in the city smothered immediately, if not five minutes ago. See to it!"

They urged their horses to a fast trot. Gongs on the Old Wall were already ringing the alarm of Riversong returning. He flew over the burning bakery, then turned north, back over the Old Wall, and dropped a rock on another building with a smoking oversized chimney, the clayworks at the corner of Potter Street and Barley Street. This destroyed the glazing kiln, which was then being used to burn mortar for rebuilding damaged walls. Because the clayworks was designed with the likelihood of accidents and explosions in mind, the fire did not spread from the broken kiln, and Riversong at first was puzzled why the warriors on the Old Wall were so dismayed.

Now I understand, the dragon said. *You make mortar and bricks with kilns, and weapons and tools with forges, and I can easily destroy these.*

He flew away to the west, rather than to the northeast as usual, and returned with a stone from the seacliffs, which he dropped right on the castle weaponmaker's forge, at the foot of the inner curtain wall.

I was saving these close stones for some effective use, Riversong remarked, before flying to fetch another.

Lord Herring hurriedly sent messengers to Baron Pelican, Commander Conch, and the Northgate tower lieutenant, ordering absolutely no sortie, and the gates remained closed. Riversong spent the next hour systematically dropping rocks on every building in the city with an oversized chimney, which broke most of the kilns and larger forges.

Now you have no forges to make weapons, and no mortar to make forges, said Riversong. *I will be sleeping in the forest eight miles up the longest road, if you decide to challenge me while you still have enough arrows to fight.*

52.

"Can we eat soon?" asked Ripple.

"The stew should simmer for another twenty minutes, and also we must wait till Rockdream and Salmon come home," said Birdwade.

"When the muffins are done, can I have one?"

"Just be patient."

"Oh, all right," Ripple said, and walked across the room to see what Wedge was doing.

Birdwade moved the covered muffin pan and grill to a cooler part of the fire. "I do not know how well these will come out, for I have never made them this way, but it will be something to give you to thank you for letting us stay here."

"Letting you stay here?" said Moonwort. "You are now our landlady!"

"I guess I am, but likely every deed in Newport will be worthless before I collect next month's rent from either you or the family downstairs. Do you believe otherwise?"

"I did at first," said Cliffbrake. "I planted the herbs out back in the common yard, or I should say, Moonwort, Coral, and Bloodroot planted them for me, after my back slipped out again. The ground is hard here. But I do not think we will live here much longer."

"What about Salmon and Rockdream?" asked Bloodroot. "They will not desert their duty."

"Their duty is to help kill the dragon, which they think cannot be done unless he makes a mistake," said Cliffbrake. "We will all be dead long before Riversong makes a tactical mistake."

Coral said, "When the dream warned me to leave the cottage, I could think of few things harder than trying to live in the wild with little Wedge, and I did not want to force my husband to choose between his family and his duty, so I favored coming here, and shared his hope that the city would endure. But now—"

Footsteps came up the stairs, the door opened, and Salmon entered the room, looked at Coral for a long moment, and said, "You want to leave the city."

"Well, yes."

"Do you know that despite the bombardment, every smith in the city is forging arrows right now? It takes but a few bricks to make a usable forge from almost any hearth."

"Does that make any real difference?" asked Moonwort. "All the arrows in the world cannot kill a dragon who stays hidden or out of range."

"No, but leaving the city is just what he wants us to do. Why do you think he has killed so few in the city, and mostly only warriors? Because he cannot devour the bodies. Why do you think he has left the ships and boats unharmed? Because he wants us to use them.''

Moonwort said, ''If Newport has something like a thousand buildings, and the dragon destroys ten or twenty each day, but we repair no more than one or two of these, how soon will the whole city be ruined?''

''Well—''

''Two or three months at the most. But he is learning more and more about how the city works. Today, he destroyed the forges and kilns. Maybe the forges were no great loss, but what if he destroyed the public fountains, or the granaries? And of course, he could destroy this house at any time.''

Taking the muffin pan off the grill and uncovering it, Birdwade said, ''These are done. Shall we set the table?''

Salmon hung up her crossbow and quiver, and asked Blood-root, who was getting bowls from the cabinet, ''What do you think?''

''I think we also need spoons and napkins.''

''You know what I meant.''

''I need to think about it some more,'' said Bloodroot. ''If I leave the city, in wartime without permission, which surely would be denied, I am committing lesser treason. Not only could I never return to Newport, but I could never work as a warrior or guard in any other city.''

Coral said, ''That is not my plan. To leave Newport, only to move to another city even more vulnerable to the same attack, seems foolish to me. If we lived in the wilderness, or in a village as small as a goblin camp, we would not have the resources that attract a large dragon, and if one chanced to come, we could hide, the way Raven's people did.''

''I remember that story,'' said Birdwade. ''The goblins were warned by their witch's dream.''

''Just as we were warned by my dream of the cottages burning,'' said Coral. ''Just days after that, the dragon hid himself right in our forest.''

When they heard Rockdream coming upstairs, Moonwort filled the serving bowl with stew, and Birdwade arranged the muffins on a plate.

''Now can we eat?'' asked Ripple.

''Hello,'' said Rockdream. ''Oh, that smells good. Birdwade, I was so sorry when Bloodroot told me about your family.''

She smiled, but her eyes were wet. ''I never realized how

much some of my customers love me. But I would rather talk about what we need to do than what has already happened.''

Rockdream sighed. "I wish I knew the answer to that. Let me hang up my weapons and jacket.''

"I have an answer,'' said Coral.

"What is it?''

"Come, let us all sit at the table, and we can talk about it while we eat. Ripple has been so patient." Coral scooped Wedge up into her arms, and asked, "You want to try eating some stew?''

He smiled, babbled, and reached for her breast.

"You can have some milk as well,'' she said, and unlaced her bodice.

"May I offer a prayer?'' Birdwade asked when they were all seated. "I pray that this meal be blessed, and that our hearts be open to receive the divine wisdom and love we need to guide us through this time of trouble. So be it.''

"So be it,'' the others repeated.

Coral took a deep breath, adjusted Wedge more comfortably, and said, "I feel in my heart that we must leave the city soon. Salmon's escape from the *Great Circle* proves that we can hide our thoughts from the dragon, and once we reach the foothills, we should be relatively safe. I think we can get to Spirit Swamp in about ten days, maybe two weeks. Then we can search for a hidden hummock where the hunting and fishing are best, and build ourselves a little village, where we would welcome any other survivors of the city.''

Rockdream said, "I keep trying to deny this to myself, but yes, we must leave the city, and your plan sounds like a good start. We should leave during the next heavy rain, and travel very lightly, for our best hope is in speed.''

Coral smiled with wonder and relief.

"Just a moment,'' said Salmon. "Is this desertion of duty honorable? Is there any way you can even imagine it being honorable?''

Coral said, "Not just our city, but our whole way of life is being destroyed. Your duty and Rockdream's are futile, and you know it. But the rest of us love you both, and we will need your hunting skills to survive in the swamp.''

"But what about my parents, and Bloodroot's family, and my other close friends, like Feathergrass, Ironweed, and

Stonewater? If the city truly is doomed, how can I leave them behind to die? How large a group can escape?''

"No larger than the group we already are," said Rockdream.

"But everyone who leaves the city does not have to do it together, even if all ten thousand of us are bound to each other by ties of friendship and family," said Cliffbrake. "You must either say goodbye to the others and go with us, or say goodbye to us and go or stay with them."

"Be careful you do not get accused of treason by the warriors in your families," said Moonwort.

"None of them would do that," said Salmon. "At least, I do not think they would."

"We can talk to them carefully, to learn what they think," said Bloodroot.

53.

Rockdream woke to the sound of distant gongs. He and Coral dressed quickly, by the light of the nearly full moon through the window. While she wrapped Wedge in a small blanket, he grabbed his longbow and quiver and roused Birdwade and Ripple in the common room. Coral opened the doors to the other two bedrooms, but Salmon and Bloodroot were still out, and Moonwort and Cliffbrake were also missing.

"They went out some time after that wizard came to see Moonwort," said Birdwade. "At least, I think he was a wizard."

They hurried down to the street, where, despite the clear sky, the wind was sudden and cold. Ripple was rubbing her eyes, still half asleep.

"There he is," said Birdwade.

The dragon's neck and wings were bright with moonlight where he twisted and turned in the buffeting wind, still clutching a boulder in his front talons. Coral saw a blue light surrounding the dragon, and a twirling column of blue fire connecting him with the ground, somewhere a few blocks away. He struggled against the wind until the column was nearly vertical, then dropped the rock, which cut off the column of fire while it fell, slowly.

Rockdream only saw the dragon drop the rock, which fell at normal speed, and the ten seconds of its fall were not enough for the wind to blow it far off course.

The boom, clatter, and rumble startled Coral out of her

trance; the wind dwindled to nothing; and the dragon flapped his wings and flew away without his usual bellow of triumph and mental laughter.

"Someone tried to fight him with magic," said Coral.

"Then the wind was unnatural," said Rockdream.

"More than that," Coral began to say, but stopped when she saw how many neighbors now stood nearby, because she did not want them to associate her or Moonwort with weatherworking or any of the other more powerful practices of the dark sorcerers of the first century.

"What happened?" asked the older woman from the family downstairs.

"The usual," said Rockdream. "He dropped a rock and flew away."

"Well, who will stand watch in the street? We did it this afternoon."

"We did it yesterday," said the man across the street.

"Why argue about it?" said Rockdream. "If you are asleep, a ten-second warning of a dropped rock will not give you time to react, and if you are awake, you may as well stand watch."

"So if we do not want to get clobbered by a rock, we must stay awake. Bah! Why did the dragon have to come at this hour?"

"We could wait awhile to see if he comes back," suggested Rockdream.

"He will keep coming back till someone puts an arrow where it counts," said the man across the street.

Meanwhile, Coral was quietly asking Birdwade about the man who came to see Moonwort.

"He was balding with a gray beard, short but big in the stomach, and wearing a patched tunic and baggy pants. I have never seen him in the bakery."

Coral thought for a moment. "Did he have an accent, like Loon?"

"I did not notice, for he mumbled so quietly, but he did have a slight lisp."

"Oh. That would be the wizard Lightbringer, who is Mother's friend, but I did not think he was in the city. I want to see which building the dragon smashed. Rockdream—" She pulled him away from the neighbors and told him what she wanted to do.

"What about Wedge?"

"I want him with me."

"Where are you going?" asked the woman downstairs.

"We have relatives in that direction," said Coral. "We want to make certain they are all right."

They walked Salmon Street to Shopkeepers Street to Turtle Street, past citizens watching the sky, past buildings the dragon had damaged before. "The only way we will know which damage is new is to hear people talking about it," Rockdream said grimly.

"We will know. That was louder than anything since the west transept of the church fell down."

They turned the corner of Market Street and saw that the main market was reduced to rubble. Three mounted warriors stood in front of a roofless row of broken columns, and even the Old Wall of the city looked damaged. One of the warriors rode up the street, ordering people to move back.

"I never saw the like," one woman said to Rockdream and Coral. "The rock hit the market roof right next to the Old Wall; I saw a blinding flash of light; and boom! The lintels fell off the columns and the whole market collapsed."

"Stand aside! Do not block the street!" cried the mounted warrior.

Rockdream thought he recognized his voice. "Fennel! Is that you?"

He stopped his horse. "Rockdream! I thought you were at Eastgate. What are you doing way over here?"

"I live way over here. This is my wife, Coral, and my son, Wedge, asleep in her arms."

"I wish I had time to talk. Stay away from the market, all right? It is a real mess. Unless you want to help dig out groaning dying bodies, that is."

"There were people in the market?" asked Coral.

"We found three so far, but they are all unconscious or dead, so we do not know who they are or what they were doing. A witch and two wizards, if you want my opinion."

"I am a witch," said Coral. "I may know some of the people."

"You may not recognize them. They are battered pretty badly. Do you know more about this than you are telling me?"

"I wish I did, but whatever they were doing, no one told me anything about it, though someone might have told my mother something." Coral shuddered. "Both my parents are missing, and I fear—I fear—"

"I understand," said Fennel. "Go ahead." He rode up Market Street another block and turned the corner, while Rockdream and Coral walked toward the ruin.

Warriors from Marketgate and Harborgate were digging through the roofing tiles. "This one is dead," someone said. Two priests were kneeling over one of the three figures on the grass. Coral immediately went to one of the other two, for though the face was bruised beyond recognition, she recognized the dress.

"Mother, Mother, why did you do this?" she whispered, trembling with tears. "This was against everything I thought you believed in."

At that moment, a breeze began to blow.

"What do you know about this?" asked one of the priests.

"Very little," she replied. "When the dragon came, my parents were missing, and I saw the—the heavy blue rope being broken by the rock, or maybe they were trying to slow the fall of the rock. I do not know."

The priest stared at her.

"You have no right to invade my mind that way," she said angrily. "You can hear my thoughts well enough to know that I am telling the truth."

"I needed to make certain you are not dragonbound," said the priest. "This one is."

"Hold Wedge for me," Coral told Rockdream, and kneeled beside the battered, groaning man. With her trance-eye, she saw his pattern of light, dim, disorganized, and frayed, and a strong rope near his stomach. "This is not a dragonbinding."

"What is it, then?"

"Do you know this man?" asked the other priest.

"His name is Cherrywand, and the black cloud at the end of the rope is a black cloud. Battered as he is, he is still trying to stir up a storm to fight the dragon, and if you invaded his mind the way you did mine, I should not wonder that he would confuse your thoughts with the dragon's. Use a more gentle approach."

"He is dying, and we must learn what we can."

"Never say that to a person in shock! Cherrywand, I am Coral. You can stop bleeding and rest. The dragon is gone."

He groaned. "—failed. He will be—"

"Yes, he will probably be back."

Cherrywand closed his eyes, and when he opened them again, he was no longer breathing. The breeze changed direction and became more noticeable.

Coral stood up next to Rockdream. "I can understand Cherrywand trying something like this, but Mother always said witches should be healers and nothing else."

"Maybe she tried to talk them out of it," he said, and adjusted Wedge, who was squirming a bit in his sleep.

The priests were looking at two more bodies.

"Father!" Coral said, and kneeled at his side. He turned his head slightly to look at her. "Do not try to move," she said.

"I cannot feel anything below—I broke my back again. Coral, is, is—?"

"Mother is dead," she said, tears running down her face. "What were you doing here?"

"Being a fool," he said hoarsely.

In Cliffbrake's mind, Coral saw an image of the dragon struck by a bolt of blue lightning, of a group of seven wizards, four witches, and a midpriest, who tried to gain the weatherworking ability of a dragonbound sorcerer by binding to each other. Had they channeled enough power to change that etheric blue rope to a lightning bolt strong enough to kill the dragon, it would have killed them as well.

"At least nothing hurts," Cliffbrake said.

"Salmon was not with you?"

"No. You do what we planned before, you hear me?"

Coral tried to control her tears. "I could not leave you."

"I am the one who must leave. Smile. I love you, even if I cannot move my arms to hold you. You do what you need to do and stay alive. Do something to make this world a better place to live in before I come back. Now help me out."

"Father, there are priests here. I—" She looked up and saw that the priests were completely distracted by the newest body, the midpriest she had glimpsed in Cliffbrake's mind. "All right, close your eyes, and imagine that you are floating above this scene, looking down on yourself, and me, and Rockdream and Wedge."

Coral waited until she saw a certain pattern of light form several feet above Cliffbrake's body, then quickly, with a small quartz crystal from her pouch, she cut the slender strand of light connecting his spirit and body. "Go in peace," she whispered, forcing herself to think of anything but how much she would miss him, lest he return to his paralyzed body. His eyes opened a minute later, but they were empty, and she closed them.

The warriors, hearing no more responses to their calls, carried out the dead bodies they had found before.

"There should be at least three more," said Coral. "There were four witches, seven wizards, and one midpriest in the circle, plus my father. They should all be buried with honor, for they died fighting for the city."

"That may be true," said the first priest, "but I cannot condone the use of such magic, even to kill a dragon."

Coral said, "They did not use the rage of a dragonbound sorcerer to create lightning, but a delicate movement of threads. Had they succeeded in killing the dragon, the lightning would have killed them as well. They thought being under a roof would protect them, but in fact, the etheric rope became physical only when the rock struck the roof, and then the market exploded. Their weapon was like a sword with a point at both ends, and no handle."

"Well, we do not want anyone else trying such a thing," said the other priest.

"Nor do I," said Coral, "not because I disapprove of it, rather, because no one has the skill. This was like sending a ten-year-old squire with a few day's archery practice into battle."

"Humans are not meant to use such power," said the first priest.

"Oh, spare me your lecture about past abuses! I heard enough of that from my mother, who died because she did not follow her own advice, or maybe because she did, until the last moment. At least, can they all be buried in the Lilac Garden, like the others who have been killed by the stones?"

"That is what we planned to do," said the first priest. "How many of them can you identify?"

Coral named as many of the bodies as she could.

54.

When the burial in the Lilac Garden was finished, it was dawn, and raining a light mist. "How are you ever going to stand guard?" Coral asked Rockdream, while shifting Wedge to her other arm. The baby was awake, and turning his head to look at the passing trees.

"When it rains, I am off duty. Seriously, that is my arrangement with Lieutenant Dusk, that, and I stand guard no more than six days in a row."

On Unicorn Street they saw small groups of people with longbows and quivers, some also with swords or long knives sheathed on their belts. On Potters Street they gathered in larger groups.

"Warrior!" shouted a woman. "We are going to kill the dragon. Will you join us?"

Rockdream thought quickly, and asked, "What is your plan of attack?"

"The herds are still alive, many of the animals at least, up on the First Saddle, about fifteen miles up the road to the mines. We are marching up there to gather them up and bring them back. When Riversong tries to stop us, we will kill him."

"Thousands of us are going," said another woman.

"Warriors are bloody cowards. He will not go," said the man beside her.

"Rockdream, do not argue with them," Coral whispered urgently. "This could get ugly." Wedge was looking at the people very quietly.

"I can see that," he mumbled, "but I certainly cannot march fifteen miles to battle after being awake all night." He gradually raised his voice so the citizens would overhear him.

"Some good that did," said the man. "You stood watch all night and Riversong destroyed the market."

"Let him be," said the first woman. "If he was starting his watch instead of ending it, he might join us."

"The warriors will not join us," the man muttered.

"If everyone talks like you, they will not."

"They must," said the first woman.

"We do not need them."

"Which is exactly why they must join us. If we kill Riversong and bring back his head without them, well, what do we need warriors for?"

Coral stopped walking and fumbled with her free hand to unlace her bodice. The citizens glanced back at her, then continued. Wedge had just nursed half an hour ago, and was not very interested in nursing now, but what she wanted was an excuse to step aside. "Lord Herring has lost control of the city," she whispered. "Do you think their plan has any chance of success?"

"The East Road passes through three miles of the forest where Riversong dared us to meet him yesterday, and to stay in the open, they must either cross a steep-sided gully, or else climb all the way to the crest of Herders Ridge. In anything less than a pouring rain, they are likely marching into another firetrap like the island. Maybe this mist will become a hard rain. I hope it does. But even then, he will do something. He always does something, and most of those who go out to fight him end up burned and in his belly."

Coral began lacing up her bodice while Wedge tugged a ringlet of her hair. "You must not do that," she said to him, and carefully loosened his hand. He babbled and smiled at her. "How am I going to keep you quiet out there? I guess I can muffle your mouth with my hand." She did this for a few seconds, then let go, and smiled, as if this was a new game she was playing with him.

They resumed walking with, and yet not with, the groups of armed citizens moving toward Castle Street, where a crowd was blocking Churchgate, cheering wildly when Lord Herring appeared on the wall above the arch of the main gate.

"Brave humans of Newport!" he bellowed, but two hundred feet away, his voice was muted by the mist, and people hushed each other to silence.

"Brave humans of Newport," he repeated, "I see that you are ready for battle. Indeed, with this hope, I gave you arms you can use effectively against our enemy. Yesterday, I had eight hundred and fifty warriors. Today, I have at least a thousand more!"

Someone shouted, "Two thousand!"

"The biggest dragon-fighting army east of the sea!" he bellowed, and everyone cheered.

"He is lying," Coral said to Rockdream's ear. "This was no plan of his."

When the cheering died down, Lord Herring shouted, "Such an army deserves to be led by the best of generals!"

He meant Commander Canticle, who was the only other warrior of high rank atop the gate, but someone in the crowd shouted, "You lead us, lord!"

"Well—" He hesitated.

"Lead us, lord!" someone else shouted.

"I am an old man, but I can still shoot a bow, and I know how to lead an army!" He raised his hands to stop the cheers. "If my grandfather could kill Mugwort with an army of three hundred, surely I can kill Riversong with an army of two thousand!"

Coral hugged Wedge close, squeezed Rockdream's hand, and released it to wipe the tears from her cheeks. "He knows he is going to his death," she whispered, but Rockdream did not hear her over the cries of "Kill the dragon!"

Lord Herring raised his arms for silence. He was getting hoarse. "Commander Canticle will be my rear general. Organize yourselves to march in a column of four to Eastgate, and double up to a column of eight outside the walls. I am coming down."

By the time he and his attendants reached the street, the army of citizens was stretched out and moving in formation. Rockdream and Coral stood aside in a doorway. "I think they have a chance," he said. "They are moving like real warriors. Huh. They are real warriors, and I—I am not."

Coral checked to see whether anyone was standing near enough to hear her words before saying, "Husband, listen carefully. They will lose this battle, and Lord Herring will not return alive, though Canticle may. I have not dreamed about this, but this is a moment of knowing. I remember now, as though it has all happened before, us standing in this doorway watching people march through the mist, and I remember what follows in the pattern. Lord Herring knows this also. I heard his thoughts."

Rockdream's face was frozen to stone. He wanted to march with the lord, to die in battle if must be.

"If you go, as tired as you are now, you will certainly be among the many who will die, and then Wedge and I will die, either when the city falls, or else in the wilderness alone, but your death in battle will not save a single Newport life."

Rockdream nodded, almost imperceptibly.

"Here," said Coral, handing him Wedge. "Hold your son."

Wedge pointed at the column of four, and said something like, "Wye-yi, wye-yi," over and over.

"Yes, warriors," said Rockdream.

10

THE REFUGEES

55.

Old Plowpuller pulled the small cart loaded with sealed clay jars slowly over the rain-slicked pavement of Castle Street to Churchgate, where Coral knocked on the door of the south tower.

"I am Coral the Witch," she told the warrior who opened the door. "I have here several gallons of the best burn ointment, which I offer to the city as a gift."

"As a gift?" he asked with surprise.

"My mother and I made it together, and now she is dead, and with the lord going off to battle—well of course I hope nobody will need this, but even on a rainy day like this, some people may get burned, and I do not feel good about making money when so many are fighting as volunteers."

"Then I thank you very much," he said, and helped her unload the jars from the cart.

Back at home, Salmon was packing with the others. At Bloodroot's insistence, she had neither marched off to battle with the citizens' army, nor gone to her dragonwatch duty on the South Wall. Deciding what to take along, and what to leave behind forever, took some of the edge from her anger, but not enough.

"What Coral said to me is true," said Rockdream. "Our deaths in battle would not save anyone else's life."

Salmon glared at him, thinking, "Had we married each

188

other, we both would be marching to battle, confident of
victory and without fear of defeat," but she did not voice this
thought.

"You truly believe that," she said.

"I must," he replied.

Birdwade and Ripple had no clothes but the dresses, aprons,
underclothes, and shoes they were wearing when the bakery
burned, but Birdwade found that Cliffbrake's clothes fit her
fairly well, and Coral's tunics could serve as dresses for Ripple
if she rolled up the sleeves.

"But Mommy, it looks funny," she said.

"Well, I look funny, too." Birdwade was wearing a pair of
woolen coveralls.

"You look like Daddy but with your face."

"I guess I do."

"We could take Whitebelly with us," said Ripple. She had
found and played with the bakery cat that morning in the
common yard.

"No," said Birdwade. "Whitebelly will be all right here.
Dragons do not eat cats."

"But I want him with us."

"No. Rockdream and Coral have to leave their horse behind,
and we have to leave Daddy's animals and our cat behind. Here
is a tunic with short sleeves. This should work better."

Ripple wrinkled her nose. "Why are Coral's clothes all
green and brown?"

"This one looks much better on you," Birdwade said, when
Ripple tried it on.

"You really think so?"

"Yes. We need one more."

By the time Coral returned home, everyone else was packed
and ready to go. They took two changes of clothes for each
person; two of Salmon's imported wool tapestries, which were
big enough to serve as tents or blankets for everybody, yet light
enough to be no great burden; the longbows and quivers of
Rockdream, Salmon, and Bloodroot, and Rockdream's shorter
sword; the smallest hatchet; two coils of rope; the best knives
and spoons and the two smallest pots; all of the dried meat,
cheese, and fruit; and the waybread which Birdwade had made
that morning. Coral packed only three of her books—two herb
books and Hornbeam's *Wisdom of the Elves*. She hesitated,
then decided to bring the lyre.

"Saying goodbye to Plowpuller was hard for me," Coral said. "If I thought we had any chance of being allowed to take him outside the walls, I would, and not because a pack animal would make our journey easier, for I know he would not, but just because—"

"The animals you work with become special," said Birdwade. "That is what Brownbark used to say. But we dare not live anywhere in the open where a horse could graze."

"What did you do with him?" asked Rockdream.

"I took him back to the stable at Eastgate, which was what delayed me. Do not worry. I gave the medicines to a guard at Churchgate, as we agreed, and returned home through Marketgate. As for the dragon, no one has seen him since last night. Since he is not circling above the army, I suppose he is lying in wait, somewhere where they least expect him."

"And maybe where we least expect him," said Rockdream. "We should go north through the forest all the way to Elk River."

"Wonderful!" said Salmon sarcastically. "How many thousand feet higher are the mountains there?"

"First we have to get out of the city," said Bloodroot.

"You mean we have two deserters to disguise," said Saimon. "No problem. We both wear your clothes and give false names. What would a Northgate guard know about sailors?"

"Maybe nothing, maybe quite a bit," said Rockdream.

56.

Two men and a woman dressed as sailors, a woman in cloak and coveralls with a small child, and another woman wearing a brown cloak over a green skirt and holding a baby, all stooped over with heavy packs, stopped at Northgate.

"Hello!" shouted Salmon. "Will you raise the bars and let us out, or must we climb the walls?"

Coral looked at Salmon with surprise.

"This is not Harborgate, and the guard might not appreciate your humor," Rockdream said.

"Stand where I can see you through the slot and I will consider it," said a warrior's voice. "Now who are you?"

Except for Birdwade and Ripple, they gave false names, and Coral said she was Birdwade's servant.

"Show me that sword," the guard said to Rockdream.

He pulled it from his belt scabbard with feigned awkwardness, lest he be recognized as a warrior and a deserter, and said, "Look, it is a short one, not a warrior's sword. I bought it honestly. I could have hidden it inside my pants."

The guard laughed. "You could not hide a pocket knife inside those pants, they are so tight."

"I am lucky to have any pants at all after yesterday. But if my friend's pants are too tight, what does it matter? Before long, likely as not, they will be quite baggy."

"The guard has better things to do than talk about your pants," said Coral.

After a moment, the guard said, "All right, I will raise the bars, but I think you are bloody fools to flee the city now. Likely as not, the dragon will be dead before tomorrow. I guess you think otherwise. You want to leave a code to return?"

"If the dragon is killed, the gates will be wide open," said Salmon.

The bars of the small gate creaked upward, and they walked through.

Of the two roads leading north from the city toward the forest, the North Road was more direct, for it climbed a low ridge after fording Big Creek, thus avoiding the many fords of the Coast Road. But it was also more exposed, and closer to where the dragon probably was, so they planned to take the Coast Road if possible.

They were stopped by the Big Creek ford, which was at least thirty feet wide, and maybe four feet deep in the center. "When I crossed it two weeks ago, it was half as wide, and no deeper than my boots," said Salmon. "This drizzle cannot be the cause, even if it has been falling all day."

"Here it is a drizzle. Up on Herders Ridge, it may be a downpour," said Rockdream.

"Can we rest awhile? My legs hurt," said Ripple.

"Not till we reach the forest," said Birdwade.

"My turn to carry Wedge," said Bloodroot, and they walked the crossroad before the creek up to the North Road, and another mile on this road back to the creek. Even here it was more than knee-deep on Rockdream, who carried Ripple across, then the others followed. Birdwade slipped, but balanced herself in time to avoid a fall.

"We should have nothing worse to wade across than puddles, from here to the end of the road," said Rockdream.

"I am glad of that," said Birdwade.

From Big Creek, the road passed through more unplanted farmland, and parallel to the edge of a small forest. Beyond the last side road, the ridge became steeper and more prominent. By this time, the drizzle was no more than a mist, and the gray sky was darkening toward twilight. Across a grass-covered gully and about a mile away, they saw the trees on the next ridge, but closer, much closer, on a sandstone ledge near the bottom of the gully, the dragon Riversong was curled asleep.

Fortunately, Wedge was asleep and silent in Salmon's arms, and they had been walking quietly. If they ran or hastened now, the dragon might hear them, or perceive their thoughts of fear, and awaken, and attack, which he would certainly do, if they had any thoughts of attacking him. The breeze was moving up the gully, so their scent would not awaken him, but if he chanced to stir and open an eye, he could not miss seeing them.

When Birdwade saw the dragon, she immediately covered Ripple's mouth with her hand, and the girl nodded, looking very pale.

Salmon, holding the baby, continued to walk straight ahead up the road, now little more than a trail, and the others followed. She thought of herself as a mindless puff of fog, and Coral did the same. Everyone walked without thinking or feeling anything but numbness, step by step, up the ridge, into the deepening gloom.

When Birdwade looked back, she no longer could see the dragon, only wisps of fog gathering over the stream in the bottom of the gully.

"Can you carry me, please?" whispered Ripple.

"My legs are as sore as yours. Hush. The dragon might hear you," Birdwade whispered back.

"Keep moving," whispered Rockdream.

"I cannot. I keep stumbling. I am so tired, and so hungry."

"We must keep moving, and it truly is not safe to even whisper," Rockdream told the girl. "I would carry you, but my back is sore from my pack. Please keep walking and do not say anything."

"All right," she whispered, and they walked more quickly to catch up with the others.

Soon, Salmon stopped and said, in a low voice, "We should cross the gully before it gets too foggy to see where we are," and they angled off the ridgecrest toward the stream. The going was easy at first, but near the bottom was a four-foot drop, where Ripple and Birdwade both slipped on the mud trying to go down. The stream was swift but small, and easily crossed, but the mudbank on the other side was hard to scramble up with the packs. Rockdream gave everyone else a boost, then passed his pack up to Salmon and climbed up himself. Like the others, he wiped his muddy hands on the wet grass before continuing.

About halfway up to the forest, the fog smothered them, and just moments after this, they heard the unmistakeable sound of flapping dragon wings coming closer. No one moved, or even breathed, except the sleeping baby, and Coral and Salmon both visualized them all surrounded by a blurred gray light that was smothered in darkness. They were puffs of fog. The wings came closer, passed overhead, then moved farther away, up the gully toward Herders Ridge, and then the night was silent.

After waiting an eternity, they moved up the slope to the forest, which was edged by prickly, impenetrable brush, which they nonetheless pushed each other through. Somewhere above the trees, and fog, and clouds, the moon was almost round, but here it was so dark, they could not see anything, and here they stopped for the night. Ripple and Coral got the largest share of dried meat and fruit, for they could least afford to lose weight, and then they all huddled together between Salmon's wool tapestries.

Coral said, "I offer a prayer of praise and thanks to Wind the Hunter, who helped us hide our bodies and thoughts from our enemy this night. May she continue to favor us."

"So be it," said the others.

Birdwade asked, "Whatever was he doing down here? We thought he would be up on Herders Ridge, with the animals and the army."

"He will be, once he sees the army," said Rockdream.

"He might attack the city, instead," said Salmon.

"Perhaps he bedded down here because it was raining too hard up there," suggested Coral.

"Whoever heard of a dragon bedding down in the open in any kind of rain?" asked Salmon. "He never does what we expect. In the morning, as soon as we wake, we should move farther into the woods, and be as quiet as we can. Remember, he can fly farther in an hour than we can walk in a whole day."

57.

They woke up to a gray morning dissolving to sunshine, and hastened deeper into the forest before eating breakfast or daring to talk. Ripple and Wedge had both caught cold, and Wedge was fussy and did not want to be carried by anyone but Coral.

"I know you do not feel good, little one, but we must be quiet in the forest," Coral said, and covered his mouth with her hand one more time.

When they stopped for breakfast, they changed into dry clothes, which made them all feel much better. The going was easy through this part of the forest, for the firs and cedars were so tall and dark that there was no undergrowth but swordferns and sorrel. About midmorning, they came to a stream as large as Big Creek was at the North Road ford, which they did not try to cross, but walked uphill to a place where it was narrower, and bridged by a great fallen cedar.

The sky began to be discolored by a thin brown haze moving from the east, and they smelled smoke, and knew that battle was raging, miles to the east, where Riversong had again set fire to a wet forest.

"What if we get caught by the fire?" asked Ripple.

"It is uphill, and the forest is wet, so it will not move toward us very quickly," said Rockdream. "But we must keep moving, and keep quiet, for the dragon may be only a few miles away."

They tried to stay at the same elevation, but the streams they had to cross kept forcing them farther up the slope, till they were into the winter oaks and laurels. The berry bushes were of course not ripe, but Coral saw a patch of yellow tubers, and here they stopped for lunch, digging up and eating some of these raw, with their small pieces of dried meat and fruit.

The afternoon onshore breeze blew the smoke away from them, and they camped early in an open glade of winter oaks, where they hung their wet clothes and the tapestries in the sun to dry.

"Do you feel bad about getting them all muddy?" Bloodroot asked his wife.

"Yes, but I would rather use them than leave them behind, and can you imagine how many blankets and furs we would have needed to carry to get the same warmth?"

They bedded down shortly after sunset, and woke feeling

better the next day; even Ripple's sniffles were gone. Just after they forded a stream and ate lunch, Coral found some wintercress, which she collected and saved, to spice their supper.

Their third camp was in a grove of firs with trunks wider than their outstretched arms, and at least twice the height of Newport's tallest tower. The rising full moon was tarnished by haze from the distant fire.

The fourth day, they startled a grunting family of wild pigs, but they did not try to shoot any of them, for they dared not make any cookfires until they crossed the Foggy Mountains, and also, they still had a good supply of provisions. "But one of those pigs would have tasted good," Salmon said, when they ate another meal of dried meat and waybread.

Now they were walking more east than north, and soon found themselves near the edge of the forest, and not just a large meadow, but open grassland stretching as far as they could see. "I guess the grass grows lower on the inland side of Herders Ridge," Rockdream said. "If we go back down into the forest, we should come to Elk River."

They saw it about an hour before sunset, a smooth flowing river perhaps two hundred feet wide, with broad flats of gravel between the water and the banks. Looming above the forest on the other side was the dull-red rock and bright snow of Rusty Peak, on the crest of the Foggy Mountains, with Miners Peak immediately to its south, and a deep gap between it and the next mountain to the north. Here Rockdream hoped to find a pass.

"At least the snow has melted where you want us to go," said Salmon.

"First we have to get across the river," said Rockdream. "Another ten miles upstream, it might dwindle to a creek, but that would take us nearer the dragon, and maybe up onto the grassland, by the time we climb high enough to cross the streams that feed it."

"We can cross here," said Bloodroot. "These logs are sound enough to make a raft."

"But do we have enough rope to tie them together?" asked Salmon.

"We have enough to tie at least three of these together. It would not hold us all, but we can ferry across."

"That would work," said Salmon.

They took turns that evening, and the next morning, cutting the best logs to length with their one hatchet.

The assembled raft was almost too heavy for five humans to lift onto the rollers, but then it was easy enough to push into the water. It proved buoyant enough to carry three adults at once, so Bloodroot, Rockdream, Coral, and Wedge went on the first crossing. Both Bloodroot and Rockdream had stout poles, but the raft was difficult to push across the current, especially in the middle of the river. When they reached the other side, Bloodroot said, "I do not think I can manage the raft alone."

In their four days of travel, they had encountered no animals more dangerous than the pigs, and seen few tracks of anything but pigs and deer, so Coral was not worried about being left alone with the baby while Rockdream went back with Bloodroot.

"We will have to make three trips," Bloodroot told Salmon and Birdwade.

"You can put the rest of the goods on the raft, and take Birdwade and Ripple, and I can swim across," said Salmon.

"This water is cold," said Birdwade.

"But it is much warmer than the ocean was two and a half weeks ago, when I was dunked in it for several hours." She unlaced her bodice, and pulled her shirt and undershirt off together. "See that you keep my clothes dry," she said, unlacing her boots and untying her pants. Naked, she waded through the shallow, then jumped in.

"Can I swim too?" asked Ripple.

"No," said Birdwade. "This is a big strong river, and only big strong women like Salmon can swim across it."

"I mean, when we get to the other side, can I swim in the shallow?"

"The dragon could fly over and see us. We have to get back under the trees as soon as we can."

When the raft was about a third of the way across, Rockdream saw Coral turn to face the forest, then stoop to pick up the crawling baby. Two, three, five brush wolves jumped off the bank and trotted across the gravel. Coral stooped again, scooped up a handful of gravel, and threw it at the advancing wolves, who then backed off, and separated, to surround her.

"Bloody death, get away from her or we will slaughter every backstabbing one of you!" Rockdream shouted. "Birdwade, get me Salmon's bow and a few arrows."

"No good to pole faster," said Bloodroot. "If we do, the current will move us farther away."

At that moment, Salmon stood up in the shallow, near Coral and the brush wolves. Even naked and unarmed, she was dangerous, for she stooped to pick up a sizeable cobble from the water's edge and hurled it at the pack leader, who gave a yipe of pain and fear when it struck him square on the shoulder. A second cobble nearly missed the other male. "Get away from her!" Salmon shouted, as loud as she could. "I am fiercer than all of you!"

The brush wolves were barking and backing away. An arrow whizzed overhead. Coral was holding Wedge with her left hand, and throwing handful after handful of gravel with her right. Suddenly, the wolves turned and ran, the former leader limping hindmost with his tail between his legs.

"I want to learn to use a bow," Coral said. "Thank the goddess they were only brush wolves. If gray wolves, or a fangcat, or a bear had come, it might not have gone so well."

"While we are at camp each night, I will try to teach you, and Birdwade also, if she wants to learn. Speaking of arrows, did you see where Rockdream's went?"

"I think—I guess I did not." Wedge, now that the danger was over, came out of his startled silence and began to cry.

"Never mind. I see it. Blood. This gravel is hard on water-softened feet."

Coral was changing Wedge's swaddling. By the time she finished this, the raft reached shore, a few hundred feet downstream. "I will get your boots and clothes," Coral told Salmon.

"Make certain they save the rope," Salmon said, and Coral ran down the beach.

"Are you all right?" Rockdream asked her.

"Just frightened, as is the baby. Can one of you hold him? I need to get Salmon's boots and clothes. This is no beach for bare feet. She said to save the rope."

"Of course," said Bloodroot.

58.

They made their fifth camp in a grove of tall white oaks whose new-grown leaves were still bright green, on top of the hill between the river and the next valley east. Here, Salmon gave Coral and Birdwade the promised first archery lesson, using a rotten log as target. Though Coral's arms were more muscular than they used to be, from carrying Wedge, she was barely able to bend the bow.

"This may take me awhile, but I will learn. I am determined," said Coral.

Birdwade, who had less trouble bending the bow, but who hurt her fingers twice trying to learn the release, was less inclined to persist.

"I understand," Rockdream told her. "Did I ever tell you about how the goblin warrior Screaming Spear tried to teach me to use a spear-thrower?"

"I just—if I had wanted to become a warrior or a hunter, I would have done so. I know a baker is not very useful without grain, but I can cook other things really well, once we can make fires, and—"

"We can worry about what work we each can do, when we get settled," said Rockdream. "For now, you are our friend, and that is all you need to be."

"Thank you," said Birdwade.

Rockdream, Salmon, and Bloodroot each took a turn standing guard that night, by the light of a moon still almost full. They heard and saw nothing but mice, and the spotted skunk who stomped into the glade just before dawn. These were no concern, for they were already hanging their packs from branches to keep such animals away from the food.

The next morning, they climbed down a steeper slope than any they had encountered before, at the bottom of which was a swift stream, narrow but deep, which they crossed on a fallen pine, with some difficulty, because the broken branches sticking up tended to snag their packs. After climbing the opposite slope, they found themselves following another fork of the same stream, northeast toward the mountains.

About midafternoon, they forded the stream, to reach a trail as broad as a road on the other side.

"This is a mammoth trail," said Bloodroot. "I did not think any mammoths were left in the north range of the Foggies."

"The miners talk about them occasionally," said Rockdream. "They say they are almost as big as dragons, and shaggier than unshorn sheep, not at all like the almost hairless mammoths of Goblin Plain."

"Are they dangerous?" asked Ripple.

"Yes, but not like bears or fangcats," said Birdwade. "More like Daddy's cranky old bull."

"I did not like him. Maybe we should go another way."

"We can use this road if we make a bit of noise while we walk," said Rockdream. "If the mammoths hear us coming, they will not think we are hunting them."

"But what if the dragon hears us?" asked Ripple.

"He will more likely see us than hear us, if he comes this way," Rockdream explained. "So we still have to stay under the trees, but we can make a little bit of noise, if we do not make too much."

"Do you understand?" Birdwade asked her daughter.

"I wish we could go another way."

"You are the one whose legs always get sore," said Birdwade. "This will be much easier walking."

Of course, Ripple was the first to step into a half-dried patty of mammoth dung, which made her cry, she was so disgusted. Along the trail, the mammoths had stripped the spring growth from every tree up to a height of fifteen feet, and pulled the grass and flowers from every meadow, leaving little but trampled mud.

"They mess up everything," said Ripple.

At a fork in the trail, where the mammoth herd had turned north, they continued east, where the trail came to a dead end in a large meadow walled on three sides by high cliffs.

"So much for our easy road over the mountains," said Salmon. "Now what?"

"I suggest we go back into the trees and camp for the night," said Coral. "Wedge and Ripple are both cranky, and I want another archery lesson before it gets dark."

When they rationed their supper, Salmon said, "We will have to start hunting soon, or in a few days we will be very hungry."

"We should get over the mountains first," Rockdream said. "Maybe while you are giving Coral her lesson, Bloodroot and I can find a trail around these cliffs."

"I will watch the children," Birdwade said.

Rockdream and Bloodroot took their bows and walked together from camp to the mammoth trail, and toward the downhill slope. Rockdream said, "I know if we each searched one side of the valley, we would find what we want that much sooner, but in truth, even though this was my idea, I feel too tired to make a serious climb. But if we stay together, perhaps we can inspire each other.''

''All right. Which side looks more promising to you? The north cliffs seemed lower to me.''

''Good enough,'' replied Rockdream, and that was the way they went. They found a deer trail climbing what was almost a one on one slope at first, but which soon became easier. They did not go all the way up, for the sun was already sinking below the ridge, and the rest of the way seemed easy enough.

In the morning, while they were eating breakfast, they heard heavy feet and deep grunts, and soon saw several mountain mammoths on the trail, stripping leaves with their trunks.

''Oh, they look funny!'' said Ripple.

''Let us hope they do not come too close,'' said Birdwade. ''They are even bigger than I thought they would be.''

The humans quickly packed their gear and walked away from the grazing mammoths, through the woods toward the north side of the valley. Rockdream was in front, then Coral carrying Wedge, then Salmon, then Birdwade and Ripple, and Bloodroot behind. Out of nowhere, only twenty feet ahead of Rockdream and well within pouncing distance of anyone in the group, was a huge tawny male fangcat, who had been shadowing the mammoth herd. He stared at the humans for a moment, then before Rockdream even thought of drawing his sword, he silently, fluidly, bounded away, toward the trail they wanted to use themselves.

''Blood!'' said Salmon. ''That was lucky.''

''You will not believe this,'' said Rockdream, ''but I knew he would not hurt us.''

''Do you trust that hunch enough to dare following him?'' asked Salmon. ''He has taken our trail.''

''He wants to get one of those mammoths,'' said Rockdream. ''I would not be surprised if he was trying to get us to follow him, to lead us away from his mate and cubs.''

''Now that makes sense,'' said Coral.

''All right, let us go, but be on guard,'' said Salmon.

With the heavy packs, they had to grip roots, bushes, and tree trunks to pull themselves up the first part of the trail, but eventually it became easier. By this time, there were no more fangcat marks, for he had circled away from the trail, back toward the valley. Now they were on the gentle slope above the cliffs, which climbed to a saddle, leveled off, and began going down.

"Not much of a view," Salmon said, for the pines were tall and close together, "but I think that was the pass."

59.

The eastern slope of the mountains was much gentler, an oak and pine forest gradually leveling to the marsh, which they reached late the day after they crossed the pass. Rockdream shot a heron, and they built their first cookfire since leaving Newport, to roast it. The meat was tough, but after a week of nothing but dried food, it was delicious. What they missed now was the clear water of the mountains, for the braided, muddy creek that crossed the marsh was none too tasty, even decanted and boiled.

The marsh was muddy, covered with waist-high reeds, and dotted with pools and ponds, but not flooded, and most of the streams were fordable, even the day after a cold uncomfortable rain. What slowed them now was not the terrain, but their need to hunt, and gather what edible plants Coral could find.

The fourth, or maybe the fifth day of wandering across the marsh, they saw a dark stripe ahead on the horizon, and that afternoon, they came to the twisted willows and cypresses of Spirit Swamp. Here much of the ground was still flooded with several inches of water, and soon they all had wet feet despite their boots. Coral and Ripple were the first to try wading barefoot. Though the water was cool, this was more comfortable than chafing wet boots.

"Soon we have to come to the Crooked River," said Bloodroot. "The smaller fish are said to be plentiful, and there should be hummocks or at least levees on the banks."

"I would rather stop at the next hummock we see," said Birdwade.

"We can do that if we are willing to catch tree frogs for supper and breakfast," said Salmon. "But we must catch several hundred, and carefully skin each one."

"All right," Birdwade said with a sigh.

"The hunting is not good here," said Bloodroot. "It is too wet for land creatures—"

"I am a land creature, despite my name," said Birdwade.

"And too shallow for fish or turtles."

The next hummock they encountered was no more than a foot above water level, very muddy, and Birdwade agreed this was nowhere to stop; but beyond this, the water gradually shallowed to puddles on silty ground, which rose about a foot to a sandy levee edging the river, with a sizeable pine hummock just a few hundred feet downstream.

"Praise the holy ones!" said Bloodroot. "This one is almost a hill."

"We must watch out for river lizards," Coral told Ripple and Birdwade. "They are big, and they can bite, but they will retreat if you kick or punch them in the snout."

"We should put our boots back on," Birdwade told Ripple.

"Look," Coral said, pointing to a seven-footer sprawled halfway out of the water. Its dull color and the twilight made it hard to see.

Birdwade inhaled with surprise. "I guess it is nothing to fear, after getting safely past a dragon, a wolf pack, and a fangcat."

"They are quick enough swimmers, but clumsy on land. See how short its legs are," said Bloodroot.

"It looks like a big toad," said Ripple.

Rockdream notched an arrow in his bow, which pierced the river lizard's side behind its shoulder. It struggled briefly, trying to reach the arrow with its hind foot, then collapsed. "Help me carry it ashore!" Rockdream shouted while he ran toward it. He cut its throat to kill it.

"Bloody death, why did you kill that thing?" asked Bloodroot. "I may be hungry, but not that hungry."

"Maybe we can get something better, and maybe not, but it is almost dark, and at least we have something. You can use the guts to chum up some fish."

"Rockdream is right. Let us help him," said Salmon.

After they pulled the slippery carcass onto the levee, Salmon said, "Pull the skin away very carefully, for it is poisonous, and let me gut it, for the liver is even worse."

"But none of it is quite what you would call edible," said Bloodroot. "I will go start a fire."

"We may as well cook only the best cuts," said Coral. "There is enough here to feed us all for several days, but the meat will not keep unless it is smoked and dried, and who would do that with river lizard when we can catch fresh fish in the morning?"

"The leg cuts look like bird, and the tail cuts look like fish," Birdwade said while she rinsed them. "Shall we roast or fry them?"

"I think if we tried to roast them, they would fall apart. If we fried and spiced them, they could be quite good."

"Bloodroot will not think so, no matter what we do," said Birdwade. "How is the spice supply?"

"Better than ever. I am finding things faster than we are using them up. I still have about half of what we gathered in the mountains, and almost everything from the marsh, and I think I will find some good things here come morning. We need not worry about wasting anything."

The frying was quick, and the meat tasted better than what most of the group expected.

They put the rest of the carcass up in the crotch of a big willow, to keep it from scavengers, but the next morning, when Bloodroot got up to try his luck at fishing, he found several crows feasting on the remains. They flew off quickly, before he even thought of killing crows for breakfast. The guts were gone, but more than enough meat remained.

With makeshift nets of sailor's pants with knotted legs, Bloodroot and Salmon waded into the shallow, scattering bits of river lizard meat to chum the fish. They caught about twenty fingerling catfish, three bigger catfish, and two carp, before two river lizards swam over to investigate, and they had to stop.

Meanwhile, the children were playing with Birdwade, and Rockdream was giving Coral an archery lesson. He was a less patient teacher than Salmon, but he had to admit that she had made progress, for she could notch and release the arrow with reasonable force, though her aim was still poor.

"I discovered that I can strengthen my arms by moving energy through them," she said.

"Can you visualize the arrow hitting the target?"

"I always do that, but—let me try something." She retrieved the arrows, notched one in her bow, and looked with her trance-eye at the connection between her arms, the arrow, and the marked place on the rotten log which was her target. The trace of light became fainter or brighter as she slightly varied her aim. Her release was not perfect, but the arrow did strike the target.

"Now I would have said your aim was off, but that was not bad," said Rockdream.

When Salmon and Bloodroot brought back their catch, they all helped gut and cook them.

"I think we could live here," Salmon said while they ate. "We have a dry enough hummock, wood for a cottage, reeds for a thatch roof, and plenty of fish in the river. Coral, did you get a chance to look for tubers and such?"

"No, I was practicing archery. I hit the target just inches from center several times. I found I could see the arrow's possible flight with my trance-eye, and used this to guide my aim. You may want to try it."

"I will," said Salmon.

"I thought we were going to live somewhere where the hunting was also good," said Birdwade. "These fish are much better than river lizard, but Rockdream says that where the ground is drier, there are deer, and pigs, and—"

"Leopards," interrupted Bloodroot.

"We need not decide anything yet," said Rockdream. "We can stay here awhile, or go farther east, or come back here if this place is best."

60.

They made a raft to cross the river when Salmon and Blood-root saw a deer on the other side. There the land was less flooded, and they found another large hummock to camp on about half a mile upstream, where the river made a sharp bend.

One night, two river lizards crawled up into camp, while Salmon was dozing on guard, and actually nuzzled Rockdream's elbow and Birdwade's foot before anyone startled awake and drove them away, which led to a crying baby and a frightened little girl. The next day, they began building a sleeping platform, with upright poles tall enough to support a railing and roof, and joists held in place with notches and pegs, for they had no nails or other fasteners. Rockdream and Coral, who had built their cottage on Apple Road four years before, did most of the carpentry, while Bloodroot and Salmon fished or hunted deer, and Birdwade watched the children. The third night after their rude awakening, the platform was ready to use.

"We may as well sleep on it for a few days before we bother with framing and thatching the roof, to be sure the floor is high enough," Rockdream said. A heavy rain two days later encouraged them to build the roof, which took another three days.

While they were gathering reeds for thatch, they met three other refugees from Newport, who had fled Riversong's victory over the Citizens' Army, and somehow managed to catch two pregnant goats, and bring them across the flooded part of the swamp. The man's name was Holdfast, his wife was Wren, and her mother was Ripple, same as Birdwade's daughter.

"If you are a Ripple, I must be a Wave," the woman told the little girl, and she insisted that everyone call her Wave from now on.

"Oh Mother, that is ridiculous," said Wren.

"Life is ridiculous," she replied. "I want to be somebody else."

"We lost my father and brother in the battle," Wren explained, "and ever since then—"

"Oh, enough of that!" said her mother. "That was then, and this is now, and I am certain we all have sorrows we would rather forget. By this time, Riversong is likely curled up in the ruins of Newport Castle, sleeping off a stomach overstuffed with mighty Newport warriors. Why else would I live like this? If I think about who I was and what I had, I am bitter and angry. Let me be somebody else. Let me be Wave, a woman with no past."

"I understand how you feel," said Birdwade. "The dragon killed my husband and mother, and many of my friends."

"He may have killed everyone in the city but us, for all I know," said Wave.

"Yes, and the worst part of this is being unable to say goodbye to the ones you love," Birdwade continued, "but Coral helped me and my daughter do this, and helped us hear their replies. She could do the same for you."

"No witchcraft for me," said Wave. "I know better than to trouble the spirits of the dead. The best cure for grief is time."

"If they love you, they will not be troubled, but glad to talk with you," Coral said, "but the choice is yours."

"I think we might like to stay here awhile," said Holdfast. "We can trade you milk and soft cheese, once the kids are born, and also help you hunt."

That night, Salmon dreamed of thick fog and fear, of battle and fire, of stone walls collapsing. "I think it means the dragon has destroyed Newport Castle," she whispered to Bloodroot.

"That could be, or maybe what Wave said made you dream."

"I wonder if Coral also dreamed about this," Salmon said, but when they discussed it at breakfast, Coral remembered no dream at all. "Maybe I dreamed about it because part of me wanted to fight that battle, to die in it if need be," Salmon said. "I dare not think I might have made a difference."

"Not likely," said Bloodroot.

"I agree," said Rockdream.

After a moment's thought, Birdwade said, "Never look back, and do not try to plan too far ahead. That is how I have lived through these things without losing myself."

Over the next few days, they all helped Holdfast's family build their own platform and roof. Wren and Coral were braiding thatch to the sticking, when Bloodroot shouted something from the river.

"I see sails," Coral said, glimpsing white through the trees.

Holdfast and Rockdream jumped off the platform.

"Wait! Help us down!" said Wren.

Coral was already scooting down a pole. A forty-foot riverboat, marked only with the pentacle of Newport, furled its sails and dropped anchor in the middle of the river.

"Why does it not have a name?" asked Wave. "I may be wrong, but I think we should have hidden ourselves, instead of rushing out to greet them. They outnumber us at least twice."

"No one from Newport would stoop to piracy," said Rockdream.

Salmon laughed. "Anyone who steals a boat is a pirate, and almost anyone would stoop to that, if pressed by the dragon. As for the boat's name, it is the *Starmark,* one of merchant Speartail's riverboats. Should I shout? Ship, hello! I hope you come in peace, for we have nothing worth burning or pillaging!"

"Land hello! Of course we come in peace!" shouted a voice from the riverboat.

They lowered a skiff, which one sailor rowed ashore. "The captain wants to talk with the leader of your group," he said. Rockdream and Salmon looked at each other for a moment, then Rockdream got in the skiff.

"Something does not feel quite right to me," Coral said, after they left.

The captain, Speartail's wife's sister, Daffodil, talked with Rockdream alone in her cabin. She was a small woman with graying red hair, but her manner was as stern as any tower lieutenant. "I will be blunt with you. We need a place to settle, fast, and a place on the water to hide the boat from the air."

"Do you think Riversong will come to the swamp?"

Captain Daffodil hesitated, as if uncertain just how much she wanted to tell this warrior. "All the boats are supposed to meet at a certain time and place. If the dragon knows this, he will be there as well, and then he will search the swamp for other boats."

"So the city was evacuated? That is good news," said Rockdream.

"Canticle's plan was to scatter, by land, river, and sea, so that as many people as possible escaped the city alive. We prayed for a real storm, and we got one, with enough lightning and thunder to keep any dragon grounded, and enough wind to blow this boat as far as the marsh before dawn. So far, so good, but Canticle is too ambitious. He has not actually said this, but we know he means to conquer Goblin Plain. If we had enough real warriors like you, we might be able to do it, but those goblins are fierce fighters. You seem disturbed."

"I could not fight in such a war," said Rockdream.

"Well, my crew and I talked about it some, and came to the same conclusion, so I ordered them to sail up this river to see where it went. Along most of it, so far, wherever the trees are thick, the ground is too soggy for hunting or building. But you found a good place."

"And you mean to take it over."

"Let us say we want to share it with you," Captain Daffodil said. "My crew are not all sailors, but people with a variety of skills. We have tools and amenities you could not have packed over the mountains. We even have two priests aboard. We can build a real village. I hope this offer is acceptable to you and your people, for I have no choice. I am responsible for the lives of everyone aboard my ship."

"I understand that," Rockdream said.

61.

The village of Sharp Bend took its fifty-three inhabitants less than a month to build, and was finished a few days before the summer solstice. Twelve small huts with plank walls and thatched roofs stood on platforms, concealed from river and sky by the trees, and the *Starmark* was anchored in a narrow inlet. The days became hot, the nights became warm, and the mosquitos became plentiful.

A few days after the solstice, Captain Daffodil, who was master of the village, but did her fair share of the common work, was butchering a deer with one of her sailors, Bloodroot, and Wave, when her knife slipped, making a deep stab in her right leg. "Backstabbing death!" she swore, pulling out the knife and sticking it in the dirt. "Get the priests, you bloody fools, and help me hold my leg together!" Her pants were hot with bright throbbing blood. Wave held the captain's leg while she collapsed; the sailor ran to the priest's hut, and Bloodroot went to get Coral, who was picking bronzeberries with Salmon, Birdwade, and Ripple.

By the time Coral and Salmon ran back to the village, Daffodil was lying on a platform, with her outer pants removed, and the priests were washing the wound. "I have some goldroot to pack that with," Coral called up to them.

"Keep that witch away from me!" Daffodil shrieked. She had been polite to Coral before this, but in the stress of the moment, her fear and prejudice took over. Coral nodded grimly to the priests and walked away from the scene.

By the next day, Daffodil had a high fever, and that evening the priests spoke in secret to Coral about her herbs.

"I cannot be sure about what would be best for her without examining her myself, but it sounds like she caught a sickness from the deer's blood, or else from the water you used to wash the wound, which a goldroot packing might have prevented."

"We blessed the water," said the younger priest.

"Sometimes that is not enough," said Coral. "This water is less clean than what we are used to, and I would boil it before I used it to wash a wound like that one. But we might yet save her. Is the wound swollen and white?"

"White, and greenish around the edges."

Coral frowned. "I think if she were my patient, I would lance all the swellings, and make a poltice of goldroot and sleepflower—"

"That is a proscribed herb," the older priest said firmly.

"You might have healed her with hot and cold boiled water yesterday, but now this is serious."

"Which is why we came to you. If we could have some peppermint, or cinnamon, or cloves—"

"I have peppermint, but the last thing she needs is a stimulant."

"How can you know that?" asked the older priest. "We are the ones who have worked with her. Her fever is lower since we gave her willow bark, but now—"

"If you broke her fever without also giving her at least twice as much goldroot as all that I have, she will almost certainly die before morning," Coral said angrily. "I do have experience with badly infected leg wounds. I suppose fairlady might help, but that is also proscribed."

"You keep fairlady powder?" the younger priest asked.

"No, but there are fairladies growing on the reedflat. I could make a double-diluted infusion—no, triple-diluted, just to be safe."

"It is proscribed," said the older priest. "Will you give us the peppermint?"

"No," said Coral. "It would weaken her."

Daffodil died during the night. When the priests blamed Coral for this, behind her back, because she refused to give them the peppermint, she quickly guessed why so many people in the village seemed angry with her or afraid, and went with Salmon to confront the priests.

"I would like to know why you blame me for the captain's death," she said. "You were her healers. You washed the wound with dirty water, did not pack it with goldroot, and broke the fever much too soon, and did not follow the advice I offered you. The stimulants you requested would have killed her that much sooner. Why blame me for your own incompetence?"

Before the priests could answer, Brisk, who had been Daffodil's first mate, said, "Likely as not, you cursed the captain for refusing your help."

"I know that you were close friends with her, but that is no excuse for such dishonorable slander!" Coral said, almost shouting. "I would never do such a thing, not even to you, as angry as I am with you now. Daffodil made it clear to me that her wound was not my concern, which was her right, and I accepted this, and even tried to help her chosen healers when they came to me. I think I could have saved her life, but we will never know for certain."

The younger priest said, "We heard your thoughts when

Captain Daffodil yelled at you, and you wanted to give her herbs that are not only proscribed, but poisonous.''

"When she refused the goldroot, I was afraid she would die. I was not cursing her to die!" Coral shouted. "And those medicinal herbs, in minute, nonpoisonous dosages, were the only things that might have saved her life after you gave her the willow bark. I do not believe this! If you mean to accuse me of being a black sorceress, say so at once!''

"I do," said Brisk.

"I was asking the priests.''

They hesitated, then the older one said, "We may have misjudged you. You are indeed telling the truth.''

"Is she, or are you afraid of her curse?" asked Brisk.

"We are priests of the Lord of Light and Darkness, who is embodied in the Holy Family, and we cannot be cursed, and what is more, we always speak the truth, as we perceive it,'' the older priest said firmly. "This woman uses herbs which the Church has proscribed, but she is not a black sorceress.''

By this time, most of the humans in the village had gathered around the priests' hut, to listen to the argument. Some offered Coral apologies when she stepped off the platform, but others edged away.

Salmon said, "When you first took me as your apprentice, you warned me about this kind of prejudice, but this is the first time I have seen it.''

Rockdream hugged Coral tightly, but when they got back to their own hut, he said, "You should not have risked provoking them. We are not in Newport, and you are only protected by custom, not law. This village has no laws. You could have been killed.''

"I thought it was better to bring this out into the open than to let people mutter.''

Salmon said, "I think the priests are plotting against you. Why would they ask you for peppermint or anything else, if they thought you had cursed the captain?''

Coral said, "I do not sense that they are consciously plotting against me, but my life may indeed be at risk the next time someone in this village gets injured or sick, especially if Brisk becomes the new village master. Rockdream, I am sorry, but for my sake and Wedge's, we should leave.''

Rockdream sighed. "I do not think Brisk will be chosen master.''

"If not him, then someone else no better. Husband, you did not want to live with the people from Daffodil's ship, anyway."

Salmon said, "I certainly did not, but I will miss the river. We should pick a place away from any water a big boat can reach, or we will have the same problem all over again."

"Daffodil was notorious for being hard to cope with," said Bloodroot.

"Also, I do not want to be confronted for being a deserter," said Salmon.

"The whole city was evacuated," said Bloodroot.

"You know the difference."

"Well, we do not want to risk being swept into a war with Goblin Plain," said Rockdream.

"We will find a good place," said Coral.

"Mom, do we have to go?" asked Ripple.

"Why would you want to stay?" asked Birdwade. "You do not like any of the children from the boat very well, but you do like Wedge, and Coral, and—"

"I do not like to walk so far."

"We will only be traveling for a couple of days this time," Salmon said. "The ground will be drier and much easier to walk on than it was a month and a half ago."

62.

Salmon was right about the ground being dry, but wrong about the journey being easy, for the hunting was poor and their provisions were soon used up. By the fourth day of their journey, Ripple was sick from eating too many bronzeberries on an empty stomach, and worse than that, Coral's milk supply was beginning to dry up.

That afternoon they reached what looked like the Turtle River. In the open water beyond the reeds and cattails were a multitude of river lizards swimming slowly, clasped together in pairs, and some of the unattached males were bumping the couples, trying to force them to separate.

"They look delicious," said Coral, and even Bloodroot and Ripple were hungry enough to agree.

"But how can we kill one without the others eating the carcass before we get it ashore?" asked Rockdream.

"Mating river lizards do not think much about eating," said Coral.

Salmon was already stringing her bow. "I will shoot one, and if another tries to eat it, I will shoot that one also."

"Aim for a lone male," said Rockdream.

"How about that one?" asked Salmon. "Shoot, then jump in and swim it back."

They shot, hit their target, dropped their bows, splashed through the reeds and began swimming. The river lizard stopped thrashing and swam away, leaving a wake of blood.

"We lost it," said Salmon.

Rockdream stopped swimming and stood up in the waist-deep water, shaking his head. "We drove every single one of them away from this part of the river."

"This is not the river," Salmon said, standing up beside him. "The water has breeze ripples, but not a trace of current. This must be an old loop of the river, cut off when it changed course. What was that?"

"What was what? Oh, I see it. It could be a catfish."

"Forget the river lizards. Let us go back and get our nets."

They gathered grubs from a rotten log, chummed the water, and netted enough catfish for a real feast in less than an hour. Then, while the others gutted and cooked the fish, and Birdwade watched the children, Coral searched for edible plants, and found not only plenty of swamp sorrel and tubers, but also the rootings and tracks of wild pigs.

"That settles it," said Salmon, who particularly liked pork. "This is what we are looking for. I am ready to start building."

"Wait a moment," said Birdwade. "I can agree with staying here long enough to hunt those pigs, but I do not think we can live near all these river lizards with two small children."

Rockdream looked thoughtfully at the lake, swallowed a bite of cooked fish, and said, "Maybe hundreds of river lizards are less dangerous to us than a few. We know they are here, and we will not be surprised, the way we sometimes were at the other place."

"Ripple knows how to kick river lizards in the snout, or hit them with a stick," said Bloodroot.

"I guess so, but the big ones are scary," she said.

"These catfish are delicious," Coral said, "and so are the greens and roots, and I think the hunting will be good. Nothing can be certain for us now, but this place feels familiar to me, in a way that the other place did not. I think if we start the village

I envision here, others will join us, but not so many and so quickly as to overwhelm us.''

"I know enough now to be assertive," Rockdream said. "Anyone who wants to join us must respect us."

"What can you do if they do not?" asked Birdwade.

Coral said, "I learned some things from the wizard Treeworm about how to hide a home from unwelcome visitors that I did not think of using at Sharp Bend. If the village gets larger, this kind of glimmer will no longer work, but then we would outnumber any strangers."

Salmon asked, "Are you saying that our friends, or people who would become our friends, will be able to find us, but others will not?"

"Treeworm said the spell is effective, but we will see."

63.

Most of the Newport refugees who joined Loop Lake village that summer were indeed friends of someone in the original group. Among these were Ironweed and Stonewater, who had been merchant Fairwind's bookkeeper and house-servant. They had fled the city overland as part of one of Canticle's maneuvers, and were nearly starving when they reached Loop Lake, for neither had much hunting skill.

Stonewater said, "We had a warrior in our group, and Ironweed's father was a farmer who knew how to shoot, but we have no skill ourselves, and Ironweed's younger sisters were just children. We caught cold in a mountain storm, and when the wolves attacked the next evening, we were too sick to fight effectively. They killed one of the girls and mortally wounded the other before we drove them away."

"We were not the first ill-prepared group to pass that way," said Ironweed. "The predators have lost their fear of human hunters."

Stonewater wiped the tears from her eyes and continued, "The warrior was an older man, and twisted his ankle badly in the fight, but insisted that if he bound it well, he could walk. We followed several false trails before we found the pass, two days later."

"Which pass?" asked Rockdream.

"Is there another besides the one south of Miners Peak?" asked Ironweed.

"We took the one north of Rusty Peak," Rockdream said.

"You were wise to flee the city early," Stonewater said. "We lost the rest of our group in the foothills east of the pass. When that bear attacked, the warrior was limping, and Ironweed's father was carrying the delirious girl. The warrior shot the bear in the heart, but it mauled all three of them before it died. I am not sure how many days we stayed at that camp, butchering and smoking the bear, and trying to nurse the two men, after the girl died. When Ironweed's father died, the warrior told us to save ourselves. He wanted one of us to stab him in the heart, so that he would die cleanly and quickly. He was too big for us to carry, so I—I did it. We packed as much bear meat across the marsh as we could, but all too soon we ran out. We have had little this past week but bronzeberries and birds' eggs. When we saw your fire around the lake, we were so very grateful—and to find old friends—"

"Praise and thanks! Our luck is changing," said Ironweed.

64.

Swanfeather, the warrior who had been Salmon's roommate as a squire, and her husband, Flatfish, a fishcatcher, had a much easier journey. They escaped in his skiff on a foggy night, and made it up the river without incident. "I was supposed to stand guard on a larger boat," Swanfeather said, "but Flatfish and I both had the same bad dream about this boat, so we took the skiff. When we reached the swamp, we paddled through the backwater, for we dared not meet the other boats after I deserted my duty."

Coral said, "If you both had the same dream, and the warning was clear, you did the best thing."

"I do not doubt it," said Flatfish. "Many of the bigger boats did not get away. Sometimes Riversong carried a charred piece of hull or a mast, and breathed new flame on it before he dropped it. He would tell us which boat the wood was from, and which captain and which fierce warriors he had devoured."

"Enough of that," said Swanfeather.

Rockdream asked, "When and where was this meeting of boats to occur?"

"The captain knew; I did not," said Swanfeather. "I suppose it must have been somewhere on one of the rivers."

"What meeting?" asked Ironweed. "I understood that we were supposed to scatter widely as possible."

"I do not like the way Canticle has manipulated people," said Coral, "even if he thought he had to do this, to fool the dragon."

"What do you mean, he manipulated people?" asked Stonewater.

Coral said, "There was to be a reunion of Newport people, at some time, somewhere in the swamp, which apparently only some groups knew about. Captain Daffodil of the *Starmark* believed that Canticle intended to conquer Goblin Plain, and wanted no part of either the meeting or the war."

"Daffodil? She is no good source of information," said Ironweed.

"I stood duty in Canticle's Tower, five years ago, during the turtle dispute between our fishcatchers and Goblin Plain," said Rockdream. "Canticle was opposed to the agreements, and said that if Newport ever was destroyed by a dragon, the survivors would have to conquer Goblin Plain, and it would be best if Strong Bull feared our strength."

"Rockdream, if anyone but you had told me that, I would call that person a liar," said Swanfeather.

"Really? Think about it," said Salmon. "Why reunite at all if not to build a new city somewhere else? Why put the best warriors on boats and the older ones on foot, if not to assemble the best possible fighting force? Ironweed and Stonewater's warrior must not even have known about the meeting, or he would have told them before he died."

"I am not sure even Canticle could be that ruthless about his command," said Rockdream.

"I think he did his best to save everyone he could," said Swanfeather.

"Canticle is stubborn," Coral said. "Once he thinks he knows what is best, or at least what is necessary, no one can dissuade him. In these uncertain times, many people may mistake his stubbornness for good leadership and follow him, even into a dishonorable war."

"You are truly convinced of this," said Flatfish.

"I am not Canticle's enemy, but in some way that I do not yet understand, I am his opponent," Coral said.

"Canticle is trying to continue living the old way," said Rockdream. "He wants to build a city, well defended, but eventually both attractive and vulnerable to dragons, on conquered goblin land. His are the kind of brave if sometimes dishonorable deeds that have made most of the history of humans east of the sea. But Coral pulled me aside from the flow of history, and suggested that we try something else. We are not refugees and exiles here, but settlers trying to make a new home for ourselves. We are trying to live a more natural way, not exactly the way goblins do, but inspired by their small camps. We do not need the wealth and population that would attract a dragon. We may succeed or we may fail, but at least we are not repeating old mistakes. We are trying something new."

THE END

**The story of the survivors of Newport
will continue in
*The Goblin Plain War.***

APPENDIX ONE

CHRONOLOGY

Year
1. Turtleport, first human settlement east of the sea, founded by Windsong the Mariner and her people, political exiles from the Middle Kingdom.
10. Coveport founded by a group of monotheists, religious exiles from the Middle Kingdom.
14. Settlement of the Two Rivers Valley begins. Some trouble with goblins.
22. Midcoast founded.
23. Southport founded, by commercial interests from the Middle Kingdom.
28. Death of Windsong.
30. First Goblin War begins. Many goblin peoples unite to oppose the spreading of the humans.
33. Isle of Hod pirates trouble Southport and Turtleport.
38. After eight years of war and many deaths on both sides, five goblin high chiefs and many chiefs sit the peace circle with the human Lords of Coveport, Midcoast, and Turtleport, and many keepholders and village masters. All lands of the Two Rivers Valley, and all lands west of the Foggy Mountains within a hundred miles of the Turtle River Delta, are to be human, and all other lands in the region are to remain goblin. Goblins from the Elk Coast, north of Turtleport, move to Goblin Plain, and goblins from the Two Rivers Valley move to the Moon Valley, or else east of the Silver Mountains.

44. Bracken, a dragonbound wizard on the Isle of Hod, kills his dragon to gain great power, but the storm he creates devastates Hod Town.

50. Rockport founded.

57. Auroch, a dragonbound witch living in a remote forest near the headwaters of the Bigfish River, is killed by neighboring villagers, but her dragon, Mugwort, escapes.

62. Mugwort attacks and destroys Turtleport. The survivors resettle in the Two Rivers Valley.

66. The Human War begins, Valley monotheists opposed to Turtleport orthodox.

70. A group of priests and priestesses from both churches reach a compromise. The monotheists' Lord of Light and Darkness is said to be embodied in the eight gods and goddesses of the Holy Family. The one is worshiped through the eight, and the eight through the one.

71. A private army raised by a younger son of the Lord of Midcoast, supposedly to attack Mugwort, instead founds a city at the mouth of the Moon River, thus breaking the great peace circle.

72. Humans win the Moon Valley War; few goblins survive.

107. Human traders build a camp east of the Silver Mountains, with goblin permission, but when this quickly grows to become the city of Upriver, the goblins become alarmed.

117. Blue River goblins attack Upriver.

120. Humans found several keeps in the Dragonstone Mountain country to prevent these goblins from joining the war. The warrior Wentletrap, an exile from Rockport, joins the Upriver army. A brilliant tactician, he is soon appointed general by Lord Starkweather.

123. Pip the Elf persuades the Blue River goblins to sue for peace. She and Wentletrap gather a private army, kill the dragon Mugwort, and found Newport.

124. Wentletrap and Pip's daughter, Blackberry, born.

139. The dragon Redmoon destroys Southport.

141. Blackberry's son, the future Lord Herring, born.

144. Wentletrap and Pip leave Newport to journey to the country of the elves, but do not return. Blackberry's husband Stock, who was one of Wentletrap's original warriors, becomes second Lord of Newport.

149. A forty-foot female dragon tries to attack Newport and is killed.

156. Another, slightly larger dragon flies over the city twice but does not attack.

177. Coral born in Newport.

178. Rockdream born in Newport.

179. Lord Stock's Comet.

180. Herring becomes third Lord of Newport.

181. Some goblin battles in the Dragonstone Mountain Country.

182. The dragon Riversong destroys Moonport.

186. Rockdream becomes a squire. His older sister, Glint, dies.

189. Coral lives with the wizard Treeworm that summer.

194. Rockdream passes his warrior's test and stands dragon-watch in Canticle's Tower. His meeting with Coral the Witch. The Turtle Crisis. Salmon, spurned by Rockdream, marries Bloodroot.

195. Rockdream marries Coral, becomes a gate guard at Eastgate. He and Coral build a cottage near her parents' cottage.

197. Coral becomes pregnant. At the end of winter, she and Rockdream journey with High Shaman Drakey to Goblin Plain.

198. After two weeks at Beartooth's Camp, they return to Newport. Sighting of two dragons by Captain Catch-Plenty of Godsfavor. Wedge born in midsummer. Lord Herring's Comet followed by a hard winter.

199. The dragon Riversong besieges and destroys Newport, killing Lord Herring, most of his family, and most of the population. General Canticle's evacuation of Newport. Rockdream's people build Sharp Bend Village, are forced to leave this by other refugees, and build Loop Lake Village.

APPENDIX TWO

WENTLETRAP'S DYNASTY

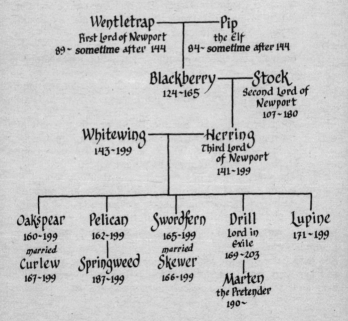

Wentletrap
First Lord of Newport
89 ~ sometime after 144

Pip
the Elf
84 ~ sometime after 144

Blackberry
124 ~ 165

Stock
Second Lord of
Newport
107 ~ 180

Whitewing
143 ~ 199

Herring
Third Lord
of Newport
141 ~ 199

Oakspear
160 ~ 199
married
Curlew
167 ~ 199

Pelican
162 ~ 199

Springweed
187 ~ 199

Swordfern
165 ~ 199
married
Skewer
166 ~ 199

Drill
Lord in
Exile
169 ~ 203

Marten
the Pretender
190 ~

Lupine
171 ~ 199

Note: only people named in the text are included. Lord Herring had many
more grandchildren.

APPENDIX THREE

THE HOLY FAMILY

SKY, the Father, whose globe is the sun.

THE NAMELESS MOTHER, whose globe is the world.

THUNDER, the First Son, the King, whose globe is the twelve-year star.

CLOUD, the Second Son, the Wizard, whose globe is the dimmer twilight star.

MOUNTAIN, the Third Son, the Priest, whose globe is the slow-moving star.

WIND, the First Daughter, the Hunter, whose globe is the moon.

FIRE, the Second Daughter, the Warrior, whose globe is the red star.

LAKE, the Third Daughter, the Lover, whose globe is the brighter twilight star.

In the Rose Garden of Newport, the statues made by Spiral the Sculptor included all three sons, and the oldest two daughters. She died before putting the final touches on Fire the Warrior, and her work was so perfect that Lady Blackberry refused to even consider hiring another sculptor to finish the set.

INDEX OF NAMES

BROWN FOX, goblin boy, son of Screaming Spear and Antelope.

CANTICLE, human man, tower lieutenant, afterwards commander and general.

CATCH-PLENTY, human man, captain of the *Diving Pelican*, from Godsfavor.

CHAINFERN, human man, healing priest.

CHERRYWAND, human man, wizard.

CICADA, goblin woman, shamaness, Beartooth's wife.

CLIFFBRAKE, human man, gardener, Coral's father.

COALJAY, human woman, tower lieutenant of Eastgate.

CONCH, human man, tower lieutenant, afterwards commander.

CORAL, human woman, witch, daughter of Cliffbrake and Moonwort.

CROSSING, human man, Lord of Midcoast.

CURLEW, human woman, warrior, Baron Oakspear's wife.

CYPRESS, human woman, warrior, Dusk's wife.

DAFFODIL, human woman, captain of the *Starmark*.

DRAKEY, goblin man, high shaman of Goblin Plain.

DRIFTWOOD, human man, merchant.

DRILL, human man, Baron of Newport, Herring's fourth son.

DUSK, human man, warrior, afterwards tower lieutenant of Eastgate.

EDGE, human man, warrior.

FAIRWIND, human man, merchant, owns the *Great Circle* and the *Golden Turtle*.

FANG, goblin boy, Beartooth and Cicada's son.

FEATHERGRASS, human man, mariner, Loon's husband.

FENNEL, human man, squire, Rockdream's roommate, afterwards a warrior.

FINITE, female housecat, Moonwort's cottage.

FLATFISH, human man, fishcatcher, Swanfeather's husband.

FLEDGELING, human woman, warrior at Canticle's Tower.

FORECASTLE, human man, merchant.

FROGSONG, human woman, fishcatcher, Vein's wife.

GLINT, human girl, now dead, Rockdream's older sister.

GLOWFLY, goblin woman, shamaness, Screaming Spear's daughter.

GRAY LIZARD, goblin man, warrior at Beartooth's Camp.

GRAYWOOL, human man, fishcatcher with a leg injury.

GREEN, human man, sailor aboard the *Happy Gutter*.

HERRING, human man, third Lord of Newport, son of Stock and Blackberry.

HOLDFAST, human man, herder, Wren's husband.

HORNBEAM, 2nd c. human man, wizard, friend of Pip the Elf.

HOOK, human man, blacksmith, Sparkle's husband.

HYSSOP, human boy, son of Vein and Frogsong.

IRONWEED, human man, Fairwind's bookkeeper, Stonewater's husband.

LIGHTBRINGER, human man, wizard.

LIGHTSTRAW, human woman, sailor aboard the *Golden Turtle*.

LOON, human woman, minstrel from the Four Lakes Kingdom.

LOVERING, human man, legendary king of Jade Forest.

LUPINE, human woman, Baroness of Newport, Herring's daughter.

MALLOW, human woman, priestess.

MANTLEHARP, human man, warrior of Eastgate.

MAPLEWING, human woman, warrior of Eastgate.

MARGIN, human man, warrior of Canticle's Tower.

MARTEN, human boy, Baron Drill's son.

MOONWORT, human woman, witch, Coral's mother.

MUGWORT, male dragon, destroyer of Turtleport, killed by Wentletrap.

NOTCH, human man, warrior of Canticle Tower.

OAKSPEAR, human man, Baron of Newport, Herring's first son.

OLD ONE EAR, male fangcat, killed by herders.

ORCHID, human woman, baker, Birdwade's mother.

PELICAN, human man, Baron of Newport, Herring's second son.

PINCHGRIP, human man, warrior of Eastgate.

PIP, early 2nd c. elf woman, Wentletrap's wife, Blackberry's mother.

PLOWPULLER, Rockdream's gelding horse.

RAVEN, pre–1st c. goblin woman, shamaness of an Elk Coast camp.

REDMOON, female dragon, destroyer of Southport.

REDMYTH, human man, Middle Kingdom warrior, Windsong's husband.

REDTHORN, human man, portmaster of Newport.

REED, human man, captain of the *Great Circle*.

RIPPLE, human woman, Wren's mother, changes her name to Wave.

RIPPLE, human girl, Birdwade and Brownbark's daughter.

RIVERSONG, male dragon, destroyer of Moonport.

ROCKDREAM, human man, warrior of Canticle's Tower, afterwards of Eastgate.

SALMON, human woman, warrior employed by Fairwind.

SCALLOP, human woman, warrior, Rockdream's mother, Bane's wife.

SCREAMING SPEAR, goblin man, former chief of Beartooth's Camp.

SCULPIN, human woman, captain of *Happy Gutter*.

SEES FAR, goblin man, warrior of Beartooth's Camp.

SKEWER, human woman, warrior, Baron Swordfern's wife.

SORREL, human woman, patient of Moonwort and Salmon.

SPARKLE, human woman, weaver, Hook's wife.

SPEARTAIL, human man, merchant, owner of *Starmark*.

SPINEBALL, human man, farmer.

SPIRAL, human woman, mid–2nd c. sculptor.

SPRINGWEED, human boy, squire, Baron Pelican's son.

STARMOSS, human man, priest, afterwards midpriest.

STOCK, human man, second Lord of Newport, Herring's father.

STONELIGHT, human man, midpriest.

STONEWATER, human woman, Fairwind's house servant, Ironweed's wife.

STRONG BULL, goblin man, high chief of Goblin Plain.

STRONGHORN, goblin boy, son of Beartooth and Cicada.

SWANFEATHER, human woman, warrior, Salmon's friend, Flatfish's wife.

SWORDFERN, human man, Baron of Newport, Herring's third son.

SWORDROT, female dragon, destroyer of Cherry Blossom City in Godsfavor.

TERRAPIN, human man, captain of the *Golden Turtle*.

THRUSH, human man, first mate of the *Happy Gutter*.

TREEWORM, human man, wizard living on the Elk Coast north of Newport.

VEIN, human man, warrior of Canticle's Tower, Frogsong's husband.

WAVE, human woman, Wren's mother, herder.

WEDGE, human boy, Rockdream and Coral's baby.

WENTLETRAP, early 2nd c. human man, first Lord of Newport, Pip's husband.

WHITEBELLY, male housecat, Orchid's bakery.

WHITEWING, human woman, Lady of Newport, Herring's wife.

WINDSONG, human woman from the Middle Kingdom, founder of Turtleport.

WINDWATER, human woman, warrior, Rockdream's archery teacher.

WOAD, human man, King of the Middle Kingdom, Windsong's enemy.

WREN, human woman, herder, Holdfast's wife.